the
tall
man

the tall man

Phoebe Locke

WILDFIRE

First published in 2018 by WILDFIRE
An imprint of HEADLINE PUBLISHING GROUP

1

Cataloguing in Publication Data is available from the British Library

Hardback ISBN 978 1 4722 4925 8
Trade Paperback ISBN 978 1 4722 4924 1

Typeset by Palimpsest Book Production Ltd, Falkirk, Stirlingshire

Printed and bound in Great Britain by
Clays Ltd, Elcograf S.p.A.

MIX
Paper from
responsible sources
FSC
www.fsc.org FSC® C104740

Headline's policy is to use papers that are natural, renewable and recyclable
products and made from wood grown in sustainable forests. The logging and
manufacturing processes are expected to conform to the environmental
regulations of the country of origin.

HEADLINE PUBLISHING GROUP
An Hachette UK Company
Carmelite House
50 Victoria Embankment
London EC4Y 0DZ

www.headline.co.uk
www.hachette.co.uk

For Mum, Dad and Dan,
with love

From 'Making the Movie: The Difficult Journey to the Truth' by Federica Sosa, published in *Variety* magazine, July 2019

When I first embarked upon this project, I was cautious. Although my previous documentary had been the subject of much critical acclaim, I needed to find another story which would grab me – consume me – as that one had.

The Banner family's story first came to my attention during an extended stay in London. The case was much in the news at the time; in fact, as the impending trial drew closer, it was unavoidable. The headlines chilled me: a senseless murder; a family haunted by one member's demons; an urban legend which had sunk its claws into an innocent child and turned her life upside down. I knew immediately that this was a story I wanted to tell.

Never, at that tentative sketching stage of potential, did I foresee the difficulties that my team and I would encounter. For every knot we untied in this tragic story, there was another one waiting; another secret looped up and feeding on the very fabric of this family. We compiled pages and pages of interviews; we began to look at events from all points of view, trying to find our way in. And looming over it all, always, was this playground tale, this dark figure of the Tall Man.

Many of the difficulties involved access. Not everyone concerned in the tale was alive to share their part. Often we had to rely on material left behind; on second-hand accounts. While these can be more enlightening than an interview, it was so incredibly frustrating, as a film-maker, not to be able to pick up on a certain point – a thought or a choice of word or an act itself – and ask *Why?* To ask, *Was this real to you?*

Much of what is in the film is now public knowledge, thanks to the trial and to the constant media attention. People became obsessed with the ghosts and the darkest deeds of the Banner family. With the Tall Man and the grip he held over them. I set out to cover the trial, to get behind the headlines and the ghouls and to uncover the cold truth about a murder. But to hear it told by the people involved shed a different light on those events. This story is not one of tabloid gore and shock; it is one of grief and guilt and the terrible secrets which nestled for years at the heart of not one but two families. It is about the legacy of a dreadful legend, a story that begins and ends in the darkest woods.

It has haunted me ever since.

It began near the end of summer, when the days were long and hot and school seemed a distant, baseless thing to fear. Sadie and Helen were walking their bikes beside the river, looking for a place to sit down and eat their sweets – Toffos for Sadie, Opal Fruits for Helen, everything exactly as it always was. Sadie had hit a root as they cycled through the woods and her palm was scraped raw where she had struck out at a tree, trying to stop herself from falling. She examined the graze again, the tiny flecks of bark embedded in the skin.

'Hey, there's Marie,' Helen said, the side of her mouth full of chewed sweet.

Helen's older sister was sitting on one of the peeling benches that lined the river bank, two friends beside her. Sadie stopped looking at her hand.

Marie had recently turned twelve, and she had also begun to wear a training bra. Sadie had seen it herself, pegged on the washing line at Helen's house alongside all the regular washing, with its small soft cups and its thin satin straps. She looked at Marie, sitting on the bench and kicking up dust with her trainers, and wondered, with a sudden rush of heat, if she was wearing it then.

Marie, glancing up, noticed the two of them standing there. A smile tightened the corners of her mouth before spreading slowly. She nudged her friends and then waved them over. The wheels of their bikes clicking and the taste of toffee turning sour in Sadie's mouth.

'Hey, girls,' said one of the friends, a dark-haired girl with freckles splashed across her narrow nose. 'Want to play a game?'

'It's not a game, Justine.' Up close, Sadie recognised the girl on the other side of Marie as Ellie Travis, the elder sister of a boy in her class. She had pale blond hair, a hank of which was caught between her face and the arm of her glasses. 'I told you what my brother said.'

'Don't listen to anything James says,' Helen said cheerfully, her shyness now beginning to fade. 'He talks absolute rubbish.'

'She's not talking about James.' Marie rolled her eyes. 'She's talking about Thomas. He's the oldest, and it was his job to tell Ellie about the Tall Man. And because I'm the oldest, now it's my job to tell you.'

Sadie watched the way Justine's eyes narrowed at this, her mouth twitching into a smile. She took a lolly from her pocket and unwrapped it, her gaze drifting from Sadie's shorts up to her T-shirt and then to her face. When their eyes met, Justine did not look away.

'Who's the Tall Man?' Sadie asked.

'He lives in the woods,' Marie said, leaning forward to take the packet of Opal Fruits from Helen's hand.

'He sees everything,' Ellie added, pushing her glasses back up her nose.

'He's a murderer.' Justine leaned back with a grin. 'He comes in the night and he takes you away.'

'He took a girl from my street five years ago,' Ellie said, her hands working anxiously at the hem of her shirt. 'That's what I heard.'

'That's not true,' Helen said, her arm sliding through Sadie's. 'Stop trying to scare us.'

'It is true.' Marie flicked a balled-up sweet wrapper at her sister. 'But don't worry. Now you know about him, you'll be safe.'

'Not just safe,' Justine said, cracking the lolly with her small, white teeth. 'He can make you special, too, if you ask him.' She got up from the bench, making a show of consulting her watch – a purple and yellow patterned Pop Swatch that Sadie had been eyeing through the window of the jewellers in town for weeks. 'I've gotta go. Stay tuned for more tales of the Tall Man, kiddos. I think he's going to like you.'

Marie stifled a snort of laughter, but Sadie noticed that Ellie kept her eyes on the ground, fingers still seeking out the loose edge of her top.

'Does he really kill girls?' Helen asked, her eyes wide, and at that Ellie got up from the bench.

'I don't like this any more,' she said. 'I don't want to play.'

5

Justine shrugged. 'So go home. We don't need you now anyway.' And she smiled at Sadie and Helen, ignoring the look Marie shot her. Only Sadie looked at Ellie as Ellie shuffled away.

'In answer to your question, Helen,' Justine said, picking up her bike from the ground and swinging a long leg over it, her denim shorts frayed at the edges, the pocket torn. 'Yes. He does. He killed his own daughter.' She pushed lazily at a pedal, moving away from them down the riverbank. 'She didn't do what he wanted,' she called over her shoulder, and then she was gone.

1

It felt wrong almost immediately. They walked towards
the sound of the music, the grass scratching at their calves,
and he wanted to turn back.

'Are you OK?' she asked, slipping her hand into his.

Miles glanced at her. She'd dressed differently that
morning; a daisy-print sundress with a white cardigan pulled
over, not the dungarees or baggy jeans, the thin-strapped
vest tops she usually preferred. He appreciated the effort.

'Yeah,' he said. 'I'm OK.'

He still felt sick. Sympathetic, perhaps – he'd heard that
was a thing. Sadie kept reading things out to him in bed at
night, a constant stream of *Did you know* and *Wow, this
is weird* and *Listen to this*, and it was all conflicting and
bizarre and witchy, comparing the baby to fruit and saying
how playing it music in the womb would make it smart.

He thought of the sneer on his mother's face when, an

7

hour ago, he had mentioned this in an attempt to lighten the atmosphere. How she had reached out to refill Sadie's teacup and then his. *Yes, I'm sure classical music will ensure the poor sod grows up with half a chance.* The way his father's hand had clamped down over hers on the arm of the chair. *Frances, love.* And the way his mother had sighed, blinking firmly once and then twice, before offering them the plate of biscuits. *I'm sorry, Miles. You're both just so young.*

'They'll come round,' Sadie said, squeezing his hand and then letting go, shading her eyes as she looked at the festival in the distance. There was a stage set up in the centre of the field, stalls lined up on either side. Clouds of smoke rose, the scent of burning meat drifting towards them as they left the makeshift car park and headed up the hill.

He loved her for saying it. And they *would* come round, he was sure of it. How could they not? Their only son was going to have a child, their first grandchild – and yes, perhaps, he and Sadie were too young, with only the first year of university under their belts, but everything happened for a reason, didn't it? Sometimes things were meant to be.

Sadie slipped her cardigan off and tied it round her waist. 'At least it's done now,' she said, putting her arm round him. 'We can enjoy the afternoon, anyway.'

With Sadie, it was meant to be. This much he already knew.

He wondered what his parents were doing at that moment, though he was fairly sure he could guess. His father would have removed the good gin from the cupboard, brought down the thick crystal glasses which were his mother's favourite. They would be drinking in silence on the patio, and then, later, his mother would pace back and forth across the kitchen, preparing dinner and airing her views. Then, perhaps, she would call Miles.

'I guess we need to tell your parents next,' he said. He felt her stiffen beside him.

'I think I'd better do that bit,' she said, turning away. 'I don't think they'll be very pleased.'

'Not like mine, you mean?' He leaned down to kiss her bare shoulder but the joke fell flat even as it left his mouth, the memory of his parents' horrified faces resurfacing.

He'd known that it would be difficult. He remembered the moment Sadie had told him she was pregnant, him sitting on the edge of her narrow bed in halls. He'd been out the night before, a bar crawl with the rest of Sociology Soc, and he'd been scrubbing at the faint stamp of a club on his hand with his thumb. Sadie had stayed in for the previous two nights, saying she had a stomach bug. The stomach bug had turned out to be something else entirely. A something which was now curving her flat belly out in the slightest of slopes, a something which next week they would apparently see in black and white on a hospital screen.

'Hey,' she said, stopping him at the edge of the festival. Her eyes fixed on his. 'We'll be OK,' she said, her hands travelling down his sides now, tracing over his ribs. Her touch making the hairs on his arms stand up, his mouth dry.

9

'I know,' he said, dipping his head to kiss her. Her teeth sinking into his lip as she smiled.

He followed her towards the crowd, the hem of her dress rippling in the breeze. He was scared, of course he was. He was finding it difficult to imagine that in a year's time, there would be three of them in the car, three of them wherever they ended up. It was much easier, for now, for him to focus on his studies – that was something he was at least in control of. Something practical and important that he could do for their future, for Sadie, for the baby. It gave him a funny, hot feeling in his chest.

They passed the first stalls at the edge of the festival: jams and cakes and cheese from local businesses, wooden ornaments and candles in glass jars. Someone on Sadie's course had told her about the festival; Miles had dutifully passed on the hot tip to his flatmate James and several people from his course. He cringed looking at these middle-class, middle-aged offerings and hoped that they had not come.

'The band that's on after this is meant to be really good,' Sadie said, leading him past the stalls without a glance, and suddenly everything was OK again.

He knew it was a cliché to say – he'd tried once, drunkenly, around a pub table with his flatmates and had been roundly jeered at – but he'd never felt the way he did about Sadie before. She was beautiful, yes. That much was obvious to anyone. And funny, too, though perhaps not everyone got to see that side of her. Her spikiness put some people off – he'd heard Lila, James's latest girlfriend, refer to her as 'a cold fish' (he was possibly being generous; Lila had been whispering and the word was just as likely to have been *bitch*). But Miles had been intrigued by the defences Sadie put up whenever she first met someone. It had only made him more determined to get past them.

He reached over and smoothed a strand of hair behind her ear, the wind attempting to tug it free again. 'You were great back there,' he said. 'With my mum and dad, I mean. Thank you.'

She turned her head to look at him, her mouth turned up in the small, secret smile he loved best. 'It's me and you now,' she said. 'Isn't it?'

And he knew that it was.

They reached the stage area and Miles stopped and craned up on his toes, looking for James and the others in the crowd. 'Come on,' Sadie said, pulling him through a group of teenagers and working her way up the edge of the field. 'Let's get closer to the speakers, I bet that's where they'll be.'

His friends had begun to treat Sadie as if she were made of glass or something highly explosive, falling over themselves to offer her a chair or a better view of the screen. They'd been ready to commiserate when he told them the news two weeks previously – had patted him on the back, nodded solemnly as he spoke. *I'm excited*, he'd added, and that made them recalibrate, buy shots. Now all they asked was when the scan was, how Sadie was feeling, whether they planned to find out the sex when they could. He saved up the rest of it to think about alone in his single bed, on the nights when Sadie retreated to her own room – her room that, he was all too aware, she'd have to give up as soon as she decided to tell the university she was dropping out. How would they live; how would he study and provide for them? He thought often of the fact that he had never even held a child – had no brothers or sisters, was the youngest of his cousins. How did you do it? He'd heard something about supporting the head, that was supposed to be important. And there was talk of burping them, a term he found baffling. He would have to buy a book on babies to read in private. Several, probably.

There was no sign of James or anyone he recognised, though Miles wasn't especially disappointed. After the awkward and uncomfortable morning at his parents', the feeling of being alone with Sadie – of being a team of two against it all – was warm and protective, a bubble he wanted to stay in for the rest of the day.

'I'll get us some drinks,' he said. 'Want to come?'

'I'll wait here.' Sadie looked around her. It was a good spot, right at the edge of the crowd with a clear view of the stage. There was a stretch of grass beside them, cables running down towards a generator, and then a copse of trees bordered the field. 'I'll keep an eye out for the others too,' she added.

Miles made his way to the closest refreshments stall and bought himself a pint and Sadie a Coke. He wandered back towards her, briefly considering a hot dog, and then saw a glimpse of a familiar T-shirt ahead. Neon green, the sleeves slightly too short – he looked at the back of the person's head, saw dark curly hair, and knew that it was James in his favourite (and ancient) Teenage Mutant Ninja Turtles T-shirt. Miles slipped into the crowd towards him, trying to keep both drinks from spilling as he shouldered his way through. The next band were starting, people edging forwards, and Miles lost sight of James once and then twice, finally surfacing into a gap a row or two behind him.

But then the person in the green T-shirt turned and it wasn't James at all – a man twenty years his senior, grey peppering his beard and the shirt itself plain apart from a small Adidas logo on the breast. Embarrassed, Miles turned away.

Scanning the crowd, he was surprised at the distance he had put between himself and Sadie; it took him a moment or two to locate her. She was still on the edge of the field but she had moved into the line of trees. He could see her head tilting the way it did when she was listening to someone – a friend, he assumed, presumably whoever it was that had recommended the festival to her in the first place. He took a step or two closer but couldn't see who was there in front of her, the shadows swallowing them and the crowd jostling Miles back towards the stage.

Sadie was saying something to whoever it was but, with a sudden pang of dread, he saw fear on her face. Saw her backing away from that patch of shadow, a hand clamped protectively over her stomach. Her face had drained of colour, her eyes wide like a child's.

13

Miles pushed through the crowd, his pint sloshing furiously in its plastic glass. The sun dazzled him as it came out from behind a wisp of cloud and someone's elbow caught him in the ribs as he shoved his way past, the band's opening chords shrieking through the speakers. He saw a flash of Sadie again, that slack-jawed fear still on her face as she stumbled back, and then the singer stepped up to the microphone and the audience surged forward and she was lost to him.

He pushed past a group of girls, tripping over a bag, and then, finally, he was out of the crush, the edge of the field ahead. He turned to his left and saw Sadie there, her back still to him, her attention on the trees in front of her. As he closed the short distance between them, he registered that she was alone again. He reached out, his hand clasping her shoulder, and she turned sharply, her face softening when she registered that it was him – though the fear (*it was terror*, a voice in his head corrected him; *ugly, uncontrolled terror*) in her eyes remained, her hand still pressed tightly to the place where their child was growing.

'Are you OK?' he asked. 'What just happened?'

She turned away, though not, he noticed, before casting another look behind her into the shadowy recesses of the trees. 'Oh, nothing. Drunk guy, you know what it's like. Come on. Let's go in a bit closer.' He opened his mouth to say something else but she was already moving, the now half-empty Coke taken from his hand.

It was not as if this hadn't happened before. Sadie was beautiful, Miles reminded himself as he followed her back

14

towards the safety of the stage; men often stopped her in crowds and bars. So why, he wondered, was his heart still pounding in his chest? He looked back at the trees again, now dappled warm and gold by the sunlight. He could see through them into the fields beyond. No one.

He glanced at Sadie. Her eyes were locked on the band, her head nodding slightly to the beat. She took a sip of her drink, her other arm still folded across her middle.

It was the way she had looked, he realised. She had been afraid, he had seen the terror pass across her face. The nakedness of it was perhaps what had frightened him so deeply, and yet it was more than that; it was something else that he had seen there too. It came to him as the band began their second song and he saw Sadie glance again at the trees: recognition. Familiarity. Sadie had been terrified, yes, but it was not as new to her as it was to Miles.

2

2018

The crew meets Amber Banner for the first time in her
hotel room in West LA. She's dressed in a plush robe,
her hair (mostly *her* hair) piled up in a knot on top of her
head. The covers lie tangled at the end of the bed, the
sheet exposed, one pillow drooping slowly towards
the dusky carpet. A room service tray sits in the middle,
a stack of pancakes sponging up their sugar dusting as a
plate of melon weeps pinkly. In the corner, two abandoned
plates – the syrup on them hardened, the cutlery akimbo
– give off a fetid, warm smell.

She sinks on to the edge of the mattress and sighs. She
watches them file in, edging round the puddles of dropped
dresses, the obscene crotch-up curls of tangled tights and
pants. The small table is heaped with gift bags and baskets
and flowers, cards scattered on the carpet below, the fruit
browning. She smiles.

The smile makes Greta feel like she is a child at the zoo, approaching the tiger's enclosure.

'Amber, I'm Greta. We spoke on the phone all those times.'

Amber considers her, head cocked slightly to one side. Her fingers fiddle with the cord of her dressing gown.

'You're young,' she says, finally. Her eyes caffeine-twitch back and forth across the two guys, the fluffy mic and the flopped-out reflectors. She waves a hand and Greta pulls up the marshmallow pink stool from the desk and sits down awkwardly, a sheaf of papers pulled out from under her arm and smoothed across her thigh.

'We were hoping to film you getting ready,' Greta says. 'I know you have a busy morning.' The car is probably waiting outside, the driver checking his phone while the studios Amber will soon be visiting start to whirr into life; lights angled towards stages, armchairs pushed into place, an eager audience cattled into a line outside as the sunlight spreads across the pavement. Breakfast TV: Greta's worst nightmare. She interned on a daily magazine show in London, back in the day, and managed to earn herself a paid running job after a month. She remembers calling her parents, at home in Michigan, to tell them – twenty-two, six months out of uni and a step closer to the career she'd said she'd have when she left them. She knew they'd never taken it personally that she'd swapped Dearborn for England at the first opportunity, but how good it had felt to tell them: yes, it was worth it. It's all going to plan. And if she skipped a few details about what the job actu-ally entailed (an endless cycle of moving furniture, moving

17

guests, getting yelled at, getting it wrong) then that was OK too. Because it *had* all gone to plan, eventually – and here she is, nine years and many jobs later, with Amber Banner staring back at her to prove it.

Her phone buzzes in her bag and she fumbles for it among the loose memory sticks, parking stubs, balled-up napkins and sticky suncream tubes. Amber watches her the whole time with a catlike disinterest.

Greta checks the message: Federica. How is she? Apologise for me. Can't catch a fucking flight.

It's 2 p.m. in London; Greta can picture Federica pouring two more coffees, her hand tangling in the hair at the base of her girlfriend's neck as she puts a cup down beside her laptop. Federica trailing out on to the balcony, anxious about the first week of the shoot – though not anxious enough to actually attempt to catch any of the many flights leaving London's airports over the next couple of days. Instead there will be these excuses, and it will be Greta who has to make sure things start smoothly, build all of the rapport. Greta who will have to try and chip away at the 'ice princess' façade that Amber Banner has adopted in the British media – the chilly calmness that has horrified so many – and find some hidden depth, some unknown truth on which to build their film.

Amber sits serenely as Tom leans in to check the light levels, his freckled hand hovering beside her cheek. Her eyes are clotted with last night's mascara but her skin is clean and smooth, barring some faint scarring on her left cheek. In the early morning hotel room light, her face angled away, she looks editorial-perfect. Greta remembers the photo of Amber that's tacked up over Federica's desk back in London. Printed out from a newspaper on to A3 paper, the image that has been shown on channel after channel, front page after front page over the last couple of months – Amber on the steps of the courthouse, her hair swept back into a demure ponytail, a crisp, collarless white shirt buttoned up below her elegant neck. The pop of flashes blurring the edges of the frame, hands thrusting microphones towards her. And that tight-lipped smile curling her mouth, her gaze at the camera defiant and unwavering. The ending of a story that has been splashed across the tabloids' pages – and the beginning of another.

'I have to be at the NBC studios in half an hour,' Amber says, yawning so widely that Greta can see the syrup-fur on the back of her tongue, the fleshy red sides of her throat. 'Yeah, it's OK if you film. I don't care about that stuff – you can film me whenever.'

Greta can feel Luca and Tom setting up behind her, Julia, their new production assistant, notable in her absence. Julia was another promise made and abandoned by Federica – another call she forgot to make, and by the time Greta got round to doing it herself, Julia had accepted another job and their flights to LA were booked for the following day. She, Tom and Luca will have to muddle through as a team of three; will have to spend the next five days permanently damp with sweat as they lug their equipment from location to location and try to keep up with Federica's endlessly morphing vision for the film.

She tries to get out of the way as Luca attempts to find a position for the boom which won't cast a shadow into shot. 'So, Amber,' she says, trying to free the edge of her flip-flop from the loop of bra-strap it's managed to catch on as she picks her way across the carpet. 'Are you still OK with the schedule we spoke about? OK to cover all those areas with us? I know it's not easy to talk about everything that happened.'

She can't help asking this, though Federica would be annoyed. Amber is legally an adult – just – and has signed her contract. All of this has been covered, by Greta, by Federica, by the network. But Greta can't help herself. She can't stop wanting to offer Amber an out, even when it's apparent that Amber is not interested in one.

'Are you still thinking ten episodes?' Amber leans over and touches a slice of melon, as if she might take it. Her fingers linger there, her eyes watching Greta.

'It depends how much material we have,' Greta says. 'Hopefully, yes.'

Amber pulls her fingers back. She wipes pink on to the dressing gown. 'Is my dad still saying he won't talk to you?'

Greta's phone rings, a welcome excuse for her to ignore the question of Miles. She slips out into the hallway and answers Federica's call just before her voicemail kicks in.

'How's it going? Is she OK?'

'We literally just got here. She seems fine. Happy.'

'Are you filming her getting ready, like I wanted?'

'Yes.'

'Great. Perfect. I love that – the idea of watching her put that public face on. I bet she looks a lot younger without the make-up, right?'

'Yes, kind of.' Greta's not sure she does. She's become so used to looking at images of Amber Banner, of reading transcripts and reports and opinion pieces on the things that she's done, that it's often easy to forget that she is an eighteen-year-old girl. An eighteen-year-old girl who was filmed laughing with her lawyer as she waited outside the courtroom. An eighteen-year-old girl who had reportedly signed with a talent agent less than forty-eight hours after being released from police custody. A girl first seen by the world in a blurry photo taken on a phone, her pale top sodden with blood, a smear of it drying near her mouth.

'Look,' Federica says. 'I know we've set out the schedule with her – and all that stuff's fine – but it would be good if you, you know, tried to get deeper. Throw her a couple of curveballs with your questions, try and catch her off-guard. Oh, also – when you have a minute alone with him, remind Tom that it'd be a good idea to leave a camera rolling now and again. When you guys are just hanging out with her and stuff.'

Greta chews her lip. 'You mean film her without her knowing?'

'I mean, when you put it like that, it sounds bad. Don't, like, hide cameras in her room or anything. But you know

21

how it is. Usually the best stuff comes out of their mouth just as you cut. So . . . maybe sometimes let her think you're done a little sooner.'

Greta is silent, the phone hot against her ear. The hallway, with its embossed wallpaper and striped carpet, seems to stretch on forever.

'Look, the thing is, Greta . . . There's more talk in the tabloids here about her book deal. Rumours of seven figures, although I'm not sure that's true. It's definitely happening though. And that's fine – a book's not a film. The book is going to be Amber's version, Amber's side – her *edited* truth. We've got to get something more. There's more to it than her version, I'm completely sure of it. And we've got to get it out of her if this is going to work.'

'OK . . . I'll try.'

'I'm sorry I'm not there yet. I know it's a shitty time to pull the "personal stuff" card, but this couldn't wait. I'll explain when I see you. And I trust you. I know you've got this. This is gonna be your big break, believe me.'

'It's OK. I hope everything's OK.' She flushes, embarrassed. The sound of Amber's laugh drifts under the door. 'I should probably get back in there.'

When she returns to the room, Amber is seated in front of the mirror, applying make-up while Tom films her. Luca has found a suitable position beside the nightstand, where American papers from the last couple of days are stacked along with British tabloids brought from home. Amber's arrival in the States has meant a fresh wave of press, the whole story recounted over and over. While the British media haven't always been kind to her – Greta remembers vividly a column in the *Mail* about the ways in which Amber Banner represents everything which is wrong with 'young people today' – the Americans, late to Amber-fever, seem to have taken to her and her terrible story, her tragic start in life. The magazine at the top of the pile has a photo of her arriving at LAX, head down, movie-star sunglasses on. *Amber Banner arrives in Hollywood!* Luca glances up at Greta, rolls his eyes.

She lets the ghost of a smile tug at her mouth and then moves away from him. 'So, Amber, are you looking forward to today?'

Amber shrugs, grinding a brush into an eyeshadow palette. She puts it to her eye without blowing away the excess and grey powder dusts itself across her cheek. 'Not exactly. But it's nice to be able to talk about things. Now the trial's done.'

'To set the record straight?' Greta hates the way she's changing her own voice, conscious that it might be used in the film. It sounds like she's reading lines even though she's feeling her way through this, trying to guess what Federica wants when Federica isn't even on the same continent.

Amber smiles at her in the mirror. Greta can tell how much Tom, behind her, likes that shot. He leans closer, lingers, and Amber seems to humour him because she pauses a moment too. And then: 'Exactly,' she says.

3

2000

Miles woke with a sense of dread, as he always did now. Funny, he thought, half-asleep, to be able to think 'always' about something that had only been happening for less than a week. But it really had only been that long; he could count the days in his head. Ten days since Amber had been born. Three since Sadie had told him that their daughter was cursed.

It felt often as though his life were on fast-forward; as though he had only blinked since that moment when Sadie had told him she was pregnant and yet now their baby was here. Now they were out of halls and into a tiny family housing flat a short walk from campus. And it had all been fine, it had all been exciting – those months with Sadie's belly swelling, one and then both scan photos stuck to the fridge with magnets; a picture of the two of them at the registry office in pride of place on top of the TV.

Cushions bought from a charity shop to brighten up the plain brown sofa, their dingy bedroom filled with stacks of tiny white clothes. He was doing well at his course, too, found himself waking up early each day to read, his favourite mug filled with coffee on the windowsill beside him, Sadie sleeping curled around his imprint in the bed.

And then Amber had been born, and everything had changed.

The first couple of days after the birth, he'd felt raw and jittery. There had been a moment right after Amber had been handed to him, Sadie's face waxy and pale, her blood pooling on the floor, when he had been convinced that he would lose her. An emergency transfusion after her emergency caesarean, Miles pushed out of the way with their baby in his arms. The violence of it all had shocked him, he'd felt its reverberations for days. The drained, haunted look on his own face surprising him each morning in the hospital bathroom's mirror. But Amber fed well, slept well, a thatch of fair hair covering her soft skull. Slowly, the anxious feeling of edging towards a sheer drop began to leave him.

Then, on their first morning back at home in their flat, she had said it. Sadie, propped up against a pillow to feed while a half-asleep Miles bumbled his way to the toilet, had looked down at her daughter and said *I'm sorry*.

He hadn't paid any attention then, but when he returned, Amber was lying on his side of the bed, whimpers working their way into a cry, while Sadie sat and stared at the corner of the room. He glanced over though everything was as they had left it – an old chair pushed aside to make room for the changing table, a stack of folded clothes abandoned on it. He looked at Sadie again, her gaze locked on the chair, her bra and vest top still peeled down on one side. Amber's crying got louder.

He'd said Sadie's name then, his heart thumping in his chest. The relief when her eyes flicked to him was overwhelming but short-lived.

'They'll come for her,' she'd said, though her voice was calm. 'She's cursed like me.'

And then she had looked down at their week-old daughter and back up at Miles. 'I'm sorry,' she'd said, and then she'd gotten up from the bed, Amber wailing now, and left the room. Miles had soothed the baby, listening to Sadie clanking pans around in the sink. When she'd shouted that she was going to buy milk, the front door closing behind her before he had time to reply, he had gone to the telephone and called his mother.

'It's a difficult time,' Frances had told (dismissed) him. 'You have no idea. She'll be fine.'

But she was not fine. Or rather, she could not be. For though she had not repeated the claim, he kept finding her studying the baby. He kept finding her checking the windows, deadbolting the door in the middle of the day.

Worst, though, was the whispering. It had happened only once (*that you know of*, a voice added unkindly in his head) but he found he could not stop thinking about it. Late home from his lecture, delirious with lack of sleep, he had let himself in to the sound of Amber crying again. Finding

26

her in the milky-stained bouncer, also bought from a charity shop, he had picked her up, the crying driving him half-mad within minutes. He'd thundered past the open bathroom door and burst into the bedroom. He'd expected Sadie to be asleep, was already annoyed with himself for being angry; already deflating as Amber abruptly fell silent, her small wet mouth nuzzling at his shoulder.

Sadie had not been in bed. Sadie had been standing with her back to him, a hand braced against the wall. Sadie had been stooped slightly, leaning over that same chair – and she had been whispering.

'*Not her*,' he thought he made out, although afterwards he would think that he had imagined this. He would think that he had imagined, for a second, the sight of not one but two shadows on their grubby, damp-speckled wall.

He had not imagined, he knew, the fury in Sadie's eyes as she turned and saw him there, and he certainly had not imagined the way she had slammed the bedroom door in his face – though five minutes later, when he was in the kitchen settling Amber with a clumsily assembled bottle of formula, it was as if it had not happened. Sadie had come into the room and begun chopping an onion and a carrot, ready for the shepherd's pie they'd agreed on that morning.

And so, yes, he had begun to wake in the night with a sense of dread. It felt familiar and almost comforting, an old friend, and so on that particular morning, he almost closed his eyes again and let it wash over him.

Instead he turned over, his hand flopping on to the cool

sheet on Sadie's side of the bed. The light in the room was feeble and grey and he could hear Amber beginning to stir in her Moses basket – but Sadie was not in her place, the corner of the duvet turned neatly back.

He got up, the dread beginning to swell into something more urgent. Amber began to whimper in her sleep but he left her in the basket, blinking hard to reject the last traces of sleep as he went out on to the landing.

He knew straight away, he'd tell them all later. He knew, he *felt* it. He went through with it anyway; he walked through the flat, listening to their baby's cries begin to spiral from disgruntled to distress. It didn't take long to see that everything else was still and silent, any trace of her already evaporating. The front door unlocked, her key left on the table.

It didn't take long to realise that she really was gone.

4

2018

At lunch, Amber presses her fingers into the teetering burger; the bread compliant, the blood torrential. She sinks her teeth in, her eyes meeting Greta's, gherkins crunching. She replaces it as she chews and both of them watch the cratered bun rise slowly back, a string of cheese stranded on the edge of the plate oozing on to the glossy wooden table. She seems unbothered by the camera – it could almost be that she's forgotten it's there until she turns to offer a chip to Tom.

'How do you think that went?' Greta asks her, pushing her own salad aside.

Amber shrugs, taking a long slurp of her soda. 'Everyone was really nice,' she says when she's done.

'Do you find it hard to talk about what happened like that? To keep raking it over?'

She picks up her burger again and considers it. Another

29

string of cheese slowly unfolds and begins its inevitable journey towards the table. The blood hits the plate with a slow ticking sound. 'No,' Amber says eventually, glancing at Greta. 'No, it feels good that I can talk about it now.' She shrugs again and takes another nip at the burger. 'This is amazing.'

Greta glances around the restaurant. Half-empty; the lunchtime rush an hour or so away. No paparazzi here, something she's grateful for at least. She knows Tom wants that footage. She can already picture it in the edit; probably in black and white, probably with Federica's voice-over. Maybe even slow motion; the camera flashes exploding against the tinted car window, the photographers' mouths stretching and closing as they call out to Amber, as she turns away. It might even be used on the opening credits.

Amber is watching her, a smile playing about the corners of her mouth. She can tell, Greta thinks. She knows Greta has no idea what she's doing. Both of them have been abandoned here, but only one of them is floundering. Amber leans back in the booth and yawns. Greta clears her throat.

'It doesn't ever bother you?' she asks. 'Being known? People stopping you in the street? Doesn't it ever feel weird that people know more about your early childhood than you do? People have written dissertations on it.' She's exaggerating – it's one person. One person who comments religiously on any online article about the Banners, who has their own website about the family and their story.

One website of several, true – but the only one that has a full-length thesis available for download. A recent research day also led Greta into the more unnerving world of Amber and Sadie Banner fan-fiction; forums and stories and whole novels posted online about the doomed mother, the cursed daughter and the Tall Man.

Amber laughs, and Greta's heart begins to quicken. Federica will like that laugh, short and bitter. She'll probably use that clip immediately after something from one of the talk-show interviews filmed this morning; one where Amber is sweet and extra British, one where the tears fall softly and snot-free. Probably the one where the presenter had to reach for a Kleenex herself, the make-up artist rushed on to stage as Amber left it during the commercial break. Yep, Federica will enjoy that, especially with the silence that follows now, Amber staring out of the window. The public and the private. The thoughts twitching beneath the surface of Britain's newest infamous face.

Britain's most in-demand murderer.

They drop Amber at her hotel, where she has booked herself back-to-back appointments at the spa. In the car, she grasps Greta's hand in the back seat.

'Shall I go blond? Like, proper blond. I was thinking, you know the kind that's almost silver? Kind of purpley white?'

Greta, her own highlights long neglected and sliding past her ears, makes a noncommittal sound. 'It's a cool look – a lot of upkeep, I guess.'

Amber's face wrinkles and she looks away, Greta's hand left to flop back down. When they pull up outside the hotel, she clambers out and cracks a bubble in her gum. 'See you guys in the morning?'

'See you in the morning,' Greta agrees, resisting the urge to tell Amber that new hair will make inconsistencies in the film, that it'll piss Federica off. Why not have new hair? she thinks. Why not piss Federica off? Amber is the only thing about the production that can't be planned or controlled and this, Greta knows, is beginning to frustrate the famous Federica Sosa. She saw it in the last days back in London, after Amber ducked a phone call or five from Federica, after a planned meeting was rescheduled twice and then cancelled. A celebratory dinner between director and subject quickly disintegrated after Amber drank four cocktails and announced she wanted to go dancing instead of to the fancy members' club Federica had planned. So it's no surprise to Greta that Federica's 'personal issue', of which there are many, has proven important enough to pass responsibility for this stage of the project to Greta. Greta, who needs this film to succeed and who, as far as Federica is concerned, has an excellent track record in managing (*manipulating*, a small voice suggests) difficult subjects like Amber (*they were not like Amber*, the voice insists, and she is forced to dismiss it).

Back in her own cheap motel room, ignoring the thumping of the headrest next door and the wailing of sirens collecting a couple of blocks away, she checks her email. Nothing new – which is, in itself, a new thing – but then it's evening in London, Federica probably pouring the first or possibly second vodka and tonic for herself. She rereads an email from Hetty, her housemate, sent yesterday and opened in the middle of the night when Greta couldn't sleep. As with all of Hetty's emails, it's straight to the point – a birthday dinner next week for their other housemate, Lisette. She types a quick reply agreeing; she'll be back in London by then, though she already knows she'll be pulling nineteen-hour days researching, reviewing footage, trying to help Federica find the mysterious *thing* that will make this film the seminal take on the Banner case, as well as being at all the shoots with Amber. She'll make time for the dinner, she tells herself. She's only lived in the houseshare for six months, while Hetty and Lisette have been there for three years together – it's nice to be involved in things. And it's important, she reminds herself. Important to have something *else*, something other than this. She's made that mistake before.

Email sent, she clicks into a new tab and opens the team's shared drive. Tom's icon is in the corner; he'll be working through the footage from the day. Meanwhile, Federica has added her own revised notes to the folder, her uniquely inconsistent version of shorthand finally – worryingly – comprehensible to Greta.

She can't quite bring herself to read them yet, so while she waits for Tom to upload their new material, she clicks through some of the earlier prep work done back in London. Folders and folders of notes and case studies, gathered by both her and Federica. Early interviews and recordings, police photographs. She flops on to her stomach on the creaky bed and loads one of the interviews Federica conducted, labelled correctly for once: *Garrett 23/02/18 FS.*

David Garrett looks as oily as his voice sounded when Greta called to schedule the interview. He fidgets in the coffee shop's plastic chair, the harsh white spotlight picking up greasy patches on his nose and forehead, dark patches spreading under the arms of his shirt.

'Tell me what your position was at the time of Sadie Banner's disappearance,' Federica says from somewhere beside the camera, no doubt two coffees in and fidgeting too.

Garrett clears his throat. 'I was detective constable and I was assigned the case after the officers responding to the call deemed the disappearance suspicious.'

'Can you tell me a bit more about your initial findings?'

'It wasn't especially unusual. No sign of a struggle or anything like that. Husband goes to sleep and wakes up to find his wife gone – not exactly something we've never seen before.'

'You thought she'd left him?'

'Initially, that was the general opinion, yes. She had taken a bag, some clothes.'

'And what made you decide that this might be something more sinister?'

Garrett shifts in his chair again, just as an email notification pops up in the corner of Greta's screen. She jumps, eyes skimming over the previewed text. Re: Your Recent Order with JustEat. She crosses it away, returns her attention to the video.

'Well, there was the fact that the baby was only ten days old. Initially, we were worried that Sadie might have been suffering from postnatal depression or postnatal psychosis, and that her personal safety might have been at risk.'

'That theory didn't last long?'

Another nervous cough – that will work well. They'll probably narrow the shot, let the frame close in on him. 'Well, we never abandoned it entirely,' he says, fiddling with a sugar sachet. 'But initial talks with the health visitor, the midwife and her GP didn't mark her as a risk in that respect. No warning signs, at least. And meanwhile, we . . . found other areas of potential concern.'

'Could you tell me about those?' Federica asks. Greta gets up and goes into the en suite to wash her face, letting the tinny voices drift through to her.

'Well, the husband became . . . a person of interest.'

'Why?'

'It seemed obvious very early on that he was holding something back. There was a certain . . . reluctance to his interactions with us.'

'You didn't think it was the strain of being left holding the baby?'

'Maybe at first.' Greta comes back into the room, rubbing her face with the gritty towel. David Garrett pronounces certain words strangely; she noticed it the first time she saw this clip. *Mebbe.* 'I'll be honest,' he says, finally abandoning the sugar packet. 'I was a hundred per cent sure that he was guilty. We just couldn't pin it on him.'

'You thought Miles Banner had murdered his wife?'

'Yes, ma'am. I would've bet my house on it.'

Federica lets the silence sit a little longer than probably felt comfortable, at the time, and Greta knows she'll leave it like that in the final edit, too. Let the audience in on the joke, let the moment swell. Finally, she releases him:

'It must have come as quite a surprise then?'

And Garrett is a good sport, he laughs. 'Well, yeah,' he says. 'I spend fifteen years of my career regretting that one murder I couldn't prove, and then the victim strolls back through her front door one day.'

5

2016

On the morning of her daughter's sixteenth birthday, Sadie Banner dressed carefully. Not too formal, but something nice, she had decided. Something to mark the occasion. She tried not to think of all the birthdays she had missed, all the times she had not written or even remembered (though this, she knew, was not true. She had *always* remembered). She tried not to think of all of the birthdays she'd spent mourning, afraid, alone (though this, she knew, was also not true. She had *never* been alone). She tried not to think of anything at all, as she often did, and she showered and dressed. Just as she was supposed to.

She made her way downstairs, bringing with her the glossy carrier bag of Amber's birthday gifts as Miles had asked her. The stairs creaked under her unfamiliar weight, alarmed. The house was often clear in its hostility. With every sticking door, every shrieking floorboard, she heard it: *Intruder*. She couldn't disagree.

She could hear Miles in the kitchen, the sizzle of batter hitting the pan. Pancakes, of course; Amber's favourite, she reminded herself, because over the last six months, knowing her daughter – her likes and dislikes, her habits, her catchphrases; it reminded Sadie of poring over *Smash Hits* to learn every possible fact about a favourite popstar – had become like an exam for which she was constantly cramming. She was finding that even the things that she did know were protean, could not be relied upon from one day to the next. For a while, when Sadie had first come home, Amber loved crepes – but now the pancakes had to be small and fat, American style. Everything she liked was American now: the labels she wore, the music she listened to, the shows she watched incessantly on TV and on her laptop. She'd even started to talk with a slight accent, just a twang, and Sadie couldn't tell if it was on purpose or if it had happened by osmosis from all the hours of *Gossip Girl*, *90210* (a remake of *90210*! How old that made her feel!) and *Pretty Little Liars* her daughter watched.

Her daughter. It felt strange to claim such a phrase, even in her own head.

The hallway floorboards creaked too as she made her way towards the kitchen, where Miles sang along to Frankie Valli on the radio. Sadie rounded the corner and saw him, his back to her as he flipped a pancake and gave the remaining batter a little whisk, his hips wiggling.

It was the first sunny day of spring and the light coming through the kitchen window was buttery and bright. He turned to slide the cooked pancakes on to the stack beside him and saw her standing there. He was dressed in his pyjama bottoms, his grey T-shirt spattered with batter, his hair sticking up one side. He was the only thing that had not, that never, changed. It had unnerved her when she first arrived, and still she found it difficult. For a second she could imagine that it was the first morning when she'd woken up in his room in halls and wandered out to find him in the kitchen, although that time he had been frying – burning – bacon, and his T-shirt had been spattered with Snakebite from the night before. She could imagine that none of what had gone between had happened at all.

But only for a second.

He smiled at her; he was getting better at that. Quicker, at least – the fear and the assessment that passed across his face each time he looked at hers more and more fleeting. She tried to smile back as he came towards her, spatula in hand, and kissed her – beside the eye, as if he'd dithered between her forehead and her cheek and left it too late to choose. 'Good morning,' he said.

'Morning,' she said, surprising herself by daring to slide an arm around his sun-warmed back; allowing herself to breathe in the sleepy, floury smell of him with its undercurrents of aftershave and sweat. He drew back, taking the bag of presents from her. 'I remember the good old days,' he said, 'when I'd have to stay up late figuring out how to wrap a pink plastic trike or a Barbie horse and carriage.' She saw him realise too late how this comment might be interpreted as a jibe and so she smiled again to release him from it. He set the bag on the table, taking his time to rearrange the individual parcels – MAC make-up and DVDs, a perfume costing what seemed to Sadie an obscene amount – so that they fanned out of the bag enticingly. Satisfied, he returned to the hob and ladled another dollop of batter into the pan.

It had hurt, of course, though she knew he hadn't meant it to. Reminiscing was not supposed to be a thing to be avoided; memories were supposed to be embraced, welcomed, sought, not jerked back from like solitary shards of glass sifted from an anonymous shoal of sand. It wasn't his fault that those harmless memories of pink trikes and plastic horses were not hers, that they filled her with terror. It wasn't his fault that she had abandoned the both of them. It wasn't his fault that she had come back.

She went to the fridge and looked inside, because that seemed to be a thing that people did in kitchens. She'd rarely cared about food when she'd been gone, had bought bread and junk food when she remembered, ate soup from cans most nights.

'I bought blueberries,' Miles said. 'She's still into blue-berries, right?'

'I think so.' Sadie took a blueberry and placed it on her tongue; popping it against the roof of her mouth. Sour. Sensations were starting to take her by surprise again. All of these superficial life *things*, suddenly switched back on.

She decanted the blueberries into a bowl with some raspberries she vaguely remembered buying two or three days ago. They were imploding, caving under their own ripeness. When she tipped them into the bowl, they left clots of themselves behind, the carton streaked viscerally. She took the bowl over to the table with a pot of thick Greek yoghurt, another of Amber's (temporary) favourites. Though it had been years since she had been young, when she watched Amber eat she had to bite down on her tongue or the soft insides of her mouth to stop the same words spilling out that her mother always slid across the table to her – *Better not eat too much of that Got to watch that figure You won't always look like that They do low-fat versions you know.* She knew Amber could sense those words held back. Not that this would be unusual; it often felt that there was a whole other dimension within this house: Things Held Back, a shadowy other-life where they conducted most of their internal family business, where they had filed the previous sixteen years for safekeeping. Amber had so far proven very good at playing along – but Sadie sensed it there, beneath the surface; a distrust, a building fury. There were two of them in this house now.

'Morning.'

Sadie felt a tensing around her heart as she turned. Her daughter stood in the doorway, wrapped in her fluffy dressing gown, flannel pyjama bottoms tucked into fuzzy Ugg boots. Her face in the morning always shocked Sadie anyway – it was so rare to see her without make-up, her eyebrows their normal blondish fuzz instead of painted on thick and dark, that it often took a minute to compute that it was Amber looking back at her. Looking back in that unblinking, impassive way Sadie was still not used to. Looking back with a face so similar to Sadie's that when they had first set eyes on each other that night six months ago, they had only been able to stare at each other. It sent a spike of fear through Sadie.

Amber's highlighted hair was scraped up into a lopsided knot on the top of her head and she yawned widely, fanning the air near her mouth in a showy sort of way.

'Happy birthday, baby girl!' Miles said, sweeping past Sadie to envelop Amber in a bear hug that lifted her off her feet.

'Thanks, Dad.' She rolled her eyes as he put her down, but it was affectionate in a way that Sadie was finally learning to read. 'Oooh, presents!'

Their daughter turned her attention to the bag of gifts, pastel paper drifting to the floor around her. She examined each item briefly, an occasional squeal thrown in, before it joined the growing pile on the table. They were all things from the list she'd printed off for Sadie a month ago – no surprises. Amber did not like surprises and Sadie felt she could hardly blame her.

When she was done, she glanced up at them and smiled. 'Thanks,' she said, and, to Sadie's surprise, Amber came to her first and hugged her tightly – *properly* – so that she could breathe in the flowery, slightly sweaty scent of her hair and the smell of her skin.

'You're welcome,' she said, vertiginously tearful, and then, 'Happy birthday.'

Amber had already moved on, was already stretching up to throw her arms round Miles's neck as she planted a kiss on his stubbly cheek. Sadie stood back, feeling strange and warm. When Amber chose to shine her light on you, however briefly, it was so bright it stunned. It left Sadie wrong-footed, like stepping from the sunshine into a dark room, her brain struggling to catch up.

'And now birthday breakfast for the birthday girl!' Miles said, proudly setting the plate of pancakes on the table with a small bow.

'Aww, thanks, Dad!' Amber loaded a plate, a furious stream of syrup upended over everything. 'Yum.' Forking a corner into her mouth, still standing up, she made for the door. 'I'm going to get ready for school.'

'Well, I thought—' Miles started, but Amber was gone, her plate spirited away, her footsteps thudding across the ceiling above them. The room felt curiously stagnant without her in it, even as Miles deflated into a chair and began forlornly forking pancakes on to his own plate.

'Coffee?' Sadie offered, and he turned to her and smiled. He was glad she was there, she realised, with a crushing sense of relief. She was there. She was there, and Amber was her daughter, and she was at home again.

Her parents were doing their best to look serious on the rickety plastic chairs, her dad leaning forward as if he didn't want to miss a single word Mrs Barclay said from the other side of her desk. Her mother had forgotten to change out of her decorating clothes and a blotch of white bloomed across one shoulder of her old shirt. Both of them were listening to her teacher with furrowed brows, lips pressed together – from the outside, it looked as though they were the ones in trouble.

Sadie watched them through the scratched glass of the classroom window, squeaking the toe of her shoe against the lino floor. The corridor was cool and quiet and so far she was alone. But a single strip light at the end of the hallway had begun to flicker and she knew she should keep an eye on it. She glanced behind her at the place where the corridor met another, its lights already off. The shadows were still – for now – and she returned her attention to the scene inside the classroom.

She could see the moment when her parents went from anxious to angry. They had come here expecting a fight or a broken bone and instead the 'incident' Mrs Barclay had referred to in her clipped voice had turned out to be this.

Sadie. The first whisper creeping up the corridor behind her. Sadie glanced at the flickering light again but it showed no sign of giving up. It soldiered on and the shadows were kept at bay. When she returned her attention to the window, all three of the adult faces inside were turned towards her.

In the car on the way home, her mother kept hitching her seatbelt forward so she could turn and look at Sadie.

'Feeling OK, sweetheart?' she asked, once or twice, and Sadie had to work hard to nod and smile instead of rolling her eyes.

They waited until dinnertime, though that was not unexpected. Anne and Robert Frederick preferred to let their problems fester in the hope that eventually, with enough normal life pressing down on them, they might moulder into nothingness. Into whatever it was that a family grew in.

But this, clearly, was too much even for them to ignore. Over their spaghetti bolognese, orange flecking her father's shirt and a tide of rejected carrot fragments slowly washing up against the edge of Sadie's plate, they looked at her again. The mushrooms she ate first, ignoring them.

It was Anne who finally decided to speak. Her fork

Phoebe Locke

going down with a meaningful thunk, Robert hurrying to
slurp up the mouthful of spaghetti he'd taken.

'What happened today?' she asked. 'You tell us your
side of the story.'

And Sadie carefully put down her own cutlery and
pushed back her chair. 'I don't remember,' she said, and
then she went to her room.

She did remember, of course. She remembered all too well,
lying in bed with both lamps and the overhead light on.
One of the lamps was new – a lava lamp bought from
the incense-scented shop in town where a curtain of beads
separated each tiny section from the other. Her mother
hated that shop, just like all the other mothers, but she
had taken Sadie there to cheer her up after her first filling
at the dentist (she had not once, as Sadie had expected,
reminded Sadie that she had told her so; she had even
bought her a cola-flavoured Mr Freeze on their way to
the appointment. It wasn't a blue one – the sky itself
would freeze over before Anne Frederick let her child eat
something coloured such an unnatural shade of blue – but
it was a victory nonetheless). Sadie had chosen the lamp
hastily, afraid that the offer might suddenly expire, and
now she spent hours admiring it, the soft globs of purple
drifting through the sickly pink.

The other lamp had been on her bedside table when
she was small – a china toadstool house with windows
cut out and a door left ajar so that light could creep out
when it was switched on. It had been abandoned under

46

her bed but recently she had found need for it even though she was too old to have a nightlight.

She lay there with the lamps on either side of her and the ceiling light with its dusty lampshade giving out its reliable warmth. The shadows crept in anyway. They leaked out from under furniture and crept across walls. The whispers snuck in between the rushed hushing of her own breath and she tried to tell herself that she could not hear.

Thinking instead of her abandoned dinner and her parents, in all likelihood still sitting silently at the table, she turned on to her side.

School had felt safe. It wasn't the same as going into the woods with Helen's hand in hers, Justine and Marie taking it in turns to tell stories of the Tall Man. When they were alone in the woods, wind whispering through the trees, it felt as though anything could happen. It felt as though he could step out from the shadows at any moment, take any one of them away with him. But the school, with its greasy windows and its rows of desks, was a normal place. No one was special there. She spent most days looking out at the playground and beyond, at the clouds scudding across the grey sky. Wondering if the stories could be true; if the things she sometimes heard in the darkness of her room at night were real. Wondering if she wanted them to be.

They were studying the Victorians this term, which she had quite enjoyed. Looking at old black-and-white pictures of women in bustled dresses, men with ruffled collars and hats. Imagining cobbled streets lit with puddles of weak streetlight, fog crawling round corners. Sometimes she dreamt of a tall house with steps up to its front door, a face that was not hers looking back at her from a mirror with curled golden edges. The clicking of heels down an alleyway, the smell of something sweet and awful.

There was no Helen at school that day – Sadie had decided she would call at their house on the way home to see if she was OK. Helen was often off sick; she seemed to attract every bug and cold that went round. But Sadie couldn't help wondering if Helen had started to hear her name being whispered from the shadows, too.

It was Tuesday, which meant Art, and Mrs Barclay had asked them to draw pictures of the factories and mills they'd been learning about using chalk and charcoal to shade in where the light could and couldn't reach. Everyone liked Art and for once it was quiet as the class leaned over their work. Dusty-fingered, the edges of the construction paper curling, their pictures emerged. Sadie sat and watched as smoking chimneys grew and crooked windows were etched in all around her but on her own piece of paper there was only smoke and shadows, a swirling mass that seemed to take flight every time she looked at it.

She put her hand up, straight and tall. 'I made a mistake,' she told Mrs Barclay. 'I want to start again.'

'Go and get some more paper,' Mrs Barclay had tutted. 'And be quick about it.'

At the back of the classroom was a door which led into a long, narrow store room. Cheap MDF bookcases lined the walls, stacked with art things and exercise books and the plastic zip-up folders they were supposed to carry their homework around in. Boxes of pencils and paintbrushes and clammy lengths of cobweb which clung to the thickly painted walls.

Sadie hesitated just inside the door. There was a single bare bulb in there, swinging gently in the draught from the classroom. Its white light calm and even on the poured concrete floor. The corners and the edges remained independent, their own shades of shadow; the light was too feeble to cast them out. When she took a step towards the bookcase with the stacks of drawing paper on its shelves, the door creaked closed behind her and the shadows grew.

She faltered for a moment but the mountain of paper was tantalisingly close and already she felt in her the thrill of creation. It had been this way for a while, the idea of making something or of writing a story a pull so powerful she found herself angry when, with paper and tools in front of her, the thing did not pour itself immediately out.

And so she forgot about the creeping darkness and came closer to the shelf. She chose a piece of paper that was a bit bigger than the others, picturing Mrs Barclay absent-mindedly sliding the guillotine's blade across its board over and over, the pages piling up at her feet. She forgot about the creeping darkness until the bulb blinked, once and then twice. Her hand slipped back from the shelf. She looked towards the end of the room, where chairs and an old, broken easel were stacked up against the wall. The darkness there was long and stretching, the light swinging wildly now so that the shadow of the easel towered over the floor and then crept back into its corner.

But it wasn't the easel's shadow that lurked in the corner, was it? Her heart stopped as she saw the shadow slowly detach itself, long fingers uncurling. A nose and a chin in profile, high, high up the wall – turning slowly in her direction.

The paper fluttered to the floor.

Listen, *said the voice. Sadie's hand stuttered across the shelf and found a pot of plastic-handled scissors. She was listening.*

She felt breath against the back of her neck, a shadow stooping down over hers. The light flickered and then, with a spark and a clap, it went out. Sadie, said the voice.

Sadie stood very still, feeling the darkness move around her. Don't be afraid, *she told herself.* You asked him to come, you asked him. *But as the breath fluttered against her skin again, she squeezed her eyes shut despite the dark.* Sadie, *said the voice again, and then cool fingers whispered across her cheek. She could hear the paper on the shelves fluttering wildly, the jars trembling.*

I can make you special, if you ask.

Sadie was not ready to be special. She tried and tried to keep still, but when the smooth, cold hand closed around her arm, she couldn't stop the scream from escaping. She couldn't stop her own hand, hot and damp around the scissors' handles, from lashing out, from striking hard into him as he held her.

And then the screaming was not her own. Then she opened her eyes and saw the storeroom door open, the room flooded with light. And Mrs Barclay was standing in front of her, the scissors with their green handles poking up from her doughy arm. Blood running in a slow, fat trickle towards her fingers with their chalk and charcoal stains. Eyes on Sadie, wide and watching and afraid.

And then Sadie had been alone again.

She wondered if she was alone now.

She stared up at the ceiling, listening to the silence of the house. And then she reached over and slowly, one by one, she turned out the lights.

6

2016

Sadie was early to everything now, determined not to be late or unreliable. While she'd been gone, time had been her own and something she rarely thought about; it was difficult now to adjust to its strict shapes, its unrelenting march. But she was trying. *If you're coming back*, Miles had told her that first morning, his face ashen with shock and his eyes swollen and bruised with lack of sleep, *You have to take it seriously. You have to be her mother*. And so she did take it seriously; she treated it like a new job in which she was trying to impress both her bosses. She knew that it would be a long time until her probation was over.

She pulled into the leisure centre car park at seventeen minutes to ten, seventeen minutes too early. This seemed reasonable, at first, not long to wait, and she settled back in her seat, listening to the cooling engine tick. There were hardly any other cars so late at night and the fir trees which lined the car park twitched and whirled in the wind. She sat in the car and listened to herself breathe. She tried not to look at the trees.

Twitch and whirl. The shadows stretched out in the orange streetlight; they reached out, unfurled. Dark shapes danced across the asphalt and took flight. The engine tick tick ticked, the seconds becoming elastic again. She closed her eyes. It didn't help.

She'd been surprised that Amber had agreed to Miles's suggestion of the charity disco for her birthday. It was for under 18s, which meant zero access to alcohol and Sadie had been certain that Amber would turn her nose up at the idea. But then Amber was not easy for Sadie to predict, not how she'd expected. Though the physical similarity of mother and daughter was undeniable, Sadie was pleased when traits belonging to Miles alone made themselves known in their child. She had noticed too how Amber was kind to Miles, humouring his suggestions even when they were obviously uncool or unexciting to her, and Sadie took this as a good sign. When she did catch a glimpse of herself flitting across her daughter's face, she tried to pretend that it was a trick of the light.

She opened her eyes and looked up at the building. When she'd left sixteen years ago, it hadn't existed – it and its car park had been another yellowing field. Now the town had crept out, in ways she was still noticing, whole estates of identical bright-bricked houses springing up in places she only realised had been untouched once she had passed them. Had she really expected to come back and find things unchanged? She wasn't sure now.

She still thought most days of the night she had arrived on their doorstep.

It had been late, later than she'd intended, and she wasn't sure if she was relieved to see a light on in the living room. She had brought nothing with her – this had seemed important. She'd seen the house before, of course, though she hadn't admitted as much to Miles. She'd had to check, had to be sure. She'd needed to know that it was just the two of them living in that house, that it was only Sadie who would be returning to it, no unwelcome guests accompanying her. She'd thought that it was finally time, that it was finally safe for her to go back to them – but she'd learned the hard way that it was important to be sure. The shadows had an unfortunate habit of returning to her.

Walking up the short drive, she'd taken in the car, the peeling, sun-faded unicorn sticker in the passenger window. A folder lay in the footwell on that side, curling hand-writing she did not recognise on its label: *D&T coursework* ☺ She remembered the way she had stood outside the front door, listening. The Sadie she had been wanted to keep on walking, to creep around the side of the house and look in through the windows – to see for herself, from a safe distance. Instead she had rung the bell.

Now, the automatic doors to the leisure centre jerked open, light flooding the pavement. Another car pulled into the car park, full beams cutting through the dark, and she couldn't help shrinking away, turning back towards the trees. Old friends were harder to leave behind than she'd expected.

The group of kids who'd spilled out of the doors slowly separated enough for her to make out Amber among them, arm linked through Mica's. Sadie was pleased with herself for remembering Mica's name. And there was Alisdair, too – Amber's other best friend. They had been a gang of three since Amber was at playgroup and it was important that Sadie remembered that.

She often wondered what they must think of her; the returned mother, the crazy woman back from the wilderness. She wondered what they knew, though she wasn't all that sure exactly what Amber knew, either. She had tried to ask Miles in those early days, wanting to understand how much he had explained to her about why her mother had gone – and, really, how much did Miles even understand? She had listened as he recounted his memories of that week in their tiny flat after Amber had been born, and at first she'd felt sorry for him. It must have been terrifying, especially for Miles, who'd been full of the positivity that only someone who'd lived an entirely happy and shadow-free life could maintain. She'd felt guilty at first, seeing how she had taken that from him. But as he talked on, she'd felt that familiar darkness rise up in her, her patience evaporating.

'I *had* to leave,' she'd found herself saying. 'I did it to protect her.' And he had been quiet after that.

The group were still lingering outside the leisure centre,

drifting slowly closer to the car so that Sadie could make out Amber more clearly. She had added details to her face that weren't there when she left the house: a dark lipstick, almost purple; a sharper contour to each cheek. She had also removed the shorts she'd been wearing, the tight black T-shirt just long enough to perhaps pass for a dress. If you weren't *really* looking.

Beside her was a tall girl Sadie didn't recognise. Dark-haired, head down as she talked eagerly to Amber, her arms folded across her front. Lilac jeans and a pretty, diaphanous white T-shirt; the kind of girly outfit Sadie knew Amber wouldn't be seen dead in. She watched the girl watching Amber as she spoke; Amber occasionally glancing at her or nodding to show she was listening, here and there leaning towards her with a giggle, a tilt of her head. Uninterested but not unkind. With a shy wave goodbye, the girl broke away from the group and climbed into the passenger side of the other car, headlights still full beam and blinding as it swung out of the car park and away.

Sadie watched her daughter's attention move idly back and forth between the boys trying to hold it. She posed for selfies with them, leaning back into someone's chest, laughing at another's joke. But there was a flatness about her as she did, and Sadie decided that Amber was not interested in any of them.

She decided, too, that her daughter was very aware that she was watching.

The boys grew bored and loped off in the direction of

town, until it was only Amber and her friends left. Mica and Alisdair and a boy Sadie did not recognise. He walked behind as they came towards the car and she couldn't get a grip on his features as the four of them passed in and out of the pools of streetlight. When they were close, Sadie's eyes met Amber's and it wasn't until the car doors clicked open that she realised the pack had separated; that they had surrounded her.

'Hey, Mrs Banner,' Alisdair said, sliding into the passenger seat.

Amber was the last to climb into the car. Behind her, the trees had begun their writhing again.

As they drove away from the leisure centre, Sadie could feel her daughter's eyes on her in the rear-view mirror. She reached up and pretended to adjust it. Pretended not to hear the slithering whispers from the back seat, the explosion of laughter like crows bursting from a tree.

'Thanks very much for giving us a lift.' Alisdair, comfortable beside her – one long leg crossed over the other, an elbow resting proprietorially against the door.

'Oh.' She found her hands running across the worn leather of the steering wheel, searching for the words as if they were imprinted there. 'No, not at all, that's fine.' When, after a while, the silence felt like cardboard in her mouth, she remembered to ask, 'Did you have a good time?'

Alisdair turned and smiled; a tight-lipped sort of conspiratorial smile, gone in a second so that she thought she might have imagined it. 'Yes, thank you,' he said, a polite, talking-to-a-parent voice returned. 'It was really fun. Thank you for buying our tickets.'

Sadie hadn't bought them. Sadie had a pitiful amount in her savings account, scraped together in ways she didn't like to think about now, and Miles seemed to find every attempt she made to contribute physically offensive, turning away at the earliest opportunity. She didn't want Alisdair (or Amber) to know that. 'You're welcome,' she said.

She watched the headlights slicing through the street ahead of them, the beams picking out the edges of cars and hedges before abandoning them to the dark again. She could hear the whispers in the back seat again; Mica, Amber and the boy whose name she didn't know or hadn't remembered. They prickled over her skin and she flushed, embarrassed. She felt like a kid, like she had been presented to Justine and Marie all over again and was trying her very hardest to say the right thing, to be what they were looking for. Like then, she didn't know what to talk about or how to talk to them; if she was supposed to talk at all. Did Mica's mother talk to them when she occasionally brought them home from school? Did Alisdair's dad linger in the living room when the three of them were there, watching films at his house; did he stand and chat and ask them things? Or were those parents seen but not heard, slipping easily from place to place as they cared for their children in as unimposing a way as possible? She didn't know. She didn't know how to fit in. She never had.

'Mum,' Amber said, the vowel drawn out and bored-sounding; the final 'm' tugged up by a laugh, quickly extinguished. 'You missed the turning.'

Her palms felt damp against the wheel now. 'Sorry,' she said, making an untidy three- and then five-point turn. She drove slowly, the beams hiding more than they showed, the shadows shifting and unwieldy. She wished she was at home. She couldn't remember which house was Mica's and the road was narrow, cars parked on either side.

'This is me,' Mica said, as if sensing her discomfort. 'Thanks, Mrs B.' She kissed Amber on the cheek and then stretched forward to Alisdair in a wave of expensive perfume and the sweet chalky smell of make-up, her nails blood-burgundy as they gripped the seat.

'Actually, I can walk from here too,' Alisdair said, and Sadie tried to argue but the sounds she formed were feathery and fleeting, a hand lifted weakly in protest. 'Don't worry, I can cut through the back there,' he said, the car door open and those long legs in their skinny jeans unfolding out.

When they were gone, the whispers in the back became softer, the giggles sharper. The boy had been sitting in the middle and he didn't slide into Mica's vacated spot. As Sadie turned the car back on to the main road, Amber bumped towards him with a laugh, her bare knees slipping sideways; her head tilted towards his.

Sadie wanted to stop the car. She wanted to get out and feel the night air bite into her skin, the early warmth of the day evaporated.

She didn't want to think about the woods, about

Justine's torn shorts or the clack-clack-clack of the charms Helen had threaded on to the spokes of her bike wheels. She didn't want to think about the Tall Man.

He can make you special, too, if you ask him.

'Mum.' Amber sounded embarrassed, no longer laughing. Sadie looked at the road and had no idea where they were.

'Sorry,' she said, weakly. 'Did you say something?'

'You missed the turning again.' Amber's voice was flat now. 'Ages ago.'

'Sorry, sorry.' She slowed, pulling the car into a dusty lay-by and swinging it into a slow U-turn. The road was empty and the darkness liquid. She avoided her daughter's eyes in the rear-view mirror. Amber slid away from the boy in the back seat and stared out of the window.

He spoke as she drew closer to the first turning in the road, the spidery hawthorn trees with their first white flowers catching the headlights like stars. 'It's the one after this,' he said, and his voice was surprisingly deep and languorous. 'By that streetlight there – see?'

'OK.' She tried to keep her voice easy, normal. She could feel Amber simmering behind her. She turned on to the dirt track, her headlights dipping as the car jolted, and followed it through the rape fields, the lights of the town to her left.

The farmhouse was low and flat-roofed, one light on at the front. Outbuildings crouched in the shadows and a single swing sat crookedly in the parched grass, its frame rusted and peeling.

'Thanks for the lift,' the boy said, opening the door (making his escape), but before he could get out, Amber reached out and grabbed a fistful of his T-shirt. She pulled him towards her and kissed him; not a long kiss, but a hard, unflinching one, and as she released him, her eyes slid sideward to meet Sadie's in the mirror.

When they were back on the road, Sadie said, 'You're drunk.'

Amber simply shrugged, alone in the empty back seat. Neither of them had thought to suggest she climb into the front.

Sadie tried again; tentative, on unfamiliar ground. 'You're too young to be drinking, Amber.'

Just a laugh this time; a small, bitter sound. Her daughter's face turned away from her.

Sadie relented. They drove on.

'Urgh.'

Amber rolled on to her back and pulled the duvet over her face. The sun was streaming through the window; she had forgotten to close the blind before she fell asleep. She lifted her head, glancing down at her body under the cool white canopy of the duvet. She had also forgotten to change out of her clothes. Or – she turned and glanced at the pillow; the ghost of her face smeared there – take off her make-up.

She lay back down and did a quick assessment. Mouth thick and a little furry; a faint taste of whisky lingering. She felt otherwise pretty OK, considering. She was fairly sure hangovers were a myth. Just another thing that existed only in her mother's head.

Eyes closed, she tried to go back to sleep. But now she was thinking about last night, running it over in her head. She'd had fun. Everyone had had fun. Hadn't they?

Mica and Alisdair had spent a lot of time together. They always seemed to spend a lot of time together lately. Plus there had been that throwaway comment from Alisdair about some gig the two of them had been to – Amber didn't remember receiving an invitation to that.

She knew exactly why it was happening. Since Sadie had come back, her two best friends had changed around her. It was like they expected something from her – like they were waiting for her to talk to them about how she was feeling about it all. Amber had no intention of doing that. That stuff was private, it was hers. If Mica and Alisdair thought she was going to start opening up about how sad it was to be abandoned as a baby, about how weird it was to suddenly call someone who was basically a total stranger 'Mum', they obviously didn't know Amber at all. And Amber couldn't shake the feeling that perhaps the reason they had changed was that they were too weirded out by the whole thing (and who could blame them?) or – worse – that they felt sorry for her. She couldn't bear that.

On the other hand, Alisdair had stolen the whisky from his dad's drinks cabinet for them. And Mica did buy her the black crop top she'd been eyeing up online for weeks.

She fished around under the pillows and found her

phone. She'd dropped it at a party a month ago and the screen was spiderwebbed with cracks, the photo of herself and Mica she kept as her background splintered from the centre. She unlocked it; a missed call from Alisdair a couple of hours ago, when he would have been on his way to his early shift at the bakery in town. She relaxed a bit more. Still number one.

She had a text too, from Jake – that was kind of a surprise, after how totally weird Sadie had been the whole car ride home. Sweet dreams followed by a blowing-kiss emoji. She rolled her eyes. So predictable. Delete.

There was a knock at her door and she flopped the duvet back off her face. 'Yeah?'

Miles poked his head in. 'Morning, baby girl. Can I interest you in some bacon?'

'Always.'

'I thought as much.'

'I'll be right down,' she said, and when he closed the door she got up and stripped out of her clothes. She pulled on clean pyjamas from the drawer, rubbed a baby wipe over her face and pulled her hair into a neater ponytail. She checked her reflection in the mirror above her dressing table. *Much better*. She knew Miles didn't like to think about her growing up. She often wondered if it was because she looked so much like Sadie. If he'd begun to think she might leave him too.

Downstairs, Miles had opened both of the kitchen windows and the sharp green smell of cut grass threaded through the greasy steam rising from the frying pan. A lawnmower buzzed somewhere down the street. Amber pulled out a chair and watched him as he finished the bacon, dressed in his old, threadbare robe with the splashes of bleach down one side. His hair wet and slicked back from the shower. He whistled along to an old song she sort of recognised on the radio.

'Madam.' He handed her the finished sandwich, made exactly the way she liked it: slabs of white bread hacked thick from the loaf, ketchup spilling out of the edges.

'Thanks, Daddy.'

He pulled out the chair opposite and started in on his own (brown roll, brown sauce), the paper open beside him. Its pages drifted up in the breeze every so often; fluttered back down each time it retreated.

'Where's Mum?' The word unfamiliar in her mouth, which was strange. It wasn't as if they had never talked about her. Yet now she was here, an actual person instead of a vague sort of nebulous concept, it felt wrong. Now that she was here and it was supposed to be normal – unlike in the first few days, when Miles had acted as if there were a unicorn sitting on the sofa and that any sudden movement or sound might scare it away – it felt odder than ever.

'She's not feeling great.' He looked at her and winked. 'She's only got herself to blame though.'

Amber glanced at the counter; a new empty wine bottle in a row of empty wine bottles, waiting for her dad to take them out with the rest of the recycling. There were always bottles there now and they always made her think of the nursery rhyme, sent it circling through her head. *Ten green bottles hanging on the wall.* It was usually in her mum's voice even though she knew she couldn't possibly *actually* remember Sadie singing it to her. *And if one bottle should accidentally fall.*

Miles glanced up. 'Oh, speak of the devil. Ears burning, honey?'

Amber looked at Sadie and then back at her sandwich. She wondered if Sadie was angry with her about last night – which seemed kind of hypocritical, with the row of bottles standing sentry on the side. The wind picked up; the paper's pages skittering up and over, the window sucked open with a shriek. Sadie went over to it and tugged it shut, followed by the other for good measure. The sudden silence felt loaded but then most of them did, in this house now, and so Amber carried on eating.

The fridge screamed next, its door tugged open by Sadie, who leaned against it for support as she studied the shelves. Miles met Amber's eye over the table and smiled. As if the two of them were the parents, the ones who knew better, and Sadie their teenage child. As if it wasn't completely obvious that it was Miles and Sadie now, that it always had been, and that it was Amber who was surplus to requirements. She dropped her sandwich back on to the plate and pulled the paper towards her, ignoring him.

Sadie, giving up on the fridge, poured herself a cup of coffee from the cafetière on the counter and sat down at the end of the table, leaving two seats between herself and the others. She wrapped her hands around the mug as if for warmth and looked tentatively at both of them before looking away.

'Well, this is nice,' Miles said, beaming at them both. 'Saturday morning breakfast with my girls. What a treat.'

Amber was annoyed with him and his optimism wore on her sometimes but it was also irresistible in its invincibility. She remembered making him cry once when she was a kid, the memory one of her most vivid. A stupid thing – Amber tired after a day playing at a friend's, Miles insisting that it was time for bed. *I wish my mum was here*, she had shouted and the words had hit him like a slap – she had actually seen the impact, his jaw dropping from the hurt. He'd turned away before she could see him cry, but she had heard the tears there, she remembered the sound of them clearly. *Go to bed, Amber*, he had said, and she had done as she was told. She had done what he had told her ever since, because the image had stuck with her, the starkness of seeing Miles's brave face, glass half-full persona slip the most frightening thing she could imagine. Miles was all she had and five-year-old Amber had been determined that she would not be the one to break him ever again.

And now she had come to treasure that optimism of his, to see it as special. Because, even in the face of everything, Miles actually thought that they could be a normal family again – and so maybe, eventually, they would.

'So how was last night?' he asked. 'Did you have a good time?'

She nodded. 'Yes, thank you. And thanks for paying.' She remembered to look up at Sadie too, and was curiously warmed by the surprise and pleasure on Sadie's face when she did.

Miles took a gulp of his coffee. 'So who turned up in the end?'

'There was me, Mica, Alis, Jenna, some of the boys from my class, and Billie came, she's really nice—'

Sadie leaned forward, her confidence growing. 'Is Billie the dark-haired girl? I wondered who that was.'

Amber didn't like this. *Stalker, much?* But she made herself smile. 'Yep, that's her. She moved here at the start of term. She's in our form.'

'That's a point,' Miles said. 'It's just her and her mum, right, Ams? I bet her mum doesn't know anyone in town yet, either.'

Amber cringed. As *if* he was trying to matchmake Sadie with some poor other randomer. 'I guess not,' she said, shrugging.

'Maybe you should go round there,' he suggested to Sadie, who didn't look like she was listening. 'That'd be nice. I'm sure she could use a friend.'

'Mmm.' Sadie took a deep gulp of coffee, staring out of the kitchen window.

'And what have you got planned for the rest of the weekend, Ams?' Miles reached out to dip his last mouthful of roll in a blob of ketchup that was congealing on Amber's plate. 'Much homework?'

She probably did; she couldn't remember. She wasn't

sure why she'd think of it now when there was all of Sunday and the ten minutes before she left for school on Monday morning in which to do it. 'Me and Alis are going out when he finishes work this afternoon,' she said. 'Is that OK?'

'Your grandparents are coming round tomorrow,' Sadie said, frowning.

'I *know*, that's why I said we're going out *this afternoon*.' Amber could barely stop her top lip curling in irritation. It was so transparent; Sadie trying to make a place for herself in the house by putting Amber into hers. And then there was Miles, across the table, practically humming with happiness. So she had to smile, she had to hastily soften the sarcasm in the words still hanging in the air. 'I'll help you guys tidy up when I get back. Maybe I could make those cupcakes Nan likes.'

'That sounds great.' She could actually feel Miles's smile without even seeing it; the warmth reflecting on her skin. He reached out and took her plate as he stood. 'Well, have a nice afternoon with Alisdair. I'm going to have to lock myself in the study to get these essays marked.'

'Thanks, Dad.' As he left the kitchen, she glanced at Sadie, who was staring out of the window again. They were not often alone, even now. Six months since that morning when Miles had woken her an hour before her alarm, kneeling by the side of her bed. Forcing the duvet back when she tried to pull it over her face. *Amber, you need to listen to me.* And then the creak of a chair in the kitchen below. And she'd known, she'd known even then, the electric weight of *knowing* jerking through her and pushing sleep aside. *Dad, who is that? Who's downstairs?*

Amber pushed her chair back and stood up from the table. She helped herself to a mug of coffee – maybe she'd been a bit quick to celebrate her lack of hangover – and then hesitated with the cafetière in hand, looking at the back of Sadie's head. She should ask if she wanted a refill, that would be a normal thing to do. Somehow she couldn't heave the words out.

She'd been excited at first, of course she had. It was hard not to be, with Miles practically jumping on the bed like he used to on Christmas morning when she was a kid. With her mum – her *mum* downstairs in the kitchen, waiting for her. Her mum had come back for her.

But then Amber couldn't help remembering why she had left.

Tuesday, 15 May 2018, 01:39 PDT
From: Greta Mueller
To: Federica Sosa
Amber invited to speak at *Glamour* event Thurs –
revised shooting schedule attached. Some good stuff
shot today. Her *Dr Phil* appearance is online now – not
sure about geoblocking but link below.

Tuesday, 15 May 2018, 02:13 PDT
From: Federica Sosa
To: Greta Mueller
What's she like?

Tuesday, 15 May 2018, 02:23 PDT
From: Greta Mueller
To: Federica Sosa
Guarded, mostly.

Tuesday, 15 May 2018, 02:25 PDT
From: Federica Sosa
To: Greta Mueller
Can't say I blame her. Has she spoken much
about the mother?

Tuesday, 15 May 2018, 02:28 PDT
From: Greta Mueller
To: Federica Sosa
A bit. I'm trying not to rush her.

Tuesday, 15 May 2018, 02:31 PDT
From: Federica Sosa
To: Greta Mueller
Pffft she should be used to it by now! Remember who
we're dealing with here. Don't feel like you need to get
the kid gloves out.

Tuesday, 15 May 2018, 02:32 PDT
From: Greta Mueller
To: Federica Sosa
Feel very conscious that she's only eighteen. I need to establish some kind of trust with her, I can't just start throwing questions at her. Otherwise I think she'll only shut down even more.

Tuesday, 15 May 2018, 02:33 PDT
From: Federica Sosa
To: Greta Mueller
Fine but don't be too gentle. We need that stuff.

Tuesday, 15 May 2018, 02:33 PDT
From: Federica Sosa
To: Greta Mueller
The pretty young murderer thing is all v well but it's been done. The other stuff is way more interesting.

Tuesday, 15 May 2018, 02:34 PDT
From: Federica Sosa
To: Greta Mueller
This isn't about tabloid horror, it's about a haunting. You get that, right?

Tuesday, 15 May 2018, 02:35 PDT
From: Federica Sosa
To: Greta Mueller
That's a great line. Remind me to use that.

Tuesday, 15 May 2018, 02:38 PDT
From: Greta Mueller
To: Federica Sosa
Sure. I think it's going to take some careful handling to get her to talk about Sadie or the Tall Man in any kind of meaningful way though. Whenever interviewers here have asked about it, she's been pretty wary. Like she's afraid of saying too much.

Tuesday, 15 May 2018, 02:38 PDT
From: Federica Sosa
To: Greta Mueller
She must know that's what they want to hear about though.
You think she's saving it all for the book?

Tuesday, 15 May 2018, 02:41 PDT
From: Greta Mueller
To: Federica Sosa
I think she's afraid that if she says she believes in the Tall Man, she'll be written off as mad – but if she says she doesn't, maybe the press will lose interest.

Tuesday, 15 May 2018, 02:43 PDT
From: Federica Sosa
To: Greta Mueller

That makes sense. And that's another reason we've got to find that way in with her. Whatever it is – we need to be the ones she trusts. The ones she finally opens up to. I'm watching that interview you just sent and there's just this thing about her I can't put my finger on. There's more to this, I know it.

Tuesday, 15 May 2018, 02:45 PDT
From: Federica Sosa
To: Greta Mueller

It's like she's not even *glad* she got off.

Tuesday, 15 May 2018, 02:47 PDT
From: Greta Mueller
To: Federica Sosa

Is that surprising? It would have a horrific effect on anyone, surely. Even if she didn't deserve to go to prison for it.

Tuesday, 15 May 2018, 02:49 PDT
From: Federica Sosa
To: Greta Mueller

Call me a cynic but I don't get guilty or scarred from
her. I get a total blank. No emotion.
She's completely chilling to watch.
It's going to be perfect.

7

2016

They made it through Sunday; through Miles's parents. This was the fifth time they had visited since Sadie's return, and it had, she supposed, got a bit easier. Relatively speaking, anyway. John and Frances Banner had never been particularly fond of her – the girl who had gotten pregnant at nineteen and trapped poor old Miles – and her mother-in-law's fury at her abandonment of her family was only eclipsed by her fury at Sadie's return. Who could blame her? Sadie didn't. She had no idea what Miles had told them about any of it and he always dodged her questions. *It doesn't matter what they think*, he kept saying. *This is about us. The three of us.*

Poor old optimistic Miles. Already, to him, they were a three again.

She hadn't known what she would find when she returned. She'd spent a long time thinking, researching, checking. She'd felt sure that Amber was old enough to be out of danger. But deep down, a small voice had wondered if leaving would have saved her at all – and another part of her (quieter and tucked away) wondered if the danger had ever even existed. If the warning she had been given that first week of Amber's life had been a lie.

Don't. Don't think of the girl.

The little girl, sitting in that chair in the corner of the room. The baby sleeping in the basket beside the bed.

She stood up. She was not to think of the girl.

She went upstairs to seek reprieve and the memories were indeed quieter up there. In the hallway, she looked around at the walls with their pinstriped paper, the finger-streaked mirror above the stairs. There were photos – mostly of Amber, but of Miles as well, and she studied them, as she had before, in an attempt to understand all the things that had happened while she had been gone. She studied Amber's face and tried to see in it something she recognised—

The little girl said . . .

The little girl lied, she told herself. They all lie.

It didn't help. She saw again clearly the night she had finally left that flat, Amber only ten days old. Miles snoring beside her as the floors and walls creaked, the shadows creeping closer. The baby kicking her legs in the Moses basket and Sadie lying on her side to look over the edge of the bed at her. So small – it had always taken her breath away. So quiet too, lying there, eyes wide open and gazing back at Sadie like she was the sun or the moon. Feet scuffing the little mattress, the tiny fingers on the hand tossed carelessly up beside her head slowly curling inwards.

And then in the corner of the room, another small scuffle.

A whisper of a giggle.

She had sat up and the girl had been there again, just as she expected. Sitting on the chair – it was too tall for her, her feet in their clunky old-fashioned shoes and their lacy socks swinging back and forth above the ground. Her hair had come loose from the daisy clips on each side, curls falling round her face, and her skin was pale and waxy, a smudge of mud across her cheek. Her dress stained dark. Sadie had known what she would see if the girl turned round. She'd tried to keep her pinned with her gaze, begged her silently. *Don't turn round.*

'The Tall Man takes daughters,' the girl had told Sadie, as she had done on her previous visits, but this time, she'd looked sadly at the Moses basket beside the bed.

'Please,' Sadie had said, and the girl returned her attention to her, those pale wide eyes in that bruised-looking face. Sadie had heard a scratching sound coming faintly from somewhere in the flat.

'The Tall Man takes daughters,' the little girl had told her, Sadie already moving away from the bed, away from Amber. 'But sometimes he needs help.'

The words echoed in Sadie's ears now as she stood in the hallway of the house her family had grown up in without her, looking at the photos of the life they had lived in the years she had been away. She had heeded the girl's warning, she had left Amber safely with Miles and led the Tall Man and his shadows away. So why, then, did it feel like this house was still heavy with them, that eyes watched her from every corner?

In a fit of movement – sometimes she thought that if she moved quickly, she could surprise the house into obedience; ward off its hostility – she reached up and tugged the pull-cord of the loft hatch, the door flipping down and the ladder sliding neatly into place.

She climbed halfway up and then went back down, into Miles's study, for a torch. There could be electricity up there, she hadn't thought to ask. She would not chance it. She could not risk the dark.

Clambering into the hatch, she sat on the edge for a minute, letting her eyes adjust. Enough light filtered up from the hall to pick out shapes; old and broken furniture stacked up against the walls, sheets cast over some of it. She clicked on the torch, the beam bouncing through the dusty dark. It couldn't reach the corners, the shadows pooling and impenetrable. She felt as if they were just there, just out of sight. The Tall Man and his girls. Waiting to step out into the light, if only she'd let them. She flicked the torchlight away.

Against the opposite wall were boxes, neatly piled in rows. All of these things that she hadn't had to think about – school books; Christmas decorations; fancy dress outfits – labelled carefully and stacked away, all these building blocks of their past for her to unpack and understand. It was disheartening and for a while she sat and looked at them, her legs penduluming back and forth without building the momentum to carry her on.

Was that someone else breathing somewhere in the dark? The small, snuffly breaths of a child, perhaps, steady and wet. She waited for the trip-trip of small feet across the bare boards. She waited for the small tinkle of a laugh – because there was always that laugh, its silvery notes seeking her out.

She waited. She did not turn around.

A creak of a floorboard behind her, that flutter of breath again. Soon those small fingers would reach out, close around her arm or shoulder, the giggle spilling into her ear—

She jerked round, torchlight dancing over the rafters.

But there was only silence, only the shadows – and the shadows were still.

She turned back and looked again at the labels on the boxes, reciting them under her breath. *Papers – Miles. Trophies – Amber. Doll's house. Doll's house furniture. Clothes – Sadie.* She stared at that one for a moment or two. Taped up inside it was a whole different Sadie, one who had existed only briefly, and she often felt desperately homesick for her, as if that person was a flat she had inhabited until whoever had rented it to her had decided they wanted it back. She knew that box would hold countless band T-shirts and strappy tops, lumberjack shirts, denim skirts and several pairs of combat trousers. A studded belt, perhaps even a crusty old tube of hair mascara. She wanted to spread them out on the floor and lie down on them, breathe in their smell of damp laundry room and spilt lager.

Except that now they would just smell of cardboard and dust. She had abandoned them, like she had abandoned Miles and Amber, and they had collected the smells of a life lived ordinarily.

And now she was back.

She averted her eyes, letting them rest under a bike frame without wheels. A small, crouched shadow wavered there and reflexively her hand turned the torch in its direction. The light picked out the edge of a face, a face turning towards her, its eyes downcast, mouth opening—

She held her breath. Counted carefully in her head as she waited for it to unfold, to take its first steps towards her. It melted back into the dark and she let herself exhale, the hairs on her arms prickling.

She moved the torch's beam on to a sturdy white documents box. *Photos*.

She stood and made her way over, balancing carefully on the beams. The box was lighter than she expected and she sat down on the edge of a beam with it, the torch forgotten by her feet, the need to see inside suddenly urgent and animal. She tore off the tape and abandoned it, half-balled, beside her.

The photos were loose for the most part, some of them still in their lime green paper wallets, a couple even in an envelope with the old pharmacy's logo on it. Lots of them had spilled out, a leaf litter of faces on the bottom of the box. It would take time to sort through them all.

There was a whispering from the shadows behind her, though when she turned she saw only a doll's house, a wooden chest engraved *Toys*. More of the Amber she had left behind, the Amber she would never know. All of these things whispered, she realised. It wasn't only the shadows that had their secrets to hold.

At the top of the box of photos was the album. She lifted it out gingerly, holding it carefully on her lap. A white canvas cover, yellowed with age. On it, a pram made of pink gingham cotton; two ducks of yellow corduroy. And the words, sewn in loose cross-stitch: *Our Baby Girl*. She held it to her face, breathed in its dusty scent.

A floorboard creaked, a slight shifting of weight. She was disturbing things she should have left settled, she knew.

She flipped open the cover, a cheap, thin cardboard thing. The album itself had been bought from a newsagent's in town when she was four or five months pregnant, not long after she'd dropped out of her course. When she was feeling defiant. In denial. She'd been sure that it was a beginning for her, a new start. A new person to be: Sadie Banner, a wife and a mother. Someone who lived in the light. She'd truly believed, then, that she could do it. She'd ignored the fear that crawled through her at night, the dreams that still came, leaving her damp with sweat and short of breath. They were easier to silence when she woke to Miles's body pressed close to hers, their baby turning inside her.

The plastic layer over the first page had bubbled with

heat or age, or was never even laid flat in the first place, and blisters had formed over the image. A picture of herself, heavily pregnant, sitting up in bed. She remembered Miles behind the camera, lying on the mattress beside her, the camera angled up so that her belly looked moun-tainous, her face unflatteringly wide. So young; so *young*. She couldn't get over it, tracing those round cheeks with a fingertip again and again. Twenty years old but in her shapeless T-shirt, her unmade face, she could have been even younger. *One week overdue!* was scrawled beneath the image in her own handwriting, although she couldn't remember sticking this in, labelling it. She found herself looking into the corner of the picture even though she knew that nothing had lived there then, that her hopes were still alive and that the flat had been theirs, just hers and Miles's, for a few sacred days longer.

She turned the page and her breath caught in her chest. Her own face again, that same smile. A paper gown, hair in a plastic cap. The bed a hospital one; her arms, held in front of her in a double thumbs-up, laced with tubes, cannulas, medical tape. An emergency caesarean after thirty-six hours of contractions and yet she was smiling. *Stupid*, she told the photo. *You had no idea.*

And then, on the opposite page, as if by magic, was Amber. On her back in her hospital cot, legs frogged up by her sides. It took her hours to unfurl, Sadie thought. Hours to accept that she was no longer in the womb, that she was open and exposed and could move. Her face in the picture was pink and clean, eyes closed and fists balled up by her ears, dressed in the pale yellow baby-gro Sadie remembered picking out for her. No immediate post-birth shot for them; no arty black-and-white images of the surgeon pulling her free, gore-streaked and screaming. None of Amber, purple and fuzzed white, against Sadie's chest. Just her, tiny and alone in the plastic cot.

The Tall Man takes daughters, she thought. And then: *Stop*.

She looked at the photo on the opposite page, taken a day or two after they had come home from the hospital. Miles and Sadie walking through the meadow near their old house, the riverbank behind them. Amber in a sling on her front, Sadie's hand protectively cradling her tiny head. Miles facing the camera, hands clasped in front of him, that photo face he made sometimes – a small, thoughtful smile, chin tilted slightly up. Sadie was half-turned away, her arm obscuring the baby, her face glancing back over her shoulder with her hair caught in a sudden gust of wind, revealing the grey collar of her fleece, a slice of sun-starved neck.

His mother took that one, she thought, or perhaps his father; they had shown up uninvited the minute Miles had pulled the car up outside. Looking at the photo, she was sure she could remember the irritated call – *Smile!* – the wind whistling past them and the baby an unbearably light weight against her chest.

The Tall Man takes daughters.

That little girl voice whispering close beside her in the dark. Warning her.

She turned the page and kept on turning. There was Amber, legs finally flexing out, feet kicked stiffly up, her body tiny in the swamp of their bedclothes. There she was balanced on Miles on the sofa, her back against his chest, her tiny fists held out in a cheer by his huge hands. And there – Sadie's fingers, slick with sweat, traced the page – on her belly on their terrible threadbare old carpet, palms pressed down, eyes wide and goggling at the camera.

She was gone by then, she knew. She was gone, taking the shadows and their voices with her, just as she always had, leaving Miles to take these pictures, to care for this hopelessly small person all alone. The only shot of him after that was one taken at a party somewhere, Amber in the sling on his front now. His face drawn and shadowed, a hollow sort of panic in his eyes. She turned the page quickly, afraid to look at him for too long.

The last photo in the album was of Amber on her first birthday. Standing up, her hands gripping the edge of the coffee table, a cake in the shape of a 1 in front of her. Sadie remembered that day. She remembered sitting in the mildewed bedroom she had rented, crying, turning out the lamp to let the shadows claim her. She looked again at the daughter in the photo, and then she closed the album and brought her knees up to her chin, pressing her forehead against the cool linen. She breathed in the dusty smell of it again as if there might be something of her left there.

Around her, the shadows began their whispering once more.

8

2018

Greta shifts uncomfortably in the motel chair, her laptop
balanced on the arm. Headlights from the freeway outside
flicker through the crooked blinds and across the wall,
the air-conditioning humming irritably to itself. It's 3.45
a.m. and the first streaks of blue are appearing at the base
of the dark night sky, the motel blissfully quiet.

She clicks on to another page, downloads another interview from the shared drive. She picks up her headphones
and pushes one pod in, reaching for her beer with the
other hand. *Just this one*, she tells herself. *One more and
then bed.*

The woman's voice that fills her ear is soft, though it
catches on some of the consonants. Smoking or a cold;
maybe crying unrecorded. Federica conducted this initial
interview herself too, which is unusual – it means she
probably thought the chances of it being included in the

final cut were high. There is some introduction, though not much, and the clip is currently audio only, which means the woman does not want to have her image included in the film. Federica might make Greta or one of the other women stand in; film them in shadow, their faces turned away, and add in the audio later. More likely she will have filmed the woman's hands, perhaps her feet, and she will fill the screen with them and all their tells; the small movements and tensions that will underline or belie a sentence.

'And that's when you started to have the thoughts?' Federica asks, her voice closer to the microphone but respectfully low.

'Yes.' The sound dips; then there's a scraping noise, as if Federica is adjusting the position of her recorder. 'At first I'd catch myself thinking about the bad stuff that could happen, you know? I'd imagine myself dropping him or forgetting him.'

'And then they escalated?'

'Yes. I started thinking that he would be better off without me; I was sure of it. There were voices there, all the time, telling me to do the right thing and leave both of them behind.'

Greta clicks back on to the tab where she has the team's shared drive open, looks at this folder with its list of similar files, video and audio, named simply after their interviewee. All of these women, all of these stories. All of these beginnings that unravelled.

'And when were you diagnosed with postpartum

psychosis?' Federica asks, and as she does, Greta's phone vibrates; real-time Federica requesting an update. It's 11 a.m. in London; Greta can picture her with her second grande Americano of the day, her wide, flat feet up on the desk, shoes kicked off under it. She sent a message five hours ago, to Tom and Luca as well as Greta, announcing that she wouldn't be boarding a flight today either. Have to sort things out here. Am totally confident you guys have this under control x

Greta isn't so sure. And by the number of instructions and requests for updates Federica keeps sending, neither is she. Greta flips the phone over on the tiny side-table, tucks her own feet up under her.

'Right then,' the woman is saying. 'As soon as my partner persuaded me to go to the hospital. They knew right away. They got me the help I needed.'

Greta closes the file, looks again at the unedited footage of Amber that Tom has uploaded from today. That wry look; the weathered reaction to her mother's abandonment of her – to the way Sadie re-entered their lives and everything that came after that. The simple, flat way she spoke about it. *Can't say I blame her*, Federica had written, and Greta had thought she agreed. If she were in Amber's place, she imagines her own barriers might be on lockdown – the reality of what has happened too huge to process, the blame and the guilt too big to assign or accept. Federica sees Amber's blankness as something sinister but Greta is starting to wonder if it is instead deeply sad; a teenage girl failing to come to terms with the terrible legend her mother has left for her, with the dark and dreadful one she has created for herself.

Greta has always been resistant to the idea of analysing Sadie Banner's actions in their film, sees only danger that way. As the days pass, Federica is increasingly eager to dig up everything she can about her. About the things she said she saw, about the places she went after she left her family behind – and what might have made her decide to finally return. Greta knows that Federica is only doing this because they aren't getting enough material from Amber herself; the no-holds-barred, all-levels access they were promised so far amounting to being allowed to film Amber getting ready in the morning, being driven places, occasionally watching herself on pre-recorded TV appearances. Amber seems to imagine the documentary as her very own reality show, an exploration of her newfound infamy, and has so far shown little interest in exploring the story that brought her to this point (*why would she?* the needling voice at the back of Greta's mind asks her. *Would you?*). Federica has made it clear over her last few calls and emails that the team have to push her harder, get her to give them more – and yet Federica has no suggestions as to how Greta might do that.

Federica has given herself the task of privately researching Sadie Banner online and in libraries; no paparazzi, no autograph-seekers or talk-show hosts in sight. Greta trusts the instinct – she has to. Federica is an award-winning filmmaker, a woman famous for finding the story others cannot. But Greta can't help feeling guilty each time Amber offers her a chip or a sweet, each time Amber asks what Greta thinks of an outfit or her nail colour. Amber thinks their attention is on her but behind the scenes, across the Atlantic, the team are digging around in things they expressly promised they would not.

And yet as the morning draws closer, Greta can't stop herself from leafing through the photocopied pages that Federica has marked up, the things people have had to say about Sadie Banner and her voices. She listens to the stories of other women, she reads the notes on postpartum psychosis from therapists and physicians. And she thinks: *How could anyone ever have thought it was that?*

'Don't be such a baby.'

'Yeah.' This, from Helen, was particularly hurtful. 'Don't be such a scaredy-cat.'

The trees lurched out of the dusk again, their fallen leaves shivering in the breeze. Autumn had come early and the girls' visits to the woods had become more frequent. Sadie looked around at the creeping dark and wondered if she should go home.

She often wondered this. She never actually did it.

The things that the Tall Man wanted seemed to vary. Marie had heard that the Tall Man liked gifts, and so each afternoon after school, they gathered at a small clearing in the scrappy woods which Justine said was one of the Tall Man's special places. They buried pennies and sweets and Helen, who was particularly afraid of the Tall Man, buried her Kylie Minogue cassette.

And each time, they turned to Justine. 'Is it enough?' they asked.

And Justine would yawn or scratch at an elbow or fiddle with her hair. 'For today,' she would say.

But on this day, she simply shook her head. 'No,' she said. 'I don't think it's enough. I think the Tall Man will be unhappy with us.'

And Sadie saw the way that Marie glanced at Justine, that tight smile of hers disappearing.

'I want to go home now,' Sadie said, glancing around at the darkening woods.

Justine looked her in the eye and then leaned closer, her breath a warm blast of Peaches and Cream, the lollipop in her hand sucked down to a pip.

'Don't be such a baby,' she said again. 'Don't you want to be special?'

Sadie bit her lip and didn't reply. She hadn't told the others about what had happened in the art cupboard, or about the voice that had begun to speak to her. Justine had told them proudly that the Tall Man had visited her one night, and Sadie had felt a pang of jealousy. She had thought she was the only one.

Helen sat down on the edge of a tree stump, her breath wheezy. She'd been off school for two days that week after a bad asthma attack and had only been able to persuade her mother to let her out to play with the promise that Marie would be there 'to keep an eye on her'.

'Do you think the Tall Man will take Yasmin Hunt if we ask him?' she said. 'I hate her.'

'Jenny Hunt's little sister?' Marie wrinkled her face. 'There's no way he'd want a spod like that.'

'Isn't that the whole point?' Helen asked, arms crossed. 'He takes the rubbish ones away, and he makes the good ones special?'

'He takes away the ones who are bad,' Marie said. 'But he'll hurt the people who hurt his special ones, too.'

'Look at this,' Justine said, crouching down to open her school bag. 'I bought it off this boy in Year 9.' She pulled out a rolled-up magazine, its back page torn. She smoothed it out and Sadie caught a glimpse of the cover – an illustration of a woman in old-fashioned underwear running down some stairs, glancing over her shoulder at a figure in silhouette behind her. 'It's a couple of years old,' Justine said, flicking through the pages. 'But it's really cool.' She found the part she was looking for and handed it to Marie, the others crowding round to see.

The double-page spread was creased, another tear in the corner of one side. There was a second illustration, this time of a girl in bed, the covers pulled up under her chin. At the foot of the bed, a jagged black figure loomed up, sharp fingers reaching out for her. Terror Comes to Town read the title, but Helen pushed closer, her elbow knocking Sadie out of the way, and she couldn't make out the smaller print of the article itself.

'It's about some town not that far away from here,' Justine said, watching her. 'In the seventies, a load of kids all started having the same nightmare. Well, all the adults thought they were nightmares. The Tall Man visited them in the night and asked them to come with him. But get this, right? Sometimes when he visited them, he had other *children with him. And this article says that the kids they saw fit the descriptions of actual missing children.'*

'"One of them was twelve-year-old Pauline King,"' Marie read aloud. '"Several of the children of Stow-on-the-Wold described seeing Pauline in their dreams, hand in hand with the Tall Man. Pauline had been missing since the previous Christmas, when she was last seen by a member of the public leaving her school with an unidentified man. Pauline has never been found."'

Sadie shivered. Where did he take them – and would he take her? Or was she good enough to be special, to be protected? She glanced down at the rough pile of earth and leaves where they had buried their latest offerings, and then back at the cartoonish illustration in the magazine. Suddenly they seemed silly and small and not nearly enough.

'That's so creepy,' Helen said, wiping her nose on her sleeve. 'Maybe I don't want him to take Yasmin Hunt after all. Even she's not that bad.'

Justine shrugged. 'I can think of plenty of people who are that bad. I've got a whole list of people I'm going to ask him to take.'

Helen had taken the magazine from Marie and brought it close to her face, eyes flicking back and forth across the words. 'I don't want him in my dreams,' she whispered. 'How can I stop him from getting into my dreams?'

And even though Justine was answering her, she looked at Sadie again as she spoke.

'Isn't he already there?'

9

2016

Sadie hadn't expected it to be this way.

Her daughter was indifferent to her and her husband was keen to pretend that nothing had ever happened. There was all of this making up to do, yet no one seemed keen to figure out where and how that could begin, other than for her to just, well, be there. Play her part. Wait for the cracks to gradually dissolve by themselves. She was good at waiting, she'd had to be. But this, suddenly, felt entirely wrong.

In the months – the year – after she had left, she had rented a cottage on the coast. The deposit had been almost all of her meagre savings, and she had had to seek help from an old friend, but it had been isolated enough and far enough from Miles and Amber, and she had tried to feel relieved. At first, she had spent hours each day walking to the nearest town and its library, searching through newspapers for any story about a missing baby. *The Tall Man takes daughters.* As the weeks passed, again and again, her fear began to dissipate.

It was only later, much later, when she looked at the date and realised Amber's tenth birthday was approaching, that she began to think of other ways in which the Tall Man might reach her. It began to occur to her that he might not take Amber, but that Amber might be one of his special ones. That perhaps it was her replacement she had given birth to all along – and then left unattended and alone.

She hadn't risked going back then – she couldn't risk leading them there herself. She had only hoped that Miles, all of the goodness that was in Miles, would have been enough to protect Amber, to keep the shadows at bay. She remembered sitting in another cottage, this time on Skye and a full decade after she'd left, her laptop open in front of her. Remembered the years after that too, the way she would spend hours studying Amber's Facebook profile, her twelve-year-old daughter's privacy settings woefully lacking, and then, later, her Twitter and Instagram too. Searching for some sign, some expression on her daughter's face, some strangely worded status that would tell her that it had happened, that he had found her.

And now she was back, she watched Amber when Amber talked, laughed, slept. But it was difficult to really know, when the only Amber she could say for sure was untouched had been cut out of her with a scalpel.

The Tall Man takes daughters, she thought often, alone in the house, *but what does he leave behind?*

She swung the car into a space down the street from the school. Another kindness of Miles's; it had always been his preferred method of killing. And so she had the car each day while he trotted dutifully to the station to catch his train to work, satchel slung across his body like a paperboy and extra-large travel mug steaming in the milky morning light.

Climbing out of the car, she couldn't help thinking of those long walks to public libraries, the clunky old computers with their dial-up internet. She had watched over her family, she had. Even if she would never let them know it.

There was no other traffic around and a scream rose out of the distant burble of playground sound. She pulled her sleeves down over her hands and walked towards the school, listening, as she always did, for small footsteps behind her.

At the fence, she clung to the chain-links and watched the figures in the distance as they mooched and stumbled around the playground. She tried to seek Amber out but her gaze kept catching on others – on girls with their heads tipped back in violent laughter; on boys with their hands thrust in their pockets, shoes scuffed moodily against walls.

'Fascinating, aren't they?' The voice smooth beside her. The skin on her arms prickling into goosebumps as she turned.

It was a woman's voice and this was new. She was small and thin, dark hair cut sharply around her jaw. Beige capri pants and a Breton top, her Birkenstocked feet flecked with grass. The bangles around her wrist tinkled as she took a step back and returned her gaze to the playground.

Sadie blinked at her. 'I—'

'Which one belongs to you?' The woman smiled. *The Tall Man takes daughters.*

She scanned the playground, finally finding Amber on a bench, clicking through her phone while a girl beside her tried to get her attention. 'Amber,' she said, pointing, though whether she was confirming it for herself or this stranger she couldn't be sure.

'Oh! How strange,' the woman said, the bangles jangling again as she smoothed her hair behind one ear. Sadie waited for the inevitable warning. *She's mine now*, perhaps, or *That's not a girl there, can't you see?* But no – she was gesturing to another girl on the bench. 'That's Billie, my daughter.' The tall, dark-haired girl from Amber's birthday. Sadie watched as she rose, offering a tube of sweets to Amber, who took one without looking up from her phone. When she looked back, the pale hand with its bangles was extended towards her.

'I'm Leanna,' the woman said.

'Sadie.' Her own hand felt clammy and hot in the cool grip of Leanna's. 'It's nice to meet you.' These phrases and social routines were slowly coming back to her, a language she'd learned that had become rusty with misuse.

'We're new in town,' Leanna said, her hand returned

to her and her arms folded across her lean body. 'I worry
about her, I know that's silly. Sometimes I like to just
check up on her – I don't make a habit of peering through
playground fences, I promise!'

Sadie laughed because it felt like she was supposed to,
the sound jarring against the glittering of the bracelet and
the far-off roar of the children. 'Amber forgot her key,'
she said, surprised at how easily the lies still came. 'I
dropped it off at reception for her.'

The bell rang then, the more eager of the kids streaming
into the school's buildings while the others drifted across
the playground. Sadie took an uncertain step back.

'You know,' Leanna said, 'it's been such a relief that
Billie's found a friend like Amber.'

Sadie wished that her first reaction wasn't *Really?*

'Have you moved far?' she asked instead. The two of
them had, by unspoken agreement, started to walk away
from the school.

'Yes, from up north,' Leanna said. Her voice had a
trace of several accents though Sadie – who had had her
own fair share – could not pick out and follow the thread
of any of them. 'Listen.' She stopped walking again,
suddenly looking uncertain. 'Maybe this is a strange thing
to ask, but would you like to come over for a glass of
wine tomorrow night? Billie's having Amber over for a
sleepover – I'm sure she already told you – and, well, I
don't know any other women in town yet. I'd love the
company.'

Sadie looked around, though they were in a patch of

bright light, no shadows to be seen. It was possible, of course, that Leanna had heard the rumours, that she wanted to get up close to crazy and have the story to tell. But her face was earnest, nervous even, and Sadie thought of the eager way Billie had bounded after Amber outside the leisure centre. She thought of Miles's gentle suggestion, the other day at breakfast – perhaps this woman really did want a friend. She thought of those early days alone, that damp cottage, and how she had ached for company. She had been good, then, in those first towns. She had not allowed herself it.

'That sounds great,' she said. 'I'd love to.'

10

2018

Amber is late, just as she was late yesterday. She's also decided that today, day four of the shoot, she does not want to be filmed in her room. So Greta, Tom and Luca wait in the windowless lobby, its chairs upholstered in wet-looking velvet, the wallpaper glimmering in the dim light of the pendant lamps.

'This is ridiculous,' Luca says, after they've been sitting there for thirty minutes. 'I'm going for another smoke.'

Greta and Tom watch him leave, the door letting in a brief chink of bright light before it's sucked shut again.

'Think we should have a word with her about time-keeping?' Tom asks.

'We could ask Federica to. But it'll probably only alienate her, telling her off about stuff.'

Tom shrugs, reaching down to check through one of

the pockets on his camera case. 'I get the impression she hasn't had much of that, the last couple of years.'

'No.'

'Also not sure there's much point asking Federica to play Mum from five thousand miles away.'

She grimaces. 'Yeah, there's that.'

He leans back in his seat, satisfied that he has whatever he thought he'd forgotten. 'It's really harsh, by the way, her leaving you to sort all this out.'

'Well. I guess I should make the most of it. See it as an opportunity or something.'

'Yeah, as long as you can get her to give you the appropriate credit at the end of it.'

She smiles a humourless smile as they both consider the likelihood of that. 'Hopefully the schedule today will mean we get some better footage. It's hard interviewing her when she's just come off a talk-show set – it's impossible for her to answer without sounding really rehearsed.'

'Mmm.' Tom scratches the back of his neck, the edge of a tattoo she hasn't noticed before peeping out from his T-shirt sleeve. 'The stuff we've shot so far hasn't come across as particularly natural, no.'

She sighs. 'We'll get there. I hope. Hey, I listened to that band you were talking about yesterday, by the way. So good.'

'Yeah? I thought that was your kind of thing. They're pretty cool, right?'

'They're amazing. I love all the sampling they use. And the sax! The sax player is awesome.'

He grins, a dimple appearing in one cheek. 'I remembered you saying you liked jazz, thought you'd like his vibe.'

'It was definitely an uplifting accompaniment to my Tall Man research.'

'Bet he loves a bit of jazz, that guy,' he says, the dimple disappearing as his smile turns mischievous. 'A legend on the sax, I heard.'

'I see him as more of a double bass man myself,' Greta says, and even though she knows it's wrong, it feels good to joke. It feels good to hear him laugh in the airless lobby with its slick tiled walls.

'You'll have to ask Amber,' he says, and just like that, she doesn't feel like laughing any more. He glances at his watch. 'She really is taking the piss now.'

Greta wonders if it's wrong to hope Amber doesn't show up; as if they're at school and the lack of a substitute teacher will mean they can wander out and into the sunshine. She imagines diving into the overly chlorinated pool back at the motel, imagines collapsing on to one of the crappy plastic loungers with her book.

But then she imagines reading the first review of the first episode of this series, imagines adding it to her CV. Imagines telling her parents that another project she worked on has won an award. 'I guess I should go up there,' she says.

Tom pulls a face. 'Get the receptionist to call up again. I'm sure Amber can put her own shoes on.' His phone starts buzzing on the coffee table in front of them and he glances down at it. 'I should take that. I'm going to go and find a paper and possibly another coffee too – want anything?'

She shakes her head. 'I'm good, thanks.'

'OK if I leave all the stuff here with you?'

'Sure.'

He answers his phone as he strides across the lobby, his greeting eaten up as he pushes open the door to the bar and restaurant. The door swings shut silently and then it's just Greta and the receptionist, her long nails clacking against her keyboard.

Greta checks her own phone for the fifteenth time. For now, her inbox is quiet. Instead, she opens the browser and looks through some of the pages she bookmarked during last night's research session:

The legend of the Tall Man can be traced back as early as the 1970s. An urban legend which began circulating around schools in England, it has several variants – the most popular is that of a man who murdered his diso-bedient daughters. This version of the Tall Man can be sought out by 'good' or 'special' girls – the legend goes that girls who offer presents and subservience will be rewarded with gifts of their own. In some versions of the story, these gifts are powers, while in others, they are guardians – often said to be 'sent from the shadows'.

Nothing new here; Greta has read plenty of these summaries over the last six months. She clicks on to another one.

The first recorded instance of the Tall Man story is from a primary school in the north of England in 1972.

It was written by a seven-year-old girl, Julie Young, who during an exercise about Father Christmas described him as 'the tall man who comes in the night and gives presents to good people and takes away the bad people'. Her elder brother, Jonathan, thought this highly entertaining, and at Christmas that year, produced a handmade comic about the evil Santa, who he called 'The Tall Man'. It was a single copy, passed around a couple of friends and joked about within the Young household – Jonathan and Julie were from a big extended family, and their cousins had great fun teasing their younger siblings about the Tall Man coming to take them away if they didn't do what they were told.

She's read similar accounts before, although none quite so detailed. She adds a note to one of the many memos on her phone to look into Julie and Jonathan Young, wondering how likely it is that she'll be able to track down the original handmade comic. Federica will almost certainly ask; she might as well get the ball rolling now if she can.

This page also has several links out and Greta looks through them. One is a forum where people have posted their own Tall Man stories, pages and pages of them.

my bro sed tall man killd 2 girls on our street b4 i was born. dey found em in they treehouse an if u go there at nite u can hear em cryin
Anyone seen this story from Australia? Mother killed her daughter while she was sleeping – surely TM involved here?

my sister went missing when i was three. i think the tall man took her. i want to get her back.

Dis friend of mine acting so weird. How can u tell if TM changed sumone?

She moves on to the next link, an essay published in a psychology journal about the legend and several case studies of its effects on preteen girls. Its opening section focuses on Stow-on-the-Wold, a case from 1977 that Greta is also pretty familiar with now. A wave of children in the town suffering from the same recurring nightmare of a dark figure standing at the end of their bed, sometimes accompanied by another child. She's also read the article that made the incident more famous – 'Terror Comes to Town', published in a popular cult magazine in 1989. Greta has been trying to get hold of the author, Gina Slater, once a resident of Stow-on-the-Wold and now a journalist at a respectable home and garden magazine, for weeks – only this morning Federica announced that she was going to give her another call; another piece of important legwork that can be carried out from the balcony.

'Sorry I'm late.' It should be impossible for someone with heels as tall and thin as hers to sneak up on someone in a tiled lobby, but Amber seems to manage it every time.

'Not to worry,' Greta says, standing up. 'You all set?'

Amber's hair is freshly blown out, big seventies-style waves falling around her face – though it remains a glossy beachy blond, Amber clearly having thought better of her more drastic bleach plans. Her lips are a matte melonish peach, her dress a pretty white gypsy style, one strap sliding down her arm. She smells of floral perfume but there is an undertone of something ripe and cloying. Greta wonders if the abandoned breakfast trays are still collecting in the corner of the room.

'Anything interesting?' Amber asks, nodding towards the phone clutched in Greta's hand.

'Just emails.' Greta glances over Amber's shoulder, hoping for Tom. No luck. 'Did you sleep well?'

Amber shrugs. 'I never sleep well.' She looks at Greta and laughs. 'Oh, not like that. Not because of . . .' She shrugs again, glancing at her reflection in the mirrored back wall before returning her attention to Greta. 'I've had insomnia since I was a kid. I hardly ever sleep. Not unless I'm drunk.'

'Oh. That must be tough, I'm sorry.'

'I'm used to it.' Amber runs a nail around the edge of her top lip, gaze on the mirror again. She holds the nail up to her face, examines the excess lipstick caught under it. 'So. Let's go. What is it today? I swear, I did look at the schedule, but . . .'

'You have your interview with *Rolling Stone*,' Greta says. 'Before that we thought we could maybe walk around, get some shots of you by the beach. Sometimes it's nice to have footage of you just, you know, doing normal stuff – we can put some of your interviews in as voice-over that way, so it's not always you looking at a camera.'

'Cool.' Amber takes a step closer to the mirror, the nail scraping into the corner of her mouth. 'That sounds easy.'

'Morning.' Tom comes back through the concealed door to the bar, a paper folded under his arm. His Vans squeak on the polished floor, the receptionist looking up from her screen.

'Hey, Tom.' Amber turns away from her reflection, hair swirling out behind her. 'Did *you* sleep well?'

'Yes, thanks. You?'

'Yep.' Amber glances at Greta, a smile twitching at the corners of her mouth.

'Great.' Tom looks at Greta too. 'You ready?'

'Yep. Let's get going.'

As they step out into the sunlight, Greta tries to focus on the shoot; on the angles and the light and the thousands of variations Federica could decide she wants at any one time. She tries to remember that Amber is an eighteen-year-old girl who has recently been found not guilty of a murder charge, now capitalising on the notoriety that has brought her a seven-figure book deal and a media tour in the States. That Amber is being paid a generous sum of money to be filmed by their cameras, is not someone in need of looking after or protecting. An interviewee, a subject, a star. Not something to be afraid of.

But her mind keeps returning to a clearing in the woods, to a house full of shadows. To a photograph taken by a passer-by and splashed across the media, Amber with her clothes soaked black with blood, a police officer cuffing her hands in front of her. A dark space in the trees behind her, the light catching the bark of a dying tree and casting it as the edge of a face of bone, a toothless grin.

11

2016

They were late getting in the car, Amber lounging on her bed after school and only sauntering into the shower ten minutes before they were due to leave. Sadie sat on the bottom step, staring at the front door, listening to the roar of the hairdryer above her. Anxious or perhaps anticipating; she couldn't quite get a handle on the feeling. It was not dissimilar to the way she had felt, seventeen years ago, waiting for Miles to knock on her bedroom door in halls.

Silly, really.

When Amber came down, she smiled at her mother and said: 'Ready?'

And Sadie nodded meekly and took her keys from the table. It was easier than arguing, she told herself, and certainly did not mean she was afraid of a teenager. In the car, she glanced at Amber; freshly washed hair shining over an expensive-looking leather jacket that Sadie

109

couldn't remember seeing her wear before (this, though, did not generally mean that she hadn't).

'It's weird that you're coming,' Amber said, looking over at her. 'What are you even going to talk about?'

'I don't know,' Sadie said, starting the car and trying for a joke, 'probably you two.'

Amber raised a laconic eyebrow and turned to look out of the window.

'What's she like?' Sadie asked. 'Leanna, I mean. Have you spent much time with her?'

'She's nice.' Amber glanced down at the phone clutched in her hand and began typing furiously, her nails clacking on the screen. When she was done, she resumed her vigil of the passing houses. The road ticked under the wheels, the old car groaning through its gears, and Sadie wondered if she should turn the radio on. She wondered if the silence felt as heavy to Amber as it did to her.

'What are you girls going to do?' she tried.

'We're going to watch this sick horror movie Jenna downloaded.' Amber glanced over at her again and grinned. 'Don't tell Leanna, though? Please? She'd freak.'

Sadie felt that same thrill again, the feeling of anticipation. She remembered schoolyard confidences and arms clutched, giggles and secrets whispered with hot breath into ears exposed by wind-whipped hair. She found herself smiling nervously, her palms slick against the wheel. 'Sure,' she said. And then, because she wanted the moment to last, she added, 'I used to love scary films when I was younger.'

'Not like Dad. He's such a wimp.'

And Sadie laughed, the sound soft and solid in her throat. 'Yes, he's never liked them.' The thrill of these exchanged sentences, the linking together of them (Conversation! This was conversation!) thrummed through her.

And then she remembered why, aged eleven, she had stopped enjoying horror films, and the smile faded. She found she was afraid to look in the rear-view mirror, because in that moment, with its particular cliff-edge of fear, she knew she would find a face there.

'It's left here,' Amber said, pointing. 'And then right.' She fired off another flurry of text on her phone and then tossed it into her bag.

They pulled into a congested cul-de-sac and Sadie manoeuvred the car into the only available space.

'You're better at parking than he is, too,' Amber said, but she was out of the car before Sadie had even registered that she had paid her a compliment, a gust of night air circling in the space where she had been. She turned off the engine and followed her up the short path to the last cottage in the row; painted a pretty pale yellow, a stone trough of white camellias under its front window. Amber pressed the bell and they both watched through the bubbled glass as a blurry figure came down the stairs towards them.

And Sadie remembered (though she tried so hard not to, pushing the heels of her palms against her eyes as if this might stop the flow) calling for Helen and Marie; the three of them cycling round to call for Justine. The way they stood on doorsteps together and waited as impatient mothers called their daughters and eyed them with their crushed velvet tops and chokers and their battered bikes leaning against the front steps. She remembered the way she would crack bubbles in her gum, look right back at them. She didn't care. She thought she was special. They thought he had made them special.

Leanna opened the door to them, a roll of greaseproof paper in her hand. 'Hi!' She stepped back in an almost-bow, ushering them in. 'Sorry, minor timing disaster in the kitchen.'

As Sadie followed Amber into Leanna's hall, copying her as she kicked off her shoes on to the deep-red, tiled floor, all she could smell was freshly baked something: bread or pizza, some undertone of something rich and chocolatey. The hallway was neat and clean and grown-up and it did not help to disperse the feeling that Sadie was eleven again.

'Billie's upstairs with Jenna,' Leanna told Amber, though Amber was already three stairs up the flight, her jacket tossed over the banister. Sadie watched it droop and begin to slide towards the floor.

'Here, let me take your coat,' her host said, coming towards her and plucking Amber's from the stairs. Sadie shrugged her way out of her denim jacket, suddenly hot, and handed it over obediently.

'It's beautiful in here,' she said, watching Leanna hang their coats inside a narrow cupboard. *Too early*, she criticised herself; *all you can see is some floor and the stairs*. The walls were white, woodchip; thoroughly uncommentable-on.

Leanna smiled. 'Oh. Plenty more work to do,' she said. 'Come on through.'

In the kitchen, copper-bottomed pans glowed against the white wall and a triptych of abstract paintings hung above the wooden table. Sadie's socked feet felt damp against the tiles and she remembered the plastic bag hanging limply in her hand.

'I brought some wine.'

She wished she'd brought more; chocolates or olives or at least wine in a carrier bag that wasn't clinging thinly to the side of the bottle, the garage's logo distorted.

'That's so kind of you,' Leanna said, turning away with it. 'Let me pour us a glass. Would you like white or red? Or prosecco? A G and T?'

The choices dazzled her and she had to remember to be decisive, not to dwell. 'White would be lovely,' she said, and was pleased with herself.

She watched her host uncork the wine – taken from the fridge; Sadie's own bottle peeled from its bag and slid on to the shelf in its place. Was that polite or rude? Sadie couldn't remember. She took her glass of wine from Leanna, sluiced some around her dry mouth. She let out a small huff of pleasure, and then remembered that she was supposed to control those urges now. Leanna merely smiled and raised her glass for chinking.

'Friday,' she said, and Sadie smiled too.

She drank some more wine.

'So, how long have you been in town?' she asked Leanna, pleased with herself again for thinking of the question. She had practised a couple in the shower earlier that afternoon, trying to remember the sort of things Miles asked people when he first met them. But this one had come quite naturally, without conscious thought. She could do this.

'Oh, a couple of months now,' Leanna said, and then she gestured to the table with its wide, pale bench, rough-hewn and wild. 'Please, sit.'

Sitting on the seat, she found herself thinking of woods; the feel of a damp palm against hers; blades of grass twisted through her hair and her friends laughing beside her. She blinked, dispelling it. 'It smells amazing in here,' she said, because one way to silence the memories was to talk over them.

'Oooh. Yes.' And Leanna was up again; an oven glove in hand, a cooling rack magicked out of a nook some-where. She was dressed more casually this evening, leggings, a silky long T-shirt, a kimono sort of cardigan that swooped around her as her slender legs pecked quickly across the tiles. Sadie noticed for the first time the different shapes of mother and daughter, compared Leanna to tall, awkward Billie, and the thought comforted her. There were differing levels of distance and closeness, maybe; perhaps each relationship had its own unique DNA that threaded the two together. She and Amber were so obviously, undeniably related physically that perhaps it was only a matter of time before they began to under-stand each other too.

Wine. It made her thoughts swell and stretch, expansive and warm.

'How are you finding it here?' she asked, as Leanna pulled one, two pizzas from the oven, and then: 'Oh my God, are they homemade?'

Leanna glanced back, a waft of warmth from the oven crawling through the room. 'These? Oh, yeah. Thought I might as well knock them up for the girls instead of letting them order in. Not *exactly* healthy, but better than Domino's, right?'

She slid them on to the rack and then returned to the bench. 'In answer to your other question, it's been OK. It's never easy, is it? Moving to a new place?' She took a sip of her wine and checked herself. 'Sorry, I don't even know – have you always lived here?'

There it was; that sudden bump in the road. That lurch out of sync, the teetering over the precipice. The wishing (oh, the *wishing*; it was so close to remembering and yet it had its own particular, delicate pain). 'No,' she said, soothing her mouth with another short sip, easing the words out. 'No, Miles and I lived in Reading when we met.' A lie by omission, though better than an outright one. 'There's not much to do here, I'm afraid.' She tried not to think of those late months of pregnancy, when sleep was erratic and unpredictable, when Miles would stay up or wake up with her and they would drive around at night, trying to imagine where they might live when he had graduated and they could afford somewhere better than that family housing flat near the campus. His parents

115

had lent him the deposit for the house they all lived in now when Amber was almost two. He'd told Sadie that he'd chosen the town because it had always been at the top of her list.

'Oh, I don't know,' Leanna said, twirling the stem of her glass between her fingers. 'It feels like there's plenty going on.' She picked up her wine and held it carefully for a moment. 'Of course, we lived somewhere very remote before this.'

Footsteps thumped across the ceiling above them and Leanna glanced up, efficiently attentive and resigned at once. She got up, her wine glass abandoned.

'They look like something out of a restaurant,' Sadie said feebly, realising that she'd forgotten momentarily that the girls were even upstairs. 'I'd have no idea where to even start.'

Leanna dismissed this with an airy wave of a hand. 'I'll give you the recipe. Honestly, it's easy. One of those things that always impresses people without actually taking much effort.' She took a small sledge of metal from a drawer and moved the pizzas on to two earthenware plates, a stray charred asparagus stalk trailing. 'I'll be right back – you OK for a refill?'

Sadie would have liked a refill, the inch remaining in her glass rock-pool shallow and quickly warming. But she nodded and smiled like she was supposed to, and watched Leanna disappear into the dark hallway. The sound of her footsteps echoed up the old stairs and then Sadie was alone again.

Her eyes flitted around the kitchen, which obligingly revealed its wares. A tribal statue in the corner beside the hob looked down over the butter dish. A shelf beside the door displayed delicately engraved chopsticks standing sentry on ivory holders. The triptych above the table was red gore spattered with black, the paint so thick in places that she wanted to reach up and pick it like a scab. She looked instead at the framed photos clustered on the windowsill; mother and daughter on beaches, bridges, the edge of a forest. This was not her life. She looked back up at the scabs of paint, the scars left behind by the brush.

The footsteps coming back downstairs echoed until they fell out of sync, the two sets slipping into their own rhythm as they slapped across the tiles. Billie appeared through the door first; pyjama bottoms flapping, her hair plaited down her back. 'Hi, Mrs Banner!'

'Hi, Billie. You guys having fun up there?' She always hated how old she sounded when she spoke to them; the sleazy uncle at a party, some seventies kids' TV presenter. A kind of auditory rankness that made Amber's mouth crinkle every time she opened hers.

But Billie smiled and said, 'Yes, thanks!' in an edgeless way, her fingers sliding across the counter to snatch up a stray chunk of ham or bacon left stranded there. She turned as she popped it into her thin-lipped mouth, her hands plucking at the fabric of her pyjamas. 'Do you like our new house?'

'It's lovely,' Sadie said, taking a sip of wine and remembering not to take another right away.

'It's nice, isn't it?' Billie grinned at Leanna. 'Mum thinks it's too small and shabby, don't you?'

Leanna laughed, and the ease with which these smiles and laughs exchanged themselves makes Sadie feel cold with envy. 'Those might have been my exact words, yes,' Leanna replied, going to the fridge. 'Right, I made you girls a jug of mojitos.' She glanced back at Sadie. 'Virgin, obviously!'

'Oh my God.' The smile felt plastered to her face now, clown-leery. 'Amber's never going to come home.' The words, when they were out, felt macabre and loaded. She finished her wine and Leanna, arranging the mint-strewn jug and stained-rim glasses on a tray, noticed immediately. 'Bill, fill Sadie's glass, please?'

Billie came towards Sadie, bottle held out, and Sadie saw an alternate life, where a toddler Amber might have come towards her with a sippy cup or a toy teapot. Where a ten- or eleven-year-old Amber might have approached her with a homework sheet, asking for help. She thought of all the things that could have been; all the things she had given up without knowing each time she had stepped into those woods.

Wine. It made her frighteningly reflective; she often worried she would drop into one of those thoughts and never resurface.

'Thank you,' she said to Billie, who clunked the bottle roughly against the edge of the glass and then fumbled it back into the fridge. The tray of drinks jangled alarmingly as she headed for the door.

'See you later,' she called over her shoulder. 'Thanks, Mum!'

'Now.' Leanna pushed the kitchen door to as the music from upstairs got louder. 'Are *you* hungry? Have you eaten? I've got bread and cheese and things.'

And, to Sadie's surprise, she was hungry. She hadn't eaten; she often forgot, too unaccustomed to caring for herself. And so she watched Leanna pulling down plates from a cupboard, sliding a wheel of camembert into the oven, with something like anticipation. She enjoyed Miles's cooking – or had done, anyway, back before everything – but with him it was orchestrated and huge, even something simple like scrambled eggs requiring several bowls and pans and that furrowed look of perfectionism pleating his large face. Leanna moved through the kitchen lightly, things collected and deposited as she went, and Sadie struggled to follow the train of conversation, mesmerised by the darting of her hands. She watched the food come towards her; the mismatched pottery plates with wheels and wedges of cheese and sliced sourdough, wedges of apple and some uniformly perfect miniature tarts.

And then Leanna was sitting beside her, entirely undistracted, and the force of her attention was like a weight, like the sheering force of a snowplough. There was an expectation for words, she knew that much, and so she stumbled for them, her eyes flicking, loose with panic, again around the room.

'You've got so many interesting things in here,' she said

(decisive again; she rewarded herself with more wine). 'You must have travelled a lot?'

Leanna smiled, a knife slipping effortlessly through the brie. 'Here and there. Mostly India and the Far East. The Americas.'

'With Billie?' Sadie's eyes kept returning to those photos with their blue-sky backgrounds. *Not your life.*

'Yes, recently. But before she was born too.' The bottle appeared; more wine slicked into both glasses. She closed the fridge and sat again. 'I spent most of my teens and my twenties running away, if I'm honest.'

'Huh.' Sadie took another swig of wine, encouraged. 'I know that feeling.'

Leanna glanced at her and then away, her fingers toying delicately with the stem of her glass. 'How old were you when you had Amber?'

'Twenty.' More wine now for support; a secret second sip bolstering the first large one. 'How about you?'

Leanna was not so easily deflected. 'Twenty's young, that can't have been easy. Had you been with your partner long? Sorry, I've just realised I don't know his name. Miles, did you say?' The questions felt sharp and probing; an almond-shaped, clear-polished nail slid under the skin seeking, seeking – but in a way, this was a relief. Over the last year, Sadie had become so used to being probed, incised, found lacking, that answering was suddenly easy.

'Yes, Miles. We met at uni so we hadn't been together long, no. I got pregnant in between first and second year.'

Leanna picked up a tart but didn't eat it, holding it

elegantly between thumb and forefinger, pincered. 'Gosh. Did you carry on studying?'

Sadie was used to these questions and they were easier to answer. Already she had endured a charity event at Miles's work, his university colleagues asking 'What do you do?' and then looking around desperately for someone more interesting to talk to. She had endured his parents' ruby wedding anniversary, the cousins and the aunts with their paper plates of curling sandwiches and own-brand crisps clutched in hand, gazing at her: *Well, you look all right. Time to get back to being a mother and a wife, eh?* It was easy, now, to shake her head and think of those early days, that first decision. 'No,' she said. 'I could have, but we decided it'd be better if I didn't. I thought I'd go back when she was older. Financial reasons, really. I suppose I also wanted to concentrate on her, at least for the first few years.' There was a lump in her throat but it could have been pastry from the tart she seemed to be crumbling against the plate. Either way, she washed it back with the last of her glass and Leanna, of course, refilled it.

'You know, I really respect that,' she said, slicing off a sliver of a yellowish blue cheese and catching Sadie off guard. 'Making a choice is never easy, is it? Especially when you're young.' She fed the cheese between her neat small teeth, sucking a crumb from her finger. 'And that seems pretty selfless.'

This kindness made Sadie feel uncomfortable. She couldn't allow herself, knowing what had come after, to look back at that time through its rose-tinted light. Instead, she said vaguely, 'I suppose I just thought it had happened for a reason,' and stuffed a balled-up piece of sourdough innards into her mouth, sweeping away thoughts of those weeks. The pregnancy test on the tiny bathroom floor. The long conversations, the two of them side by side on her single bed, huddled under her smoky duvet. The way she woke one morning, the light filtering through the crooked blinds and her fingers linked in his, and knew what she would do, though it had seemed obvious in the days leading up to it that keeping the child was wrong.

The days and weeks before her visitors came to find her again, to whisper their message in her ear.

'Well, you ended up with a lovely daughter,' Leanna said. 'Amber is so sweet. So thoughtful.'

Sadie couldn't stop that first thought from slipping through again: *Really?*

Her second, as Leanna topped up her glass, was that she had forgotten she was supposed to be driving.

12

2018

With Amber safely delivered to a café in Santa Monica, where a *Rolling Stone* reporter sat with a smoothie and an impatient expression, Greta goes to the beach to wait. She checks her emails, her shoes kicked off beside her, socks stuffed damply in the toes. She watches gulls totter through the surf while joggers sheathed in fluorescent scraps chug past her on the sand. She thinks of her parents up in Michigan, imagines them sitting out on their deck, looking over the lake. A beer for her father; tea or perhaps a small vodka for her mother and a slice of her Zwetschgenkuchen on a gold-lipped plate between them, two forks balanced on its rim. She'd hoped to have time to fly up and visit them, but Federica's ever-changing schedule (and consistent non-appearance) is making that less and less likely.

She's wondering now what she'd thought would

happen. It's not as if she hasn't worked for Federica before; not as if she hasn't been left in the lurch by other directors and producers in the past. It's not as if she didn't sign up with the hope that she'd be able to shape the film in some way, make her mark on it.

'Hey.' Tom flops down on the sand beside her. He has a greasy packet of fries in one hand which he holds out to her. She takes one, soggy and disintegrating and spattered with thin, vinegary ketchup.

'Thanks. Where's Luc?'

'Walked up to the shops to see if he could find something for Elke.'

'Oh, OK.' She wonders, briefly, what it might be like to have someone to fly home to with souvenirs.

Tom slides the strap of his camera bag over his head and resettles himself on the sand. 'That journalist wasn't exactly loving life, was she?'

Greta laughs. 'Well, imagine. One year you're interviewing Madonna, the next some messed-up British kid who's more interested in the available pancake toppings than answering your questions.'

'Oh God, that poor woman.'

'Well.' She looks out at the sea, the hazy horizon. 'I can't help feeling sorry for Amber, to be honest. All of these interviews, the same questions over and over, all of those people watching. Us sticking cameras in her face everywhere she goes. Hardly fun, is it?'

Tom looks at her for a second, his face unreadable. 'I'm not sure she needs your pity, Greta.'

'Well, no.' She looks away, feeling stung. She had meant to carry on the sentence but belatedly it abandons her. A volleyball game down the beach picks up the slack, the groan as a shot is missed drifting up to them.

'Wish I'd brought my trunks,' Tom says. 'I'd love to jump in that sea right now.'

'I've always been too much of a wimp to swim in the sea. Too scared of sharks or giant octopuses or whatever.'

'Yeah, admittedly I prefer swimming in a place where I can see my feet touch the bottom. Don't think there's many giant octopi around here though.'

'Famous last words. I'll wait here with your clothes, if you like.'

'Probably sensible.' He smiles at her. 'You didn't fancy shopping, then?'

She laughs. 'My bank is probably very glad I didn't. I don't think I've been shopping for fun since 2010.'

'I don't think I've been out of my overdraft since then.'

'God, no. When people talk to me about buying a house I wonder which body parts they've decided to sell.'

'Right?' He eats another chip and is quiet for a minute. 'Sucks, doesn't it? Feels like it was only last week I was finishing uni and thinking I'd made it to adulthood. Now everyone's getting married, having kids, owning property – and I'm doing well if I remember to pay my electric bill.'

She laughs but it sounds hollow in her own ears. He offers her the chips again and she takes a couple. He pushes his hair – pale, a pretender to gold like the sand – away from his face and tips back on his hands towards the sun. She notices the freckles coaxed out by the heat across the bridge of his nose, across his collarbone.

'Suppose we better head back to meet Amber soon.' She puts the chips into her mouth at once, the thought of Federica's instructions for the day – *Try and get her to talk about her life before, her hopes for the future, see if that cracks her a bit. Also can you buy as many Milky Way Midnights as possible, they're Millie's favourites and you can't get them here* – ruining her relaxed mood.

He nods but leans back further, eyes closing against the light. 'I don't like her,' he says. 'I guess you can tell that.'

'Are we supposed to?' she asks (still chewing).

'It would help.'

She considers this, watching one of the gulls turn on another in a thunderclap of wings. A car drives slowly by, a bassline throbbing feebly from its open windows. 'It's a story that's worth telling. It's a terrible, terrible thing that happened, and it's getting lost under all this trashy tabloid stuff.' She surprises herself by adding, 'Federica once told me that you don't have to like your subjects to do them justice.'

He opens his eyes, rolls his head to look at her. They have been in Los Angeles for less than a week but already there is a strip of whiter skin beneath the neck of his T-shirt. 'Yeah, and where's Federica again?'

'She'll probably be here tomorrow,' Greta says, though she doesn't believe it.

'No, she won't. Since the verdict, she's not interest-ed. She thought Amber'd be found guilty and we'd be interviewing her in prison. This isn't the original plan, Greta, you know that. Now she's got us chasing ghosts. Literally. While she's at home trying to fix her fucked-up relationship on the network's dime.'

She takes her turn to tip her head back, enjoying the warmth on her face against the rising breeze, trying to ignore the chinks his words have made in her. 'Yeah, but the network are totally onside. Amber's hot property now. Didn't you see the email from Morris? They're bringing the pilot forward. We get something new out of her, this could be huge.'

'Yeah, maybe.' He picks up another flaccid chip, examines it, and skims it across the sand to the gulls. They fall on it, yellow beaks clacking like swords, medieval screeches piercing. The second fry passes the test; he tosses it into his mouth. 'But I still don't like her.'

She allows herself a nod. 'She is . . . kinda unnerving, I guess.'

'She's fake.' Another car passes, another burst of dulled synthetic sound beaten back by the gentle roar of the tide. 'She's not a good person.'

She stares at him. 'She's a kid. She's been through something we can't even imagine.'

Tom squashes down the paper of the fries with the flat of a hand. 'I know,' he says, picking up the scrunched bundle and looking around. 'But there's something . . . I don't know. I'm looking at her through the camera all day, right? And there's nothing there. There's no feeling in her face, just this deadness in her eyes.' He leans forward, about to stand, but thinks better of it, and looks back at her instead. 'It's like she's got no soul.'

'I think it's that she's guarded.' Federica's email echoes in her ears. *Can't say I blame her.* 'How could she not be? Who would *you* trust after all that, if you were in her place?'

Tom snorts. 'Come on, Greta – don't tell me you buy into all that stuff. She is *not* the victim. She's a fucking murderer, whatever else happened, and now she's making millions out of her sob story.'

Irritation rises in her, hot and sudden. 'You can be guilty and a victim, you know. Not everything's clear-cut. If it was, what would be the point of making a film about it?'

He smiles and shrugs, entirely unrattled. 'I guess. Sometimes I think it's easy to get lost trying to find the story in something. Sometimes people are just bad. Sometimes it *is* that clear-cut.'

'You don't believe any of it then?'

'Do you?'

Greta looks out to sea and doesn't answer. After a while, Tom stands and offers her a hand up. 'Don't get sucked in,' he says. 'You know what's going to happen. You know Federica's going to do something to pull the rug out from under her. She always stitches them up, you know that.'

Greta lets go of his hand. 'It doesn't have to be like that,' she says. Her phone chimes with yet another email.

Tom shrugs again and they begin walking back towards the car. 'Whatever else she is, Greta,' he says, ducking out of the way of two rollerblading teenagers, 'Amber's not innocent.'

13

2016

Amber watched as Sadie's taxi pulled away, her mother's head lolling towards the window. She took a drag on her cigarette, leaning further out into the night air, and wondered what Miles would say when he saw her. It was pathetic, really, she thought, that lack of self-control. She didn't understand it – she was only sixteen and she'd learned long ago how to discipline herself, how to let people only see her good side, to see her as strong and in control. She prided herself on it. Sadie couldn't even manage an evening at someone's house without embarrassing herself like a total weirdo. She had only been back six months and already Amber was bored of watching her fall through life, dragging the two of them along with her. Perhaps she should feel sorry for her. But then, wasn't it Sadie who was meant to feel sorry? Wasn't she supposed to have come back, wracked with guilt and endlessly apologising for abandoning her helpless baby daughter?

And yet Sadie had said nothing. She had shown up and been quiet and possibly silently sorry, but silently was not enough. She should have turned up begging Amber to forgive her, surely. And Amber would have. She would've forgiven her, and in doing so she would have proven that she was not that helpless child any more – that she had grown up to be brave and strong and in control, had looked after Miles as he had looked after her. But no. Sadie had shown up, and Miles had been overjoyed, and Amber had been expected to fit in and get on with it.

So yes, she was annoyed (not hurt. She wouldn't admit to hurt) – annoyed that she had spent years blaming everything on her absent mother, who would surely have made life perfect, only to find her returned and no great shakes at all. A mess, when it came down to it.

(*What were you expecting?* a critical voice inside her asked. *She ran away because she thought you were cursed. She was never going to be baking cakes and brushing your hair, was she?*)

She grated the cigarette against the bricks beneath the window, sparks scattering, and then tossed the stub into the neighbour's hedge and pulled herself back into the room. She wasn't going to think about that. She had spent a long time thinking about that Sunday afternoon, her grandmother and her alone in the kitchen. Her dad and granddad sipping beers in silence on the patio as they usually did. Amber had been eleven. Her grandmother had been drunk, on her fifth gin and tonic. 'Oh, darling,' she'd said, hands damp from the washing up as they smoothed Amber's hair away from her face. 'How could she ever have thought you were cursed?'

She wasn't going to think about that.

She stepped away from the window, the curtain drifting up on a breeze behind her. The film playing on the laptop sending its flickering light across the wall. She reached out to take a slice of the cold pizza left on the plate. Fine, it was tasty, but she'd rather have had a Domino's.

She looked around Billie's room. Kind of pretty, she supposed, but also kind of lame, with its matching fluffy rug and fluffy pillows and its silky throw thing draped over the end of the bed. Too try-hard, no personality – though that seemed kind of fitting. She stepped over a sleeping bag to the bed where Billie and Jenna were slumped, a bowl of popcorn between them. She collected the bottle of Malibu she'd persuaded Jenna to steal from the Co-op and sloshed more into both of their cups, flopping down on to the bed beside them.

Her phone buzzed on the bedside table and she glanced down at the lock screen: Mica. Sorry hon, can't ☹. She reached out and clicked the lock button so that the screen went black again. It had taken Mica two hours and thirteen minutes to reply to her, she definitely wasn't going to send her own response any sooner – though her head was swarming with questions: why couldn't Mica come and meet her in town? What was she doing? *Who* was she doing it with?

It wasn't as if there was much to do in town. Just the

same old pub on the high street, a totally gross old man's pub where they always got served (unlike the nicer wine bar, which had bouncers who couldn't be charmed). Sometimes the boys from the sixth form were there, and the girls could usually sneak into a better place if they walked in with them, their skinny boy arms slung around their bare shoulders. And it was *their* place, anyway, that gross old man's pub, hers and Mica's; they were *their* fuzzy memories, their giggle-filled phone conversations conducted the next morning from their individual snarls of duvet.

She turned her attention to the laptop, the film reaching its final chase scene, some poor whimpering girl trying to escape the killer by running in all the wrong directions. 'This isn't even scary,' she said, irritated, and stared at Jenna. 'I thought you said it was?'

Jenna flushed. 'I guess maybe the start was scarier?'

Amber liked the way a look from her could turn all of Jenna's sentences into questions.

'If this is your idea of scary, Jen, I'm seriously worried about you.' She turned away, but not before adding a small smile. A *Just kidding*. 'You choose something, Bill. I'm sure you can do better.'

Billie's panic was childlike and pleasing, her eyes wide and locked on Amber's as she tried desperately to produce an answer. 'Oh . . . I . . . Um, Jake posted something on Snapchat about that zombie film?' The mention of Jake made her cheeks flare red and Amber watched with interest. She knew Billie liked him. She had seen the way Billie had been looking at him on her birthday – the way her face had fallen when Amber offered him a lift home with her mum (and Amber hadn't even mentioned the kiss that had happened once they'd got there).

'You should text him and ask him if it's good,' she said, casually, and watched Billie's blush deepen. 'Here – I'll write it for you, if you like.'

'That's OK,' Billie said, her voice small, but she picked up her phone and began typing. So easy. A flicker went through Amber, a fluttering like butterflies in her belly.

Her own phone buzzed again, this time with a message from Leo: Hey baby. What u doin? The flutters sped up then, and she fought back a smile. She toyed with the options. She could text him straight back, get him to pick her up in his car. Get him to take her away from here.

But no. That would be too easy, and she had decided she didn't want to make it easy for him. Playing the game was way more fun with Leo, because he was turning out to be easy to play with.

She locked her phone again. She'd reply later, much later, so that he wondered where she was and who she was with. She liked to figure out these little things about people, the things that made them jealous or sad or happy. It was useful, it helped you get people to do the things you wanted. It helped you understand someone – and understanding someone was the best way to ensure that they couldn't surprise you. To stay in control.

And so she finished her drink and poured herself another one, and then she slid closer to Billie and smiled at her. 'Come on,' she said. 'Tell me the scariest story you know.'

From the diary of Leanna Evans [Extract A]

I slept surprisingly well and didn't wake until after eight, which is highly unusual for me. I stretched out, staring up at the yellowing ceiling. It needed painting, and I itched to begin, though I knew that it would have to join the endless list of things I needed to do in this house. In this town. The list seems to keep on growing but at least now I'm starting to feel as if I'm finally making progress. Settling in.

The curtains were open – I never sleep with them closed here, I like the light to wake me – and I sat up and looked out at the day. The whitewashed sky low and lazy, a haze over the street. It was still early; it would probably burn off later, but then it felt almost beautiful, a kind of filter on the harshness that existed out there. I looked out over the rows of houses and, beyond, the fluorescent yellow of the rape fields, the scrawny dark shadows of trees. It had upset me, previously, the starkness of this small town, but I am growing used to it.

I got up and showered, scrubbing at my skin until it was pink. I would have liked to have done some yoga had we not had a guest, but my time was not my own. And so once I was out and dressed, I went to the kitchen and flitted back and forth between the cupboards, wondering whether to cook pancakes or omelettes, a full English. I was like a teenager with a new boyfriend; trying to guess what someone might like. Trying to guess what Amber enjoyed for breakfast. That might sound strange, but I wanted it to be right.

I decided to wait until they were awake and to whip up whatever they fancied, just like that, the perfect hostess. The decision was a relief, and so I made myself a coffee and then I slid open the patio door and went out on to the terrace. I took a seat there and looked out at the parched strip of lawn. Parched, even in May. It was parched when we bought the house, looked scorched even in winter. I don't know much about gardens, about growing. I don't know how to undo a scorching.

When I finished my coffee, I went inside to find my book. I could have cleaned, of course (I can always clean!), but I didn't want to fluster myself before they came down. I wanted them to feel totally at ease, totally free. That is the true art of being a good hostess – an understanding of how your home and your demeanour make others feel and act. It's always important to remember that.

The book was something I had picked up in the town library; a literary number that all of the Sunday papers had gotten excited about. It wasn't perhaps the tempo I was looking for then, though I managed to lose myself in it for a while, until the ceiling creaking above me alerted me that the girls were awake. It was still early, by Billie's standards anyway – a bit after ten. I smoothed down my hair and went to the kitchen, filling the kettle. I set out the butter in its china dish, and took out the teapot. Then I put the teapot back, because that was stuffy, old-fashioned – something a grandma would do. You must understand how nervous I was, how desperate I was to get this right. For Billie's sake, if nothing else.

It was Billie who came down first, her hair all mussed up and eyes puffy with sleep. Her dressing gown is too short for her and worn in patches, but she loves it – she refuses to wear the one I bought for her two Christmases ago. And so instead it was Amber who came down in it, looking much younger with her glossy hair pulled up into a ponytail, her face pink and freshly washed.

I tried to keep my cool; to greet them as if it was normal for Billie to have a friend over to stay. I wished them a good morning; I offered them tea, coffee, juice. Amber asked for tea, pulling out a chair at the table as naturally as if it were her own. That was my first feeling of success, I think. My first feeling that she belonged here, that I had done the right thing by encouraging them to be friends. Billie declined a drink – she looked pale; I assumed that she hadn't gotten much sleep, though she was the one who suggested she and Amber top-and-tailed in her bed instead of pulling the blow-up mattress down from the attic. I liked that suggestion, if I'm honest; it had the feeling of Enid Blyton boarding school stories to it, a special kind of female friendship that I've never been lucky enough to experience. I was glad too that Jenna chose to go home just after midnight in the end. That might sound unkind, but she's not right for us.

When I asked them what they'd like for breakfast, Amber made polite noises about anything being fine, though she hadn't quite got used to Billie's straightforward honesty: 'Pancakes are Amber's favourites,' she told me immediately, although she was looking a little green around the gills herself. She's often sickening for something, despite her outwardly healthy appearance. It is a constant source of anxiety for me.

Amber, to her credit, blushed, and tried to dissuade me from going to any trouble. I quickly put a stop to that and got on with making the batter. Billie made a swift exit to the bathroom – another bug, I was sure of it then. I was already thinking of the broths and juices I would make for her that afternoon. When Amber and I were alone, I watched her drink her tea. I remember thinking that it must have been absolutely scalding, and being pleased because that's exactly how I like it too. I told her how nice it had been to meet her mother.

She said a funny thing then: 'It was nice of you to invite her round. She doesn't have many friends.'

I tried to make myself sound quietly curious; as if that wasn't such an unusual thing: 'Doesn't she?' Amber made a face, her attention on her tea. 'She's not like other people,' she told me and it seemed cruel to press her.

Upstairs, the toilet flushed, the tank groaning, and I flicked a drop of batter into the pan to test the heat. It sizzled and blackened instantly.

'This is such a lovely house,' Amber said. I remember that very clearly, too.

I thanked her and turned down the heat, ladling the first dollop of batter in. That morning, for the very first time, it *did* feel like a lovely house.

14

2016

Sadie picked Amber and the car up from Leanna's shortly after midday. Amber was quiet on the way home – tired, Sadie guessed. Her own head felt tight, the sunlight aggressive in its pursuit of them as they wound their way through the crowded avenues and back on to the main road.

'Did you have a nice time?' she asked, thinking of the small sense of comradery she had felt last night, on their way up those same roads. A tiny victory, but then they all counted, surely.

'Yep.' Amber shot a sideways glance at her. 'Did *you*?'

'Yeah, it was fun. She's good company.' Sadie wondered if it was OK to talk about things being fun or people being good company. She assumed she was still supposed to be in her repentant phase.

She chose not to mention how angry Miles had been when she'd arrived (stumbled) home. How he'd kept thrusting his phone in her face: *You didn't call. You didn't call.* How tears built in his eyes until one slipped out, unguarded, and he had to turn from her to swipe it away, a single, hollow cry of frustration slipping out too. Or how she'd thrown up in the middle of the night, a curdled mess of cheese and wine, her chest damp with sweat against the toilet bowl.

'I'm going out later,' Amber said, her thumb flying across her phone screen.

Sadie felt a twinge of dread. 'I— well, where?'

The lie was smooth and seamless and Sadie (a consummate expert) couldn't help but be impressed. 'To Mica's,' her daughter said lazily. 'Her parents are going out so I said I'd help her look after Milo.' Milo. Mica's baby brother; Sadie remembered this proudly, like a child who had studied for a test.

'Well?' Amber asked, impatient for conflict. 'Can I go or what?'

'Maybe.' Sadie was flustered, warm-cheeked as she tried to construct the correct answer. 'You'll have to ask your dad.'

Amber sank back into her seat, smug (this was a small victory of its own, her mother ceding to Miles and thus admitting her own lack of authority). Her phone buzzed in her lap and she picked it up and laughed to herself before composing her reply. Sadie glanced at her, wondering, as she always did, what she was thinking, writing, what the person at the other end of the phone thought of her. Her own perception of Amber had become so skewed that other people's were endlessly fascinating. What was she to them? Was she kind, considerate, a good friend? Or was that coolness Sadie sometimes saw in her eyes really what lay beneath? It scared her, though she knew that was wrong. She knew she should've tried harder with Amber when she'd first arrived, when she'd turned up and disrupted their whole life. She'd planned on – *imagined* – hugging her tightly, stroking her hair, telling her over and over how sorry she was about all of it. But then they had been staring at each other in the hallway and no amount of looking at Amber online could have prepared Sadie for how like her she was. And how terrifying that felt.

In the silence, she thought of Miles, too – back at home, waiting for them. He was barely speaking to her that morning and she kept switching between defiance and guilt in a way that was even more exhausting than the hangover. She had lived her own life for sixteen years now – who was he to suddenly impose curfews or demands? And then, just as suddenly, the realisation dawned again that she had been gone for *sixteen* years, almost; that he had managed to bring up their child all by himself and yet she could not be relied on to do such a simple thing as tell him that she would be late home. She could not do such a simple thing when everything between them was so uncertain – that feeling that they were still twenty, still about to tear each other's clothes off, persisted, and yet every moment was loaded with the memory of her absence; with the fact she had abandoned him. With the fact that he would never understand that she *had* to, she had done it for them. And now she was only making things worse.

She turned the car on to the drive and Miles was there on the lawn, the mower running. He leaned over to switch it off as Sadie killed the engine, straightening up as they climbed out of the car.

'Hey, baby girl,' he said to Amber, holding out an arm to direct her into a hug. 'Have a good night?'

'Yep! Billie's mum made us pizza. And pancakes this morning too.'

Sadie closed her door with the gentlest of clunks but they both turned to look at her. *Intruder.*

'That's nice,' Miles said to Amber, releasing her with a gentle squeeze to the shoulder. 'There's frittata in the kitchen, if you've got any room left.'

'Yum.' Amber headed for the open front door, her phone unlocked and the focus of her attention once again.

Miles studied Sadie for a second, and she felt another wave of nausea rise and then subside. 'I don't like it when we fight,' he said softly.

'Me neither,' she said, feeling something drawing back inside her, something crumbling. 'I'm sorry.' She was. She was always sorry.

'I'm sorry too.' He pulled her against his chest. His arms folded round her so naturally, so instinctively. Folding the past sixteen years away as only Miles could. 'I want you to have friends. I overreacted. I was scared.'

Testing herself, she leaned up to kiss him but his lips

were dry and cool and the smell of the cut lawn caught in her throat. Something was burning down the street and she felt fear crawl through her, Miles's shadow stretching across the ground while her own disappeared into it.

'You'd tell me,' he said into her hair. 'If you were . . . If things were . . . If they were here again?'

She tried to swallow, the burnt air snagging in her mouth. She nodded against the waffle fabric of his polo shirt.

'Good,' he said, a hand pressed to the back of her head, her forehead tucked under his chin. 'It's just the three of us now, isn't it?'

Friday, 18 May 2018, 03:04 PDT
From: Federica Sosa
To: Greta Mueller

Thanks for the text. That all sounds good, will look at the footage now.

How's Amber been today?

Friday, 18 May 2018, 03:05 PDT
From: Greta Mueller
To: Federica Sosa

She's had a bit of a funny day, actually. She had an interview for a French magazine – the journalist flew over here specially for it – and that seemed to go well. But some guy stopped her when we were out for lunch and told her she was the devil. It was awful.

Friday, 18 May 2018, 03:07 PDT
From: Federica Sosa
To: Greta Mueller
Did you get it on film?

Friday, 18 May 2018, 03:11 PDT
From: Greta Mueller
To: Federica Sosa
Tom was filming her at the time, yes. We were filming her on the phone to her agent.

It was horrible. You could see it bothered her even though she acted like it was no big deal.

Friday, 18 May 2018, 03:13 PDT
From: Federica Sosa
To: Greta Mueller
I think you're being too sensitive. She must be used to it by now – the kid grew up being told she was cursed! She's literally making a career out of it.

Seriously, don't feel sorry for her. Think of her fee! She needs to work for it.

Friday, 18 May 2018, 03:17 PDT
From: Federica Sosa
To: Greta Mueller
Look, you're doing a brilliant job over there. Honestly,

the stuff we have so far is great. I'm only pushing because I know this can be really special. And that could be huge for you. It could make you. And you deserve it! 😃

What r u doing up so late anyway?

Friday, 18 May 2018, 03:18 PDT
From: Greta Mueller
To: Federica Sosa
Jet lag. Plus this motel is both thin-walled and creepy.

Friday, 18 May 2018, 03:19 PDT
From: Federica Sosa
To: Greta Mueller
Amorous neighbours again?

Friday, 18 May 2018, 03:20 PDT
From: Greta Mueller
To: Federica Sosa
Not tonight. Small child crying. And I think the place has rats.

Did you see the email from A's teacher? What do you think, worth exploring?

Friday, 18 May 2018, 03:22 PDT

From: Federica Sosa
To: Greta Mueller
Urgh re rats!!!! You're kidding??!!!!

Yeah, I think it could be worth having an initial chat with the teacher. We've got that stuff from Sadie's old teacher – what was her name? Berkley? Barclay? – which is pretty creepy. Might sit well next to that.

Friday, 18 May 2018, 03:24 PDT
From: Greta Mueller
To: Federica Sosa
OK I'll schedule in a Skype call with her and figure out if there's much material in it. Also, did I send you this article? **[link redacted]** Very interesting Tall Man case in Germany in 2010. Didn't get much coverage here because it coincided with Dawn Brancheau being killed at SeaWorld.

Yes re rats! I can hear them running around inside the wall. It's nothing compared to that place in Texas though, remember? Bleurgh.

Friday, 18 May 2018, 03:25 PDT
From: Federica Sosa
To: Greta Mueller
Oh God, honey. That sounds awful. Next trip we go on, we'll have a better budget, promise.

Thanks for link. You really should get some sleep. I need you to push Amber tomorrow – maybe buy her a drink with lunch, try and loosen her up that way?

You could ask her how she felt about that incident today if you really think she was upset by it, might be a good jumping-off point for getting under her skin.

I'm talking to Morris right now and he's saying they need her to say what happened that night on camera. All of it. They want us to persuade her to be filmed going back to the house. It'd be gold.

Friday, 18 May 2018, 03:26 PDT
From: Greta Mueller
To: Federica Sosa
She said pretty categorically when she signed the contract that she wouldn't go back there.

Friday, 18 May 2018, 03:27 PDT
From: Federica Sosa
To: Greta Mueller
I know, I was there. I have faith that we can persuade her.

Friday, 18 May 2018, 03:28 PDT
From: Federica Sosa
To: Greta Mueller
Anyway, get some rest – you must be shattered. I'm sorry again that you're having to field all of this –

nightmare. And tell reception about the rats first thing!
That is totally unacceptable.

Thanks for being brilliant. I promise you this is going
to be worth it x

Friday, 18 May 2018, 03:30 PDT
From: Greta Mueller
To: Federica Sosa
Don't worry. And to be honest, I don't mind the rats so
much (!), it's the baby. Poor kid won't stop crying, I'm
starting to wonder if it's alone in there.

Anyway, I'll give crappy cable in bed another go. Night
x

Friday, 18 May 2018, 03:31 PDT
From: Federica Sosa
To: Greta Mueller
Earplugs, hon. Never travel without them.

Call you tomorrow when I know what's going on with
flights.

15

2016

Miles sat at the table and watched Amber finish a third slice of frittata. Sadie had gone to sleep upstairs, her hangover persisting. Amber had her iPad in front of her as she ate, scrolling through news stories about celebrities he didn't recognise on a tabloid site he despised. He taught about the dangers of such things on one of his post-graduate modules: the democratisation of celebrity, the tabloids' pervasive linking of weight loss or gain with status and success. And yet he let his daughter gorge on it. He watched her fingers manipulate the page, zooming in on a reality star's eye make-up; on another's cellulite, her face impassive all the while, eyes moving back and forth across the screen.

She looked up and caught him watching. 'What are you doing today, Daddybear?' she asked him, as she always did.

'I've got some essays to grade,' he said, picking up both plates and taking them to the sink. 'And then I thought I'd treat us all to a takeaway tonight – how does that sound?'

'I can't, sorry Dad. Said I'd help Mica with Milo.'

He turned to hide his disapproval. Mica's mother, Marcie, went out too much, if you asked him, leaving poor Mica holding the baby. 'Oh well,' he said, 'I'll give you some money, you guys can get a takeaway there.'

'Thanks, Dad, that's really nice of you.' Amber locked her iPad and then hesitated. 'Dad . . . Mum's OK, right?'

He dried his hands, eyes on the garden. 'I think so, baby girl. We'll have to keep an eye on her, won't we?'

She lingered a second longer and then disappeared upstairs with her iPad clutched to her chest, her chair left askew. He stood in the kitchen and listened until the house was silent and he could relax. He remembered the days when Amber was small enough to sleep during the day, when he would put her down in the afternoon and then walk through the rooms of the house, wondering where to begin. Often he would call his mother, who would send round his father, and Miles would lie on his bed and watch the ceiling as John shuffled around the kitchen, tidying and hiding the detritus of the day. Waiting for those first snuffly breaths to echo through the baby monitor, the first indignant mewl. Trying to silence the tide of electric feeling that every thought of Sadie ignited. Trying not to wonder where or what or how things could have been different.

He had never stopped thinking about her. He wondered if she knew that.

He was annoyed with himself for getting angry the previous evening. Yes, it was thoughtless and irresponsible of her not to have let him know that she would be late home – Amber, the actual teenager of the family, would never have done it, would never let him worry like that – but he needed to make allowances. He needed to accept that this was still a period of change, for all of them, and that it would take some time for them to find their way. He knew that he and Sadie were meant to be together; always had – had always known that he was the only person who truly understood her. And he'd known, he had *known*, even when he had let the doubts crowd in, that one day she would come home. Some things were meant to be. It was his job to look after her, it had been since they met. Sadie, he understood now, was still realising this. She'd been alone for so long that it was hard for her to allow the two of them in, and he needed to be patient.

A door closed gently upstairs, a small set of footsteps slipping across the floorboards above him – their room. He wondered if Amber had gone in to see Sadie and felt pleased. From somewhere far away, he could hear a baby crying. If he closed his eyes, he could almost be back there – just him alone, listening to his infant daughter cry, the pressure of knowing that he was the only one who would answer her almost unbearable.

He went up to his office and closed the door, attempting to shut the memories out. They were not helpful, he knew that. He had to forget now, forget the things they had all done. He glanced at his computer, the screensaver image he had chosen of the three of them. It was only a couple of weeks after Sadie had returned; he remembered herding the two of them together at the restaurant in town, handing the camera to a waitress. There he was in the middle, his smile wide and an arm around each of them. The waitress had caught them just as Amber had moved her head; caught her at an almost identical angle to Sadie. The similarities in their faces were striking. He wondered how hard it would have been if he had been wrong, if Sadie had never come home – if he'd had to watch their daughter grow into a mirror image of the woman who had left them both.

But she had come home. Just as he had known she would.

He moved the mouse and woke the computer, the photo dissolving. He glanced at the essay he had open, one he'd run through TurnItIn while he was making lunch. The results were in: 54 per cent plagiarised. Another student he'd have to call in on Monday. He crossed the screen away, annoyed, and opened his email to issue the summons.

He checked through his unread mail first. The same old department-wide messages about cleaning out the communal fridge, about separating recycling in the kitchen bins. Spam from two second-hand bookselling sites, and from a dating agency he had joined, in a fit of defiance, three years ago. He deleted that one without opening it, adding in the online takeaway receipts and the group email chain from some school friends who were trying to plan a get-together. None of that mattered now.

That left the emails from students – all scenarios familiar to him now after several years in the job, no excuse for an extension unturned – and then one from a sender he didn't recognise. SomeoneSpecial@gmail.com. The subject line *I know*.

It was a subject line designed to get attention and for that reason he paid it little. He felt sure he knew how it would end; some other dating agency or app, probably, with something cheap and tawdry and spammy: *I know . . . where your soulmate is* or perhaps the more direct *I know where your next great lay is waiting*. And so he clicked on it, knowing he had nothing to fear.

Realising, quickly, that he was wrong.

16

2018

'What do you think of me?' Amber asks Greta as she flicks through songs on her phone, already plugged into the stereo of their rental car. She's insisted they put the roof down, too, and Greta, who forgot to tie her hair back, is trying to navigate the entrance ramp to the freeway with strands of it snaking repeatedly over her eyes.

It's just the two of them, the boys finishing up some location shots from an emailed list Federica sent at 3 a.m. London time. It's their last day in LA and the week has passed in a blur of studio lights and the same prepared answers slipping out of Amber's mouth, all presumably dreamed up by the US arm of the talent agency she's signed to – Greta assumes in an attempt to drum up as much interest as possible in the North American rights for her tell-all book. But when it comes to *their* cameras, to their film, she hasn't had anything new to say. Greta's hoping that when they get back to London, Federica will be able to coax and cajole the answers she wants from her. She thinks that if Amber knew how much research Federica is doing on Sadie Banner's story instead of her own, it might persuade her to open up a bit. Because Federica's obsession is growing; the file of evidence they've been building up on the shared drive getting rapidly larger, the list of people Federica wants to interview longer and longer. The list of things that Amber said she would *not* discuss getting steadily chipped away at behind her back.

Greta doesn't want to go down that road. She's read and read and read about the Tall Man, about girls who thought he'd made them special, about daughters disappeared, and now she lies awake at night, watching shadows.

So when Amber, finally free of publicity commitments, asked if they could go to Disneyland today, Greta agreed. Disney, surely, can be relied upon to be shadow-free.

'What do you mean?' she asks now, safely in lane.

'Do you like me?' Amber flips down the sun visor and checks her make-up, running a finger across her newly plumped lips. *Her* hair is tied neatly back, a full ponytail which swings when she moves. 'Do you think I'm a bad person?'

Greta considers this. 'I'm not sure I know enough about you to like or not like you,' she says. 'But no, I don't think you're a bad person.'

She wonders if this is true. She sat backstage and watched Amber do another TV interview yesterday, this time for one of the daily news shows. She watched her

sit in the green room beforehand, flicking through a magazine until she found a picture of herself, and then trawling
the pages for another mention, and she watched her saunter
on to the set and settle herself in one of the matching
armchairs set up for the interview. She saw (as she's seen
all week) how Amber's voice became soft, timid almost,
and how, as the interviewer asked 'Do *you* think you're
innocent?', the tears welled up and began to fall. 'I took
her life and I have to live with that for ever,' Amber replied,
allowing one to slide slowly down her cheek, and then,
when the cameras were off, she returned to the green room
to eat the KFC she had asked for and to chat with the
B-movie actor who had waited to meet the famous Amber
Banner.

'I don't want to go back,' Amber says now. 'I like it
here.'

'Do you?' Greta hates it. She hates the endless highways
and tailbacks and billboards, the strip malls and perfect
white smiles. She hates Hollywood most of all. On the
way back to her hotel last night, she passed a woman
sitting on the edge of the street, busily slapping at a dirty
foot, trying to locate a vein among the grime and bruises.
A cluster of girls in skinny jeans clacked past, oblivious,
and a bus full of tourists sailed by, while cheerful 1950s
rock and roll pumped out of the vast souvenir shop on
the corner. It feels like everywhere she goes, a child is
crying; that everywhere she turns, a man eyes her from a
cab or a window or passing her on the sidewalk, their
gaze trickling over her skin like ice.

'Yeah.' Amber smiles at herself in the mirror and flicks the visor closed. She glances out at the city disappearing beside her. 'I'm, like, new here. Do you know what I mean? Nobody knows me, but people are interested.'

'People are interested in you in London, too,' Greta says, accurately.

Amber scoffs at this. 'Please. I'm a freakshow there. They just want to get a shot of me looking crazy. They want me to flip out and start smashing their cameras, so they get up in my face. They try and run my car off the road. Here the paps open doors for me. They pay for my stuff at Starbucks.'

This is true. Greta has seen it happen more than once over the last week. And Amber has never acknowledged it, or commented on it, and now there is no camera on her.

'Is that why you agreed to do the film?' Greta asks. 'So people could get to know you better?'

'No.' Amber shrugs. 'The money was good. Hey, slow down!'

Greta slams on the brakes, realising as she does that – for once – the road ahead is clear. Amber stretches an arm up above the windscreen, phone in hand, and snaps a photo of the road sign high above them, the lane instruction: *Anaheim*, a Mickey Mouse silhouette beside it. The sky is bright and blue beyond.

'Perfect,' Amber says, looking at the image and then opening Instagram. 'Urgh, I love this song.'

They drive in a companionable silence for a while, the

landscape wide and dusty under the endless blue. Greta tries not to think about the schedule for the next week, which Federica also set out in her email, packed full of location work, interviews, research. She tries not to think of the latest text from her, either, sent at 4 a.m. LA time: Sooooo sorry again. Disaster here. I think this could be it: over. Done. Don't know what to do. Followed, one minute later, by: Could you suggest to A that we do a school visit on Tues? I know she wasn't keen on filming there before but think it'll be a strong image – remind audience how young she is.

Seven minutes later: xxx

Greta can picture the scene when they arrive back in London. Federica puffy-eyed and sulky, endlessly checking her phone. She'll turn it on for Amber, of course, will heave her suitcase on to the trolley for her (the trolley abandoned to Greta minutes later) and move her carefully through the airport and into the waiting car, chatting all the while, letting Greta, Tom and Luca fall behind. And when Amber is safely in the hotel they've booked for her in London, the façade will fall. Then it'll be the two of them, the boys making their excuses, and Federica will pull her chair up close where her warm, meaty breath can reach Greta. The words will spill out, the details of what-ever Millie, Federica's novelist girlfriend, has found out or done (the latter unlikely; the former inevitable), and somehow this will feed back into a discussion of the project and all the ways in which *Greta* could have handled the situation better.

They've worked together twice before; once when Greta had just finished college and a friend's uncle, whose Hertfordshire estate was a popular (and profitable) filming location, got her a job as a runner on a period drama. Federica was an assistant director while the director was a formidable man in his fifties, known for wandering around the set in dark glasses, whispering acidly to his assistant but never speaking to any other member of the crew. Federica, on the other hand, with her bushy hair wrangled into a ponytail at the base of her neck, her own sunglasses always helping to marshal it back, spoke to anyone and everyone, a machine-gun patter of complaint as she walked through each room and tent: 'You – what's wrong with that reflector?' 'You – *what* is that painting doing there?' 'You – learned your lines today for a change?' She took a liking to Greta, who moved fast and never answered back, and when the poor set assistant hung the painting on the wrong wall yet again, she was fired on the spot and Greta – '*You*', a stubby finger stabbed in her direction – installed in her place.

Later, when Greta had notched up several similar and better jobs, a producer she had come to know and like (and once, ill-advisedly, allowed to kiss her in a prop storage warehouse in Shoreditch, a smell of mothballs and oil filling her throat, a broken neon arrow flashing feebly in a corner somewhere) had recommended her to Federica for a new film she was working on. Federica had invited her to her office in Soho and then, when Greta was ten minutes away, had texted to change the meeting to a coffee shop in Bethnal Green. Greta had arrived thirty minutes later, her thin floral top stuck to her back with sweat, the waistband of her jeans rubbing fiercely into her flesh. And Federica, sitting at a small wobbly table out on the pavement, dark glasses on and hair fluffed out into a sunlit cloud behind her, had simply smiled and taken a sip of her coffee. 'You'll learn,' she'd said, and Greta has.

The low-budget film they worked on then – a tiny crew of six, including Tom and Luca – had been a terrifying success. Not overnight; a cult success, followed by a moderate one, until suddenly Federica was stepping up on to a glassy stage, standing at a gold-leafed podium with an award clutched tightly in those wide, flat hands. A documentary about a notorious husband and wife who murdered hitchhikers in Texas over a period of three years, it gained critical praise for the access Federica was able to wheedle from the couple's children. Amber has already told Greta that she's seen it three times.

When Greta tells people that she worked on that film – which was originally called *A Sort of Darkness*, after something the youngest son of the couple said in one particularly harrowing interview (after sitting in on this interview, Greta drew her hotel blinds and went to bed at 3 p.m., every available blanket wrapped around her despite the blistering temperature outside), and which the distribution company eventually persuaded Federica to call *My Parents Are Murderers* – they like to tell her how much they love it. 'Like a horror film,' one friend gushed to her at a house party in a cramped flat in Camden.

'Except real!' She said it like it was a compliment, they all do. But they weren't there. They don't know.

A child is crying again, she's sure of it. It takes her a second to remember that they're on the highway, just the two of them. That the speakers are playing a song from Amber's phone, the melody high and wailing.

'We're almost there!' Amber squeals, leaning out over her door to take a photo of another sign. 'Oh my God, I'm so excited.'

And Greta's surprised to find she is too, just a little. It feels a bit like they're escaping, leaving something behind, even though she was apprehensive at being alone with Amber, the twin ballasts of Tom and Luca cut adrift. She remembers going to Tivoli Gardens with her parents on a holiday to visit friends in Copenhagen when she was small, the way the rides whirled and people smiled and the way her hand felt in her mother's.

She turns on to Disneyland Drive and wonders what Tom is doing, whether he and Luca are still working through Federica's wish list of footage (a list that includes such specific items as 'Child on beach with balloon or ball. Wind carrying balloon/ball away?' and 'Teen girls/young-looking drinking/laughing dark bar lots of neon') or whether they've given up and gone for a beer somewhere. She could text and invite them to come here, she thinks – if the traffic stays this light, they could make it in time. It'd be nice to have Tom there, maybe.

But when she pulls into a space in the vast parking lot, Amber turns, a hand flashing out white-hot against Greta's arm. 'Thanks so much for bringing me,' she says, those cattish green eyes locked on Greta's. 'It's nice of you.'

Before Greta can reply, the hand is gone again, its heat evaporating slowly from her skin, and Amber is climbing out of the car, her ponytail whipped up by a breeze as she looks around the car park in search of the shuttle bus that will take them away.

They walk up Main Street, Sleeping Beauty Castle looming ahead of them, while Amber aims her phone at buildings and characters. Outside a taffy shop, she asks a guy dressed as Aladdin if she can take a photo with him – and then surprises Greta by pulling her into frame too. There they are, the three of them with their faces close together, Amber's arm stretched right up to fit them in and her other hand gripping Greta's.

'I always loved Aladdin,' she says when they are walking away. 'That was my favourite of the films.' She glances at the photo and then at Greta. 'I used to sit on this rug we had in the house and pretend I could fly away on it. So lame.'

Greta smiles. 'My brother and I used to pretend we were the Aristocats.'

Amber considers this, eyes narrowed. 'I didn't know you had a brother.'

'Yes. He lives in the Middle East at the moment. He's a journalist.'

'Fancy. Shall we buy some taffy?'

She picks the biggest box, along with a snow globe

with a miniature version of the castle perched inside. She shakes it violently and watches the glitter settle, the last flakes drifting down the glass, and then she wanders off, leaving Greta to pay with a credit card she hopes will hold out for at least a day longer. Federica will pay the expenses eventually but it's a haphazard affair; a wad of battered and crumpled notes handed over one day, vague promises of a bank transfer another. *It'll all be worth it*, Greta reminds herself, though the thought of having to call her parents to ask for a loan in the meantime makes her sweat despite the shop's industrial-strength air conditioning.

'Let's go on a ride,' Amber says, when Greta rejoins her outside. The sun is climbing steadily in the sky, the heat dry and aggressive.

Greta agrees warily, and they wander through the park, Amber rooting through the box of white-wrapped taffy. 'It all tastes the same,' she declares after a fourth piece, her jaw working steadily at it. She hands the box to Greta. 'Why do they do that?'

Greta's wariness begins to fade as they pass signs for the Haunted Mansion and Big Thunder Mountain Railroad, Amber heading instead past the castle and into the tamer Fantasyland. She's surprised, though, when Amber laughs and says 'This one' to the old-fashioned flying Dumbos. It's a little kids' ride, the elephants slowly bobbing up and down as they turn to the sleepy organ music, but Amber clicks photo after photo on her phone and pulls Greta into line with her.

'So cute!' she says. 'You know, this used to be on the advert for Disneyland when I was a kid.'

Greta doesn't doubt it. Amber's memory is turning out to be forensic and photographic; tiny, irrelevant details about things retrieved in an instant. She thinks of those narrowed eyes: *I didn't know you had a brother.* She wonders what else Amber stores in her Greta file. She wonders what Sebastian, who has travelled to and reported from war zones all over the world, would think of his sister taking a teenage murderer to Disneyland to gain her trust.

Ride stopped, they climb into the cavity of an elephant, a mother and a fussing toddler in the one in front of them. Amber scans through her phone and Greta can't help glancing down at the screen too. Twitter: 1,350 notifications. She catches a glimpse of a couple as Amber's thumb trawls down them.

U sexy for a crazy bitch.

Hey Amber, saw you on Good Morning America. Wanted to say you're really brave.

watching @amber_banner on tv. u believe this shit? Bitch is some sick freak

Hey Amber, follow me back? ily

Amber Banner looking fierce on the cover of Hollywood Reporter today. Girl may be twisted AF but I like her style

Greta is numb to it now – she's trawled through the comments section of too many articles on Amber, has columns on her TweetDeck tracking Amber's handle and her name (because sometimes people want to draw Amber's attention to what they are saying about her – and sometimes they don't). She's seen the tide of public opinion turn over the course of the trial; Amber going from ice princess and sadistic teen murderess to brave and tragic and badass. The girl who laughed outside the court in which she was facing trial for the most horrendous crime to the girl who stood in the dock and wept as the story of the Tall Man was finally let loose. The girl who stood on the steps of that courthouse with that secret smile, free again. And the whole time, the world was watching. The world was captivated by every sordid detail. She remembers an article that ran on the MailOnline on day 34 of the trial, the day things really began to change for Amber. The way the details of the defence's case had been accompanied by a full-length photo of Amber leaving the courtroom, a box-out with details of how to 'Get the look' and links to lookalike shirts. On the same day, a feminist blog Greta loves ran a piece entitled 'Amber Banner does not have to cry for you to prove she is innocent: Resting Bitch Face and the perils of trial by media'. Greta's read all of it. Every column inch, every thinkpiece, every comment, every tweet. They don't surprise her any more.

She watches Amber's face as she scrolls through those notifications. A slight reaction here and there; a twitch of an eyebrow or the corner of her mouth. She wonders if they lodge in her memory too – the softer words sinking away while the sharper ones claw their way to the surface. You wouldn't know it from the outside – but Greta doesn't want to believe that the outside is all there is. If that is true, there is no story. She thinks of Tom on the beach. *It's easy to get lost trying to find the story in something. Sometimes people are just bad.* If Greta starts to believe that, she may as well quit now.

The ride starts, their elephant coasting gently down towards the ground before beginning its journey up. Amber laughs her strange, flat laugh. She takes photos: of the crowd below, of the skyline ahead, of the two of them together, her face close to Greta's again. After a couple of rotations, she grows bored, her phone slipping into her lap. Instead she looks out, a hand, with its new purple acrylic nails, clutching the grey edge of the carriage. She smells of perfume and fake tan and something metallic.

Greta looks out at the park too. Endless buggies and mouse-eared balloons, the organ music that drifts up to them carrying with it laughter and wheedling child voices; a smell of burnt sugar and suncream. She thinks again of Tivoli, with its bronzes and its blues and reds, the sharp-edged air and the mechanical chug of the rides. And she thinks of her brother in his buggy, a fat fist pressed against his cheek as he slept. Now he is tall and wiry and far away.

'You're difficult to read,' Amber says, conversationally. 'I never really know what you're thinking.'

'Yes, I've been told that before.'

Amber glances at her. 'I like that about you.'

Greta watches a man hoist his small daughter on to his shoulders so she can watch as Cinderella passes. It occurs to her that people in the park may recognise Amber, even without a camera trailing after her. She thinks of the way the old man forced his way past her and Luca earlier in the week, his finger right up close to Amber's face. *Devil child. Devil. Leave this place.*

The ride slows, the music stops. They drift down to the boarding platform and the bar on their carriage is released by an attendant. Amber looks at Greta.

'Let's go and get a drink,' she says.

They sit outside one of the restaurants beside the lake, two misty glasses of beer and a plastic basket of fries on the table between them. Greta leans a cheek against her shoulder, the skin there hot and taut. Burnt, after days of being so careful. She edges her chair further into the shade and glances at her watch.

'This time tomorrow, we'll be in London,' she says.

Amber reaches out and takes a chip, trails it through a pool of ketchup on the wax paper. 'Yeah,' she says. 'I guess we will.'

'Do you have friends there?'

Amber shrugs. 'Yeah. People . . . I don't know. I know people.'

'Are most of your friends still at home?'

'No. Most of them went to uni. Jenna's at home, though – like that's a surprise.'

Greta takes a sip of her beer, the fizz electric on her tongue. 'And will you go and study now?'

'I dunno.' Amber's phone buzzes with yet another notification and she glances at the screen. She shifts in her chair and then fixes her gaze on Greta again. 'What will *you* do after this is over?'

Greta looks away, out at the lake. Her nose is burnt too. 'I'm not sure. It will take us a while to finish this project. To put it together.'

'What happened to the other kids?'

Greta looks back at her. 'Which other kids?'

'From *My Parents Are Murderers*. What happened to them after the film came out?'

Greta thinks of the three of them: Otis, Danny, Hayley. Hayley used to call her all the time, at least once a week, her voice husky and shy. The boys would send messages sometimes, or write, at first at least. A card at Christmas from Otis and then from Otis and his wife and then, the final one, a third name, a baby.

'They still live in Texas, I think,' she says. 'I think they try to keep things normal. They're happy.'

'They're famous.' Amber twists her beer on its paper mat. 'You think people still recognise them in the street and stuff?'

'I don't know. Maybe. But . . .' She trails off; drinks more beer in the hope of pushing the sentence back down.

Amber raises an eyebrow. 'Yeah, I know. It's different, right? *They* didn't do anything wrong. *They* didn't kill anyone.'

'That's not what I was going to say.' (It is.)

'It's all right, Greta.' Amber sinks back in her chair, tilts her face up to the sun. 'I can look after myself,' she says, eyes closed.

Greta watches the big steamboat waddle across the water, two gangly-limbed kids on its deck waving furiously. She thinks of Otis and Danny again, the Miller boys. Fifteen and thirteen, that first day on set, eyes hard and distrusting. Hayley with her soft small mouth and the ratty twists of her hair, ends all soggy where she sucked them constantly, her feet in their scuffed white sandals edging always back and forth. Her damp hand always seeking Danny's – and then, a week in, always Greta's.

'So, you like Tom then?' Amber asks. A solitary wisp of cloud slips harmlessly beneath the sun.

'What?'

Amber rolls her head lazily to the left, eyes sliding open with a smile. 'Oh, come on. You *lurve* him.'

She thinks of Danny Miller, leaning close to her on the back step of his family's house, a smudge of chocolate at the corner of his mouth, his tongue working at a wobbly tooth. *You're real pretty, Greta.* Otis and his wife. Hayley, sucking a twist of hair.

'Don't worry about it,' Amber says. 'He likes you too. I can tell.'

17

2016

After they had sex for the second time, he fell asleep. Amber gently lifted herself into a sitting position and watched him. He had his arm thrown up over his eyes (often he slept with his face covered in some way) but she traced the curve of his jaw, dark with stubble, and then the fainter lines which fanned out from the corners of his mouth and nose. They gave her a strange, tumbling feeling in her belly. He was ageing. A man. It was *hot*.

She didn't actually know *how* old he was. She'd asked him a couple of times; he always seemed to find a way to avoid answering. He'd say: *Age is just a number, baby* or *You're as young as the woman you feel, Peachy* and he'd say these things in a cheesy, pervy uncle voice and then kiss her, in a twin effort to end the questioning. It wasn't that she cared. He was at least thirty, maybe closer to forty, but she didn't mind. It was a bit weird when she thought that he could be older than her dad, though Miles looked young, younger than he was, even considering he was only four years older than Amber was now when she was born. Sometimes, lying awake at night, she tried to imagine herself holding a baby four years from now. It was too alien, she couldn't do it. She couldn't believe Miles had – and *alone*. Alone and studying for a degree at the same time. It was incomprehensible to her. He had given up his whole life to look after her, and she had spent her whole childhood feeling lucky, feeling relieved. But now that she was old enough to understand what the world had to offer someone – what he had given up – she only felt guilty. *That* was why she kept smiling and agreeing to his lame ideas, why she never missed a curfew, never let him realise when she was drunk. That was why she tried to make his life easy.

At least now he had the thing he had been waiting for all along: Sadie. She couldn't hold him back from that.

And now *she* had Leo.

She had met him a couple of weeks before, at the club in a neighbouring town where nobody cared about ID if you showed some skin and turned up early enough. The cheap sign outside (Comic Sans) said 'The Box' but it was known locally – universally – as The Pox. It had sticky carpets and woodchip walls, and a balcony ran around the dance floor so that there was always a good chance someone slumped against it up there might drop a bottle on your head. But the prices were low and the music all right, and there were usually at least a couple of sixth-form boys hanging around. On this particular evening, though, the club had been fairly empty. That was OK; she had had Mica and Jenna with her, and they'd drunk a bottle of wine as they walked there and then a couple of shots at the bar and so they'd danced and messed around on the tacky pole at the centre of the dance floor.

She'd realised he was watching her in the mirrored walls. Sitting at a table alone, a bottle of beer in front of him, a plain blue shirt open at the collar. He saw her looking and so she smiled, Jenna bumbling drunkenly into her.

Later, he came up behind her and put a hand on her back. Taller than he'd seemed at the table, his body long and lean. 'Can I buy you a drink?'

At the bar, she held the vodka and Coke he bought her and she let him type his number into her phone and press 'Call'. 'Can I take you out some time?' he asked, and she smiled in a way that said 'Maybe'. At the end of the night, she let him queue up for her coat and then she let him kiss her, Mica and Jenna giggling on a sofa behind them. And then he disappeared into the crowd and she didn't hear from him again until a week or so later, when he called her out of the blue and asked her to meet him for dinner.

It wasn't as if she hadn't been on dates before – though she wasn't sure if a Saturday afternoon trip to the cinema with Mica's cousin counted. It wasn't even as if it had been her first time going *further* either, although admittedly it was different when you weren't cramped in the bathroom at a party or trying to find a secluded spot in the park with your friends sniggering over at the swings. She'd been worried that she would feel out of her depth with him; that she wouldn't have the power she did over boys her own age. It frightened her and yet somehow she was surprised to find herself doing it anyway.

He was hardly the perfect boyfriend. She got the impression often that he wasn't listening to her, that his mind was elsewhere – until, of course, she removed her clothes and then his eyes were fixed on her, their cool blue gaze unflinching. He forgot or didn't bother to reply to messages, rolled his eyes when she mentioned Facebook or Snapchat or Instagram. Rolled his eyes often, in fact, at most things she said – once even pressing a finger to her lips so that she was shocked into silence. But she liked him. He hardly seemed to sleep, and though he was bad at messaging he liked to call, liked to talk in whispers though only she had people at home to hear her. She liked to watch him move – the smooth way he went from room to room, his steps even and light, and the unexpectedly delicate way he ran his fingers over her skin. The way he picked through his food so slowly, slithers of meat nipped out with chopsticks and delivered into his thin-lipped mouth. And best of all, the fact he had his own flat – a small, soulless place, yes, but a place where Amber could be in charge again.

He turned on to his side beside her, the sheet slipping down over his pale skin, his long, slender torso. She slid a hand under the pillow carefully and retrieved her phone. A message from Billie: How's it going? Did you wear the new top? I've eaten a whole tub of Phish Food watching all three Toy Story DVDs ☺ Amber wrinkled her face. So lame. Billie was cute with it, though, and Amber liked having her as a sort of apprentice. She liked the way Billie hung off her every word without yet seeming to feel the fear Jenna did around Amber. Sure, Jenna did her best to hide it, but it was always there, under the surface. Amber scared her, and she didn't enjoy it like she used to. Especially now that her other friends seemed to be distancing themselves too.

Who can blame them? she thought bitterly. *Your mother hears voices and you may or may not be cursed. Super appealing BFF material.*

A message from Jenna popped up then, as if Amber had summoned her. Do u want to borrow my black dress this wkend? xxxx

On second thoughts, maybe being slightly scary did have its benefits. It was definitely better than the way she felt around Mica and Alisdair now. Better to be someone to be scared of than someone to feel sorry for.

There was a text from Miles, too, asking what time she'd be home. He'd stopped doing that so much since Sadie had turned up – not because he didn't care, or at least she didn't think so. Even though Amber knew she was the third wheel now, in the way of their grand romantic reunion, Miles had gone out of his way to do little things to reassure her. Taking her for hot chocolate and a muffin on a Sunday morning, the way he always had. Saving certain sections of the paper for her while he read the rest. Asking her to chop the vegetables for a stir-fry, because she did it better than he did. All of these routines and traditions that they'd saved up over the years, all the things that had made them – the two of them – a family. And yet he had also managed to leave space for Sadie to try and claim some part of things for her own. Suggesting that she and Amber walk together to pick up some mysteriously forgotten ingredient for dinner. Busying himself with work so that Sadie was the one available for lifts and pick-ups. He'd gone out of his way to make sure everyone felt at home, that everyone had a role and a place. Even though it was quite clear that they – Miles and Amber – already had all of the roles covered, he had tried.

So, no, it wasn't exactly that he didn't want her around. It was just, she'd realised, that he worried less. When Sadie had been gone, the idea that Amber might disappear had been the single worst thing that could happen to Miles – and it had probably seemed all too possible, too, given his wife had gotten up and walked out in the middle of the night, without leaving so much as a note. But then Sadie had come home again, and Miles had been free to be his optimistic, glass-half-full self around the clock, instead of being seized with anxiety whenever any kind of possible crisis even suggested itself. And even though she wasn't as confident as he was that Sadie would stay, Amber wouldn't be the one to take that security away from him.

She typed a quick reply to him – Before midnight, promise ☺ xxx – and wondered if she'd get away with that blatant flaunting of her 11 p.m. curfew. It would depend on whether or not Sadie had persuaded him to share a bottle of wine.

Leo stirred again beside her, starting to wake properly now, so she slid down the bed and turned on to her side so that they were face to face. His eyes fluttered open and she smiled at him sleepily.

'What time is it?' he said, and it was totally gross but his hot breath felt so great on her face.

'Nine,' she said. 'I have to go soon.'

He pouted and pulled her closer. 'Nope.'

'Yep.' She snuggled into him though she knew she'd get up in a second. She would get home early, make Miles happy. She'd have to tell Leo she was meeting a friend; going for drinks; coursework – whatever tripped its way to her tongue most naturally.

He ran a hand right down her side, shoulder to knee and then up again, put his face close to hers.

'You're amazing,' he whispered, words warm against her neck. 'Special.'

And she almost felt sorry for him.

The light clicked off in the hall, footsteps slinking past the door. Sadie hugged the unfamiliar pillow to her chest. Helen and Marie's parents were finally going to bed. Justine reached over and gripped her hand, her sleeping bag shushing them even as she spoke.

'It's almost time,' she said, her breath warm and sweet in the dark. 'You ready?'

'Yes,' Sadie said. The darkness didn't scare her. She knew he wouldn't visit her here, not with all of them together. The Tall Man had his special girls and his time with them was special too, it was not to be shared. He sought them out when the moment was right, when they were alone. She and Justine both knew this. It wasn't their fault if the others weren't ready for him yet.

She felt under her pillow for her torch. 'What if we get caught?' Helen whispered.

Marie was already up, carefully packing things into her

backpack. 'We won't get caught if you keep quiet, numpty. Stop breathing so loudly.'

'I can't control my breathing, Marie. Why are you so mean?'

'Shut up.' Justine pulled a sweatshirt over her head. 'This is important, guys. We have to do it right.'

'If we get caught, we're going to get in so much trouble.' But Helen was out of bed too, pulling thick socks over her pyjama bottoms.

'We won't get caught,' Sadie said. She knew they wouldn't. He would keep them safe.

They opened the door and sat close together beside it, listening. There was the creak of the mattress and then silence. Marie poked Helen in the ribs. 'You're still doing it,' she hissed, but Sadie couldn't hear Helen breathing. She could only hear the thud of her own pulse.

It seemed to take for ever until they heard the rumble of Helen and Marie's dad snoring. Marie stood up. 'OK, let's go.' She led the way into the hallway and down the stairs, showing them which step halfway down creaked, Helen almost stumbling as she tried to avoid it. Sadie felt something bubbling up in her like laughter. An urge to scream or sing, to run out of the door and spin around under the black night sky. They were actually doing it. They were going to the woods to find him.

The streets looked different in the dark. The houses sleeping, cars silent in drives. They stole down the side of the estate and on to the footpath that led across the fields and towards the river, the woods. Once they were in the shelter of the trees, they turned on their torches and Sadie felt she could breathe again.

'Tell us again what we have to do, Justine.' Helen hurried to keep up with them. She had had to put on her school shoes and her fluffy slipper socks bulged out of them, her dad's sweatshirt hanging down over her pyjamas. She looked like a child and Sadie was embarrassed for her. 'Will it definitely work?' She sounded breathless though Sadie couldn't tell if it was excitement or fear or asthma.

'It'll work,' Marie said, smiling at Justine. 'The boy who lives next door to Justine's nan told us about it.'

Sadie had seen the boy before. Sandy blond hair and freckles, shell-suit trousers and filthy T-shirts. Sometimes when they went round to call for Justine he would watch them from a window. She hated that house anyway, with its dusty yellow net curtains, the smell of cabbage that always flooded out when Justine's nan opened the door. Helen had told her that Justine had to live there because her mum was in prison, but Helen often got stories wrong and so it was not always a good idea to listen to her.

'And we'll see him? The Tall Man?' Helen tripped on a loose stone, her clammy hand shooting out and grasping Sadie's arm. The trees shivered in the breeze.

She thought of the Tall Man she saw in her dreams. He showed her all of his faces now. Sometimes he was soft and kind, a movie-star twinkle in his eye. He told her that she was special and that he would protect her. Sometimes he wore his other face and stayed in the shadows, his voice slithering out into the light. A pale hand with its long, elegant fingers reaching down and closing over hers.

'I heard that he took a girl in Manchester,' Justine said. 'She disappeared from her bed one night.'

'Do you think he'll show her to us?' Helen asked. 'Like those kids in the magazine?'

Justine shook her head. 'We aren't that special yet. That's why we have to prove ourselves to him.'

They reached their clearing, the place they came to give him things, to burn their letters to him. She remembered the last one she had written: I want to be special. *She remembered glancing at Justine's as the flame took hold, the paper blackening.* Never leave me. *The way she had looked up and seen Justine watching her, her eyes blazing with the flickering orange light. She had let go of the burning letter, let it flutter down to Sadie's feet. Her eyes never leaving Sadie's as she lifted her foot and stamped on it.*

There were no stars in the sky and the darkness in the woods was almost complete. Their torch beams danced across the trees, their breath hanging in the air.

'Here.' Justine drew a circle in the soil with the toe of her trainer. 'Who has it?'

And Marie knelt and unzipped her backpack, removing the bundle of sweatshirt she had stuffed in there. 'Point the light this way, Helen, you div.' She unfolded a sleeve and then the other, and there it was, the knife that she had stolen from the kitchen while her dad set up the video for them in the living room. Sadie felt the first real pang of fear then. Helen's hand slipping into hers made her jump.

'Will it hurt?' Helen asked.

'Yeah.' Justine shrugged. 'But we have to give him something if we want him to give us stuff.' She took the knife from Marie. 'Who's first?'

Nobody spoke. It didn't matter anyway. Justine's eyes were on Sadie.

She held out her palm. Closed her eyes as the blade bit in; as the wind whispered in her ear.

18

2018

The cabin lights are dimmed, the window shades drawn. Greta drifts uncomfortably through dreams, the muted sounds of the people around her (the soft tinkle of the trolley, the whispering crew in the service area in front of them) never quite drowned out by sleep. She feels guilty about leaving Tom and Luca in Economy, though when she wandered back there, an hour after take-off, both were sound asleep – Tom with his head against the wall of the plane, a rolled-up jacket wedged between his shoulder and cheek, Luca sliding down in his seat, his skinny legs stretched out beneath the seat in front of him and his sleep-mask pulled firmly down. Her own feels scratchy and over-showy on her face; a prop. She remembers Federica's email from earlier in the week: *Earplugs, hon. Never travel without them.* She's not sure they would have helped anyway.

They are halfway across the Atlantic when she feels Amber shift in the seat beside her. She pushes the mask up her face, blinking, and Amber's face is close by hers, eyes open. They stare at each other a while, the insistent air recycling endlessly from the vents above them. Then Amber turns over, tossing the blanket up over her shoulder. Greta pulls the mask all of the way off and lies on her back, looking up at the overhead lockers.

It's different to the way it was with the Millers. She was only an assistant then; she showed up to the meetings and she showed up to shoot days and she asked the questions she'd been told to ask when it became apparent the kids had grown to trust her. This time she's been involved from the start – she's been there through all of the trawling and the gathering and the dismissing, through all the pitches and the consultations and the initial interviews. She was there the day Federica had her first meeting with Amber – alone, in a wine bar in Soho – when Federica came back to the flat and beamed at Greta and Millie, a bottle of champagne clutched in her hand. *She's perfect*, she'd said. *This is the one*. Greta's heard Federica tell and retell the story of Sadie and Amber Banner and their ghosts to executives and investors and, once, a group of strangers in the pub.

It's Greta, though, who has to find the pieces for them to put together. Greta who has to search police records and land registries and electoral registers, who has to stalk various strangers through their social media in order to fill in some peripheral detail which Federica will somewhere down the line decide is irrelevant. Greta has spent months chasing a ghost across counties and countries but it isn't a man, tall or otherwise, just a mother running endlessly.

Isn't it?

She glances at the back of Amber's head again, its tumble of bleach-streaked hair. She tries to imagine her as a newborn, the cursed child. Tries to imagine what Sadie Banner saw, looking into that small face in the Moses basket, another set of breaths behind them in the darkness. She thinks of the sound file Federica uploaded to the shared drive last night, a recorded phone call. No note to say whether or not the woman knew she was being recorded or where Federica found her, whether her statements have been verified. Since the press picked up on the fact that the acclaimed Federica Sosa was filming her next project and that the Banner case was at its centre, all kinds of people have been crawling out of the woodwork, their stories offered. People who claim that Sadie Banner was possessed by the devil, who claim that she was their playmate as a toddler. People who claim that Amber Banner is not who she says she is, that the *real* Amber Banner died as a child or was spirited away. That the whole Tall Man story is a cover-up. That it's the truth.

But this woman was quiet, nervous. Without any notes it's hard to be sure, but it doesn't sound like she'd volunteered her story – more likely she's been tracked down in one of Federica's feverish bouts of research, probably with Millie in bed or out at work, Federica caffeinated and

184

jittery and determined to chase down whichever loose end she temporarily had hold of.

'You lived in Wombleton in 2005,' Federica had said, no trace of a question and her breath heavy on the line.

'Yes.'

'Next door to you, for six months, lived a woman who had previously been known as Sadie Banner.'

'No— Well, I didn't know that. When I went round to say hello, she told me she were called Jane.'

A silence from Federica, the woman too nervous not to fill it.

'But yeah, looking at the picture you sent, and the newspapers and that, she were her. Sadie.'

'Did you speak to her often?'

'No. She were a quiet one, kept herself to herself. Up at funny times of the night, 'sleep most the day, that sort of thing.'

'Why, what job did she have?'

'Bits and bobs. She were the cleaner for the pub for a while, then stopped showing up. She done a bit of waitressing too, caff over in Pickering. She told me she'd done factory work before she moved, night shifts, so her sleep were messed up.'

'Did you talk often?'

'Nope. I hardly saw her after that first time when she'd moved in.'

'Didn't you think that was strange?'

'No, she were a good neighbour to have. No trouble, polite if you did see her in the street.'

'So no problems at all?'

'Well . . .'

Greta remembers that hesitation clearest of all. When she heard it in her earbuds in the car on the way to the airport, it made her pulse speed up. The story was there, in that trailed sentence, that second-guessing. And Federica was the shark circling the cage, waiting for it to venture out. The bloodlust went through Greta despite herself, and she clicked up the volume on her phone to hear what came next. She's tempted to sit up now and play it again, even though she remembers every word.

'There were a few times . . .'

'Yes?'

'My kids used to say a bloke were watching them. Her boyfriend. Used to stand in the back garden when they was out playing and that. He'd not wave if they said hello, just smiled. Unsettled them, like.'

'Did you ever see him?'

'Once. It was at night and I were walking the dog past the house. Some bloke were closing the curtains in the bedroom.'

'That doesn't sound particularly memorable.'

The hesitation is there again, the woman's breathing slow and heavy. But the story is in motion now. There's already blood in the water.

'Well, it were late,' she says, 'and I were tired and the dog – little mongrel thing it were, pain in the arse – just stood right there on the pavement and I couldn't get it to move. It were like that, it didn't do any of your come or

186

sit or stay. It went when it went and if it didn't, well you were buggered. So I were there, tugging its lead and freezing my arse off and it's stood there, looking up at the house. Jane's house. So I look up too and I seen him there, in the window.'

'And how would you describe him?'

A longer pause then; Greta turns back on to her side and considers it. Not a hesitation. A simple search for an answer that has suddenly become evasive.

'He were a big man,' the woman said eventually (doubtfully). 'The streetlight were right here so I couldn't see much through the glass, not his face or owt. I just seen him draw the curtains and when I looked up he stopped for a second and he were looking back at me. But with the streetlight, like I say, I couldn't see his face. He were just stood there and I were stood there and the fecking dog were stood there and then he closed the curtains the rest of the way and I had ter drag the dog home.'

'And you saw him after that?'

'No.' The woman impatient now; the story out and waiting. 'Look, the thing is, when I get to my front path, I look back, even though the dog were dragging *me* then, he couldn't wait to get inside. I look back and I seen . . .'

This time Greta can tell that Federica lets the silence unspool because her interest is waning. But perhaps this is what allowed the woman to say what she said next; something that under greater scrutiny she might've had second thoughts about voicing.

'I seen that the windows were all like they'd been before.

No curtains closed. Just the bedroom light glowing out
even though I'd seen him there, seen him pull them shut.
Curtains open, no bloke there, the dog growling like no
one's business. I were half-cut, I'll admit, but I remember
it. It were weird enough for me to remember it.'

'OK.' Federica's voice carefully modulated, even Greta
unable to discern whether she took this seriously. 'And
what happened after that?'

'The next day the kids saw him watching them again.
It were hot and they were out messing around with the
hose and this paddling pool we'd got off their cousin, and
he were watching them.'

'You saw him?'

'Well . . . no. But Gemma, she's my youngest, she were
right upset about it, she wouldn't go outside the rest of the
weekend. So I went round there. I told Jane, your boyfriend's
got eyes wandering where they's not meant to be.'

'How did she react?'

'She didn't say much but then she never did. She were
sorry and she said it wouldn't happen again and that were
that. I went home.'

'And did it happen again?'

'Nope. Next day she were gone. No moving van, no
nothing. We didn't even notice 'til my mate who works
down the estate agent in Pickering told me and by that
time they'd signed up a new tenant, it were a done deal.
End of Jane. The next lot were right arseholes, let me tell
you. Music at all hours, screaming rows half the day.
Made you appreciate how good Jane'd been.'

'Have you been in touch with her since?'

The woman's answer was no. The trail in Greta's head is blinking out but already all of the things she knows about Sadie Banner have buzzed into life, gradually reshaping themselves to accommodate this new piece of the puzzle. One more square filled in on the grid. A step closer.

She rolls on to her other side, her back to Amber, and finally sleep comes to her. Though when it does, it's filled, as it always is, with the feeling of Hayley Miller's small damp hand in hers, with the sound of a child crying and crying and crying.

19

2016

On Monday, Sadie was alone again. It was not the kind of alone she was used to, but she was at least starting to feel less like an intruder, Goldilocks waiting for the return of the bears. The silence was a relief. The weekend had drained her; the endless hangover of Saturday, the like-clockwork arrival of Miles's parents on Sunday for their lunch. Miles in the kitchen, fussing over the joint, individually painting potatoes with goose fat; Sadie refilling endless G and Ts and straightening place settings. And Amber at the centre of it all; joking with her grandfather, allowing Miles's mother to stroke her hair away from her face, to clasp her chin between ringed fingers and examine her face with proprietary interest. Amber starting conversations at the table, gliding effortlessly through the silences the rest of them seemed to stagnate in.

Six visits now, and Sadie wondered if she had begun

to find her footing in this small slot of her family's routine. Even in the beginning, that first night, with Miles clinging to her and his tears drenching the grubby shoulder of her T-shirt – even with Amber, appearing open-mouthed and bed-headed on the bottom step in her pyjamas, as if Miles had invited her to meet Santa himself – Sadie had known that it would be Frances and John Banner who would prove hardest to win round. They always had.

The first time they'd come over after her return Frances had avoided looking at her for at least an hour, and Sadie had wanted to melt into the wall, curl into a corner, anything in order to help her. She'd known she should say something, but how to even begin? And so it had been stiff silences and John's false cheer forming a jolly base note to Miles's breezy small talk. Amber sitting back in her chair, watching them all with that smile. Enjoying it.

Now they were all becoming used to each other once again. There were still uncomfortable moments – John, his third G and T almost empty, cutting into the sponge that Sadie had made (Amber's cupcakes never materialising) and inquiring, 'Get up to much baking, Sadie? Where you were?' – but mostly it was the kind of discomfort she remembered from when they were first a couple, when they had had to tell them that she had fallen pregnant. Before all of it.

Well, not before *all* of it.

There was a moment after they'd left yesterday when Amber had come into the kitchen and found Sadie loading up the dishwasher, her own beaded glass of gin on the counter beside her. She straightened up, uncertain, as Amber came closer, took the tea towel Sadie had flung over her shoulder and began drying the glasses left on the draining board.

'You don't have to do that,' Sadie had said, surprised, but Amber merely shrugged.

'I want to,' she'd said, nudging the volume on the radio up – the Four Tops playing – and the two of them had finished the cleaning together.

She turned this memory over now, alone in Miles's study, and then thought of Frances and Amber together in the bright light from the patio doors after lunch, the three of them alone in the room. A mother and a mother and a daughter. Could things ever be that simple?

Her phone buzzed on the desk, her heart stuttering painfully. Leanna: Fancy lunch on Wednesday? She tapped out a reply and then turned the phone off.

She could not shake it, now, that memory of Amber up close by her. Taking the tea towel from Sadie's shoulder, her fingertips grazing the skin not protected by it. It had been hot, the kitchen muggy and the lamb bone left in the roasting dish on the counter so that its oily smell hung in the air, the last flecks of flesh curling as they dried. Sadie couldn't detach the image from one of Justine, leaning closer to her in the woods, her breath sickly sweet and her lips sticky with sugar. *He can make you special, if you ask him.* Justine drawing a circle in the dirt with the toe of her shoe; Justine sitting on the edge of a kerb, a cat winding its way around her legs. Digging a kitchen knife into the palm of Sadie's hand, blood running down her fingers and dripping slowly on to the ground.

A floorboard creaked in the next room. Amber's room, though Amber had left for school several hours ago.

She straightened herself, took a deep breath. Amber was not Justine, she was not Sadie. She was not one of them; she was safe. She had to be. It couldn't all have been for nothing – Sadie had led the Tall Man from her daughter, she had protected her. And yet she couldn't shake the feeling that something was wrong.

Another creak, closer to the wall this time, and she thought for a second that she heard the first small notes of that laugh she had left behind. She waited as the sound resolved itself into a siren somewhere in the distance, its peals wavering as they reached her.

She attempted to return to the mundane and monumental task of trying to find a job. It felt strange, as it often did, to be doing things the way everyone else did them. Searching brightly coloured job sites instead of surreptitiously asking around, checking noticeboards in the windows of rundown shops, cheap ads in local papers. She had cleaned, she had cooked, she had packed and shrink-wrapped and counted. Each time she had thought she'd found a place where she could keep the shadows to herself. And each time she had been proven wrong. She remembered the feeling of relief in that first year, her cottage near Peterhead. A cleaning job in a factory, the night shift, the workers gone. Just her and her mop, the occasional giggle from the darkened corners. A small set of footsteps echoing hers. Then the factory had been closed, Sadie reassigned by the agency to a school. She remembered the deep, plunging dread when they'd told her, how she had stammered and tripped over her words as she tried to think of a reason why she could not work in a place where children would be. *Oh, don't worry*, the woman had said, keen to be rid of her. *It's after hours, the kids'll be long gone by the time you're there.* And this had been true, at least at first. She had begun to relax again, she had even begun to wonder if he might have left her for good. But then one evening, the rickety old vacuum plugged in, she'd turned and seen the classroom door open. A little girl and her mother, a favourite teddy left behind. And as the child ran to retrieve it, Sadie had heard the Tall Man whisper in her ear. Had seen his girl step out of the shadows in her terrible bloodstained dress and wander over to the child. Her face pressed close, taking her in, while the mother, oblivious, chattered on beside Sadie.

She had packed her things and left town that night, her last paycheque left uncollected.

So yes, it did feel odd to be looking for a job again. In the months – the years – before she had returned, alone on Skye, she had limited herself to interacting only online wherever she could. Old furniture bought on auction websites, sanded and painted in her empty garage and then resold on those same sites. Shopping bought online, picked up from a collection point at dawn. She had hidden herself away and in doing so, she had finally made him lose interest in her.

And now she was letting other people in again. She

opened the computer's browser – but instead of launching a new window, an old one reloaded. Not her email account, but Miles's. His work account, the rest of the university homepage's tabs loading across the top of the page.

She hesitated. This was tempting; she knew little about Miles's life at work. He talked about his classes sometimes over dinner, told them funny stories about students coming in hungover or with elaborate and improbable excuses for not handing in their coursework. But here were emails from other members of staff, his colleagues, some friendly, some cool, and here she was, intruding, uninvited. *Not your life.*

She noticed an email about halfway down the page, an anonymous account: SomeoneSpecial@gmail.com. No subject line. Her mouth suddenly dry, heart thudding in her chest. She clicked on it.

Meet me at 3.30 at The Bell and I won't tell, it read. Next to that was a small smiley face. Winking.

At lunchtime Amber, Jenna and Billie sat on the wall outside the Science block, sharing the fancy fruit salad Leanna had packed for Billie. Amber checked the message she'd sent to Mica during the last period but it was showing as delivered, not read, and the sound of Billie's heels bumping lazily against the wall made her feel like something inside her was winding tighter and tighter.

'Jake was asking about you on WhatsApp last night,' Jenna said idly, rummaging through the Tupperware box for yet another strawberry. 'You totally blew him off after your birthday, huh?'

Amber glanced at Billie, whose cheeks had turned pink. Her heels bumped against the wall harder.

'He's totally into Bill,' she said, glaring at Jenna. 'Do you not know anything about boys?'

Billie smiled at her but the thing winding up inside Amber kept on turning inwards, her insides knotted and hot. Sometimes she felt like there was a whole other her deep in there; that one day, if she wasn't careful, it might come bursting out.

She couldn't help feeling afraid that this was something that only Sadie might understand.

After school, she went round to Leo's. He answered the door in pyjama bottoms, chest bare, and pulled her in for a kiss. The door swung shut behind her.

When he released her, she followed him into the kitchen, where the air smelled burnt though the surfaces were clean and the dishes stacked away. He never seemed to eat or make a mess. It seemed like it was only her being there that made things ever move. She watched the muscles in his back flex as he filled the kettle and got mugs down from the cupboard.

'How was your day?' he asked.

She had told him that she was a student at Miles's university – though she'd omitted to mention the fact that her dad worked there – and that she commuted and lived at home to help look after her sick mum. This, she reflected, was comfortably close to the truth and therefore absolutely OK.

'Not bad.' She slid off her jacket. Her uniform was

safely hidden away at the bottom of her bag; the outfit she'd stowed there this morning retrieved and the crinkles smoothed out in the school toilets.

'What are you learning about this week?' He leaned against the counter, watching her as she hung her jacket over the chair, the heat of his attention sending a thrill through her.

This part was too easy to really enjoy. She'd heard her dad talk about his lectures since oh, about the beginning of time, and she was sure she pretty much *had* got a degree in it by now. 'The rehabilitation of criminals,' she said airily, leaning against the counter too. 'Like, how and why people can become a useful part of society again.'

His eyes went all twinkly when he smiled. She tried not to look for too long, because noticing this made her belly feel warm inside. 'Such a clever girl,' he said, and then he held out his arm. 'Come over here.'

She let him fold her into him. Let him take her away.

Later, when they were sprawled out on the sofa, he started twisting a lock of her hair around his fingers, winding and unwinding it idly as they lay in silence. A patch of damp had begun creeping its way across the new plaster, an old leak covered too hastily. There was a smell which drifted through the flat every now and then – something pond-ish and festering. 'Do you like it here?' he asked.

'This town?' She shrugged, her skin sticking to his and to the leather of the chair. 'It's boring. Not exactly much to do, is there?'

'Where were your parents before?'

'Reading.'

'Is that where they met?'

'Yeah, at uni. Shall we put the telly on?'

He stretched over to pick up the remote, though he didn't aim it at the television. His other hand worked endlessly over that same strand of hair, her scalp pulled taut. 'Reading. How come they both ended up there?'

'I don't know.' She reached up and took the remote from him, clicked the set to life. Daytime TV chirped into the room, a woman in a hot-pink suit showing a couple into a violently wallpapered kitchen. 'Where'd you grow up, anyway?'

'Here and there.'

She rolled her eyes. 'And don't *you* get bored here?'

He looked at her with those twinkly eyes again, his mouth set in a hard line. 'I manage to keep myself entertained.'

Her stomach flipped but he just reached past her and got a glass of stale-looking water from the coffee table behind them. He took a loud gulp and then another before offering it to her. She shook her head. The couple on the television were politely unsure about their new cabinets.

'So, how's your mum doing?' Leo asked, taking another swig of water which leaked out of the corner of his mouth though he didn't swipe it away.

Amber shifted, the leather sofa sucking at her bare leg. 'She's fine. I mean, as fine as she can be.'

He took hold of a clump of her hair now, letting it fall

through his fingers and then clawing it back up. 'What did you say was wrong with her again?'

The pink-suited woman was showing a freckly child into a new bedroom now, the wardrobes unfinished. 'She gets these delusions,' Amber said. 'She's not, you know, right.' She screwed a finger into her temple, the universal sign for 'crazy'. It had been a while; you kind of had to develop a shorthand. It wasn't as if she wanted to dwell on this conversation, especially when she could feel his eyes on her. *Don't feel sorry for me*, she wanted to say, because the thought revolted her.

'What are you doing at the weekend?' she asked, changing the subject, and when she looked up at him, his face had changed. A door closed.

'I'm probably not going to be around much,' he said. 'I've got somewhere to be.'

'Oh.' She shifted into a sitting position, suddenly cold and exposed. She wanted him to touch her again, but he didn't; he carried on watching the TV as the camera panned out on the newly improved home and the credits started to roll. She wanted to touch him but couldn't seem to do it; her hands felt suddenly heavy and clumsy. 'I'm gonna be pretty busy, too,' she said instead. 'Loads of work to do, and loads of people I'm supposed to see.'

'Mmm.' He glanced over at her, leaning in to give her a quick kiss that didn't feel as if he meant it. 'You should head off. I need to go and see someone this evening.'

'Right, yeah.' She got up quickly, retrieving her jeans from the floor. 'I need to get going anyway.'

He watched her dress and she felt flushed and shaky. She had said something wrong, done something wrong. She'd shaved too quickly in the shower this morning – she could have missed some hair. Had she made a weird noise? Was she sweaty from the walk over? More likely it was the pity, because who ever got turned on by pity? When she went through to the kitchen to get her bag and boots, he followed her, as if he was trying to make sure she left. She felt a scrabbling inside her, a flutter of panic. She had to say the right thing, act the right way, to steer them back on to the right path – if only she could figure out what it was.

'Well, bye,' she said at the door. She wanted to ask him when she would see him again but that was totally desperate and she would *not* sink that low.

'Bye.' He leaned in to kiss her again, and it was a bit longer this time, an improvement, though nothing like what she wanted, not hungry or hard or needing her. 'I'll call you.'

And then the door was closing and she had to turn away. She shouldered her bag and pulled her jacket round her tighter – the sun hung low and pale in the sky today, the wind raging through the streets unchecked.

The whole way to the bus and the whole walk home, she told herself she didn't care. She told herself she didn't feel like crying; she hadn't cried in years.

20

2018

The plane begins its descent in a slick greyness that flickers past the windows as tray tables are stowed and seats start gliding upwards again. Greta feels dusty and sick, her skin and her mouth dry and her head taut with lack of sleep. She dreamt of Texas and the Miller kids again, briefly, and finally lurched her way back to wakefulness three hours ago, spending the rest of the flight huddled under the airline blanket, watching the most inane films she could find. Amber, on the other hand, only opened her eyes when breakfast arrived, tearing at Greta's unwanted croissant even as she ate her own; shovelling in the brain-like eggs between swigs of orange juice.

'Real cutlery,' she said, in awe, as the fork made its journey back to the plate again, her tongue gummy with egg. 'Real plates. This is what it's like to be rich, huh?'

And now she seems to be sleeping again, her blanket

back over her and her head tucked into a wing of the headrest. *So much for insomnia*, Greta thinks, though it occurs to her now that Amber's sleeping position is unusually still, almost rigid. She imagines Amber lying awake all this time, eyes held shut, and can't stop a shudder. She longs for the moment when she can step out of this cabin with its chilled air and its endlessly red interior.

The plane sinks steadily downwards and glasses are clinked into place in the service area. Greta's final film disappears, the screen blinking out and then producing a map of their route, and she looks out of the window instead. The countryside below stretches on in its patchwork of browns and greens, the occasional incongruous blue of a swimming pool as the houses swell and then shrink again, rows of terraces zigzagging into tight knots of towns.

Greta looks at Amber as the ground rushes up to meet them. It's almost time to hand her over and yet Greta can't help feeling that the burden is only beginning.

Federica is waiting for them at the edge of a clump of families, eager faces and banners poised, with her sunglasses on and a coffee in hand. She's found the time to have her hair cut while they've been away and it grazes her shoulders now, threads of grey worming their way through the frizzy curls. She's wearing a man's overcoat despite the warm day, the hand without the coffee wedged into a pocket. Her feet shoved into ugly black rubber clogs, her thick legs in linen combat trousers. Her mouth, sliding into a small smile to show she has seen them, is painted with a thin slash of red, the top layer already transferred to the coffee cup's lid.

'Amber,' she says, moving towards them and kissing the girl's cheeks in a cloud of Dior. Tom and Luca have all the luggage balanced on two trolleys and Federica is flustered for a second, her hands striking out of their own accord in the search for something to take or do. She recovers quickly, sliding an arm through Amber's. 'The car's waiting outside,' she says, leading her away with a quick backwards nod at Greta. Greta notices the mother of the family beside them nudging the father, a furtive finger pointed at Amber's retreating back. The eldest child, a teenage boy, swivels round, phone up and ready. 'Was that her? Oh my God, I have to get a picture!' His sister, perhaps thirteen or fourteen, is disappointed. 'She's kind of small. She's not scary at *all*.'

'Come on,' Tom says quietly beside her. 'Let's get out of here before the rest of them notice.'

'Before the pack descends,' Luca says, shuffling a cigarette from his jacket pocket as he starts to walk towards the sliding doors.

Federica and Amber are out on the pavement ahead of them, Federica talking animatedly with a hand pressed to Amber's shoulder.

'A match made in heaven, if you ask me,' Tom says to Greta.

'I'm worried about her.' She is tired and the words slip out without her realising. 'She's young,' she says, flushing.

'I don't think she knows what she's getting herself into with all this press.'

Tom slows, his eyes kind as he considers her. 'She's really done a number on you, huh?'

Luca slings an arm round Greta, ruffles her hair. 'Good old Greta, the beating heart of our sleazy little operation.' He releases her to light his cigarette. 'She knows exactly what she's doing, don't worry. That kid is smart.'

And they walk on, the car idling at the kerb up ahead.

It's 10 p.m. when Federica arrives at Greta's door. The hotel is dim and claustrophobic, its few frosted windows small and round, high on the walls. The swirling carpet is making her feel seasick and so she lies on her bed and wishes she'd insisted more firmly on returning home to Hetty and Lisette instead of accepting the cheapest room in this place, the dull oceanic roar of the M25 in the distance. Federica had said this would be easier, it would surely save Greta travel time and costs, it would mean a real team effort for the duration of the shoot (because, obviously, Greta being a tube ride across town would *really* be the thing that slowed the team down). She had promised that Greta would, yes, be able to have the evening off for Lisette's birthday dinner. And now there's the expected rap at the door, sharp and efficient.

She heaves herself up, bare feet repelled by the staticky carpet. She opens the door and they look at each other in the greenish light of the hallway. Federica's sunglasses are pushed back on her forehead now, her eyes tired and bare. The red lipstick has been reapplied to compensate.

They sit on the bed (there are no chairs) and drink cans of beer which Federica has brought with her (no minibar either).

'You caught the sun,' she says.

Greta's hand goes to her shoulder, the skin there feathery and cracking. 'Has she settled in all right?'

'Yep.' Federica laughs and takes a big gulp of beer, her wide throat toadish and exposed. 'Bit of a madam, isn't she?'

Greta smiles and says nothing.

'Thanks for stepping in,' Federica says, considering the can in her lap, her knotted fingers and their rings. 'I really appreciate it.'

'It's no problem,' Greta says, and hates herself. 'How have things been here?' She panics at the implied intimacy of this at the last second and adds, 'Is there still a lot of press around the verdict?'

Federica nods. 'Yeah, the tabs have run stories on her most days. Lots of shots of her in the States. You got into a couple of the pictures, actually.'

Greta feels a twinge of dread, tries to drown it with quickly warming beer.

'It's generally pretty positive coverage,' Federica continues. 'People seem to think it's right she got off. And if you read the comments, even the cynics are warming to her. Mostly.' She lifts the can to her mouth and then thinks better of it. 'It is a great story, after all.'

'You've been doing some more digging.'

'Yes. There's . . . There are anecdotes out there, Greta. If we look into these places we know Sadie Banner ended up, we can find a lot of . . . evidence. It's a whole new dimension for the thing.' That flat, wide smile again.

'You're starting to believe it?' Greta takes a sip of beer, bigger than she intended so that a little fizzes down her chin. 'The Tall Man?'

Federica stares at her. 'Obviously not. I just think it's interesting how people started to "remember" things after this all became public, you know? It's like mass suggestion. We can do a whole episode on this.'

'OK. I can pull some more statements from people in Wombleton.'

'Yes. And then up in Skye, too. Talk to some people there, and anywhere else we know she was. There's bound to be people who think they saw stuff now.'

'And Amber?'

'Yeah, we have to get deeper. It'll happen. There's got to be other stuff in there, you can practically hear her brain ticking the whole time.' Federica takes two long pulls on her beer, wiping her mouth with the back of her hand. 'We'll crack her. I know you can do it. Get something more than those crappy soundbites she keeps regurgitating. That lawyer got her well trained, I'll give him that.' She cracks open another beer, the bed creaking as she moves. 'I'm going to get her to say it. I'm going to get her to tell us that she believes in the Tall Man. That the Tall Man made her do it.'

'I don't think she does, though.'

'Perhaps not. But the more we talk about Sadie, about where she went, about all these people who reckon they saw or heard weird stuff around her, maybe she'll start to.'

Greta picks up another beer from the floor, even though her stomach is churning. She takes a long sip and looks away.

Federica doesn't mind her silence. 'Right,' she says. 'Get your laptop out. I want to run through some of the LA footage.'

From the diary of Leanna Evans [Extract B]

We met for lunch at an Italian place near the river. It was early and when I arrived it was empty save for the two members of staff polishing glasses, removing the clingfilm from the plates of cakes they kept on the counter.

Despite the lack of other patrons, I chose a table without a view; one tucked away at the back of the restaurant, with a bit of privacy. I thought you'd appreciate that. I ordered a sparkling water from the waiter, with ice and lemon, and when you arrived, flustered and five minutes late, I told you it was a gin and tonic. You couldn't be tempted, though; when the waiter arrived by your side, you asked for a Diet Coke.

I asked how your week was going. You looked unwell; big dark shadows under your eyes and a faint sweaty sheen on your skin. Your eyes kept darting around the room, occasionally dipping to check your phone. Your face looked gaunt in the daylight, far more so than in the more flattering light of my kitchen. You looked much older than the thirty-six – seven? – that you must be.

You were a little stiff as we exchanged the usual sort of small talk, your smile tight and your answers vague and noncommittal. I found myself toying with the single sheet set menu as I spoke. My hands felt clumsy, as if I wasn't quite sure how to manoeuvre them. I found myself waffling on about my week; how I had deep-cleaned the bathroom and started to clear out the previous tenant's things from the loft.

You looked up at that; as though something had struck a chord. 'Yes, I've been doing that too,' you said. You let out a strange sort of laugh; I can remember it exactly. Discordant, the way a broken glass in a silent room sounds, or a flat note in a cantata. And then you said, 'We've got bats in ours,' and it took me a moment to realise you were talking about your attic.

I took a sip of my drink and, truthfully, I wished it actually *were* a gin and tonic. It was an odd thing for you to say, perhaps, or maybe it was the careless way you were letting words fly from your mouth, as if you hadn't thought about them or even engaged as they formed sentences between us. You were different, this time, and I wondered if I had made a mistake. You returned to studying the menu and so I did too. There were only nine items on it: three starters, three mains, three desserts. This made me happier about your choice; it implied honesty, simplicity, that everything was upfront. Things weren't being hidden behind frozen favourites and hedged bets. I respected you a little more for having suggested the place.

We hadn't spoken for a minute or two, and so I asked you what you were planning to order. It's funny; I never used to mind silence. Now, often, I can't bear it. I was surprised to hear my own answer emerging before you even had a chance to express yours, me dithering aloud over the arrabbiata or the pizzetta. Despite my best efforts, I was nervous, and you seemed to understand that – you smiled at me and I felt calm again.

When the waiter returned, I ordered the mozzarella and tomato salad and the arrabbiata. It was extremely decisive for me and I felt pleased; you might have noticed this. I felt in control and full of energy – if I'm absolutely honest, as I have told myself I will be, it felt almost as if I was drawing it from you, that energy, while you continued to wilt. It took you a long time to order; eventually you selected a prawn cocktail and the puttanesca. They did not go together, really, and I felt almost maternal towards you, as if I should guide you.

Instead, I tried to divert your attention from the floor, which was where your gaze kept falling, as if your eyes were very heavy and it took more strength than you had to lift them. I asked about your weekend, what the three of you had been up to. I was curious about your relationship with Amber; fascinated, I suppose. When you were together it felt as though you were unsure how to look at each other – whether you should be excited or casual or careful. And so all of those feelings and more sort of flitted across both your faces, none of them settling. And then always you looked away from each other, as if you'd been strangers on the street, passing. The things that were happening in your house were strange and wrong and I could not turn my eyes from them.

Your attention fell to your phone then, as if my question

had reminded you of its existence. 'Oh, not much,' you said. 'Miles's parents visited.'

I remember that I reached out a hand and gently touched yours. That I asked you if everything was all right.

You shook your head a little too hard, your hair flying side to side with a certain violence. 'Fine, fine,' you said. 'How are you?'

I think I told you that I was fine. I was distracted; I had applied lip balm before we met and I had noticed the imprint of my coated lips on my glass. I was running my thumb around the rim, trying to erase that trace, and you lost interest almost immediately. Our food arrived and you stared blankly at it as I began to eat.

'This looks good,' you said, without a hint of enthusiasm. You picked up a fork and toyed with the edge of a flaccid lettuce leaf.

I took a moment to swallow my mouthful, perhaps you noticed me pause. The way you were ignoring me was infuriating; it made me want to snatch the fork from your hand, to swipe the bowl from the table. I had to collect myself. 'Mine's very good,' I said, eventually, and finally you brought your fork to your mouth.

We ate in silence then, for at least a minute or two, and I found I could tolerate it. In fact, it was you who felt the need to break it.

'How's Billie?' you asked me. 'Is she enjoying school?'

I was pleased. I paused to neatly fork up another mouthful of my salad; ensuring a balance of each element. I wanted to enjoy this moment; to savour it. 'She seems to be doing well there,' I told you. 'It feels as though it's a good school for her.'

'She seems like a good girl,' you said, which surprised me.

'Thank you,' I said, caught off-guard, 'Amber is too, of course.'

You laughed, and I felt a prickle of fear travel down my spine. You had gone to a different place even as you sat in front of me. You had let them back in.

'She lies,' you said, simply. You were not looking at me, instead flipping your knife back and forth on the table and watching a small line of reflected light flicker across the wall.

'I know,' I whispered, but when you looked up sharply I realised you were still with me after all. They had not claimed you yet.

'Billie mentioned that Amber had a new *friend*,' I said, regaining my confidence and feigning a sheepish expression, as if I were unsure whether I should be telling you. I saw the fear cross your face and it sent a thrill through me. 'A man. Billie seemed . . . a bit nervous of him.'

Our eyes met then, and I wondered what you saw there. If you saw someone as haunted as you are; someone desperate enough to do the thing you could not. I wondered if you saw what I saw in you. It was like a second shadow, one you'd only glimpse every so often – a certain way you moved your head, there again when you faltered over words. Perhaps I could only see it because I was looking, because I knew what to look for. I know where it hides.

And then you rubbed at your forehead, letting your hand trail down over your eye, dragging at your cheek, and then – as if there were nothing else for you to do – you finally took another mouthful of your food. You looked up at me and I felt something powerful surge through me as I smiled kindly at you. 'Thank you,' you said. 'I appreciate you telling me.'

This I batted away, the good friend. 'It's not easy, having daughters. What's that *Lear* quote?'

'"Tigers, not daughters",' you replied, without trace of a smile. You surprised me again; I hadn't expected you to know it.

'That's right.' I laughed to cover my surprise, my pleasure, and took a sip of my water. 'Feels very true, now they're getting older, doesn't it?'

You nodded, and wilted again, your fork placed down in defeat. 'I was the same,' you said, and I felt it was the right moment to push you on this.

'Were you?'

'Yes. A nightmare to my parents. Always staying out late, coming home blind drunk. I suppose I'm getting what I deserve.'

I sipped my water, and I ate my salad, and I thought to myself: *Not just yet.*

Tuesday, 22 May 2018, 23:31 GMT
From: Federica Sosa
To: Greta Mueller

Don't take this the wrong way but I didn't get a great vibe from you just then. I'm worried you're not completely on board with what we're doing here.

Tuesday, 22 May 2018, 23:35 GMT
From: Greta Mueller
To: Federica Sosa

I'm sorry if it came across that way. I'm tired, that's all. It's been a long week.

Tuesday, 22 May 2018, 23:36 GMT
From: Federica Sosa
To: Greta Mueller

I appreciate that and I appreciate you stepping in, but you have to also understand that I am giving you a big opportunity here. It'd be nice to see a bit more enthusiasm.

Tuesday, 22 May 2018, 23:38 GMT
From: Greta Mueller
To: Federica Sosa

Federica, I *am* enthusiastic about the project, and I'm truly grateful to you for letting me be part of it. But it's difficult to get excited about going behind an eighteen-year-old's back, no matter who she is. Some of the things you were saying earlier made me a bit uncomfortable.

Tuesday, 22 May 2018, 23:39 GMT
From: Federica Sosa
To: Greta Mueller

Oh not this again, FFS! You know what she did, right? I don't exactly think she needs a new mother figure in her life, and I certainly don't think you could handle the job if she did. I'm sorry if this opportunity is making you 'uncomfortable'!!!

Tuesday, 22 May 2018, 23:41 GMT
From: Greta Mueller
To: Federica Sosa

I'm not trying to mother her. I'm only trying to be ethical and fair in the way we treat her. We have a contract and she trusts us.

Tuesday, 22 May 2018, 23:43 GMT
From: Greta Mueller
To: Federica Sosa

It's late, and this is coming out all wrong. I need to get some sleep. I'm sorry if I've offended you in any way this evening – believe me, it wasn't my intention and I really am grateful for the chance you've given me.

Tuesday, 22 May 2018, 23:47 GMT
From: Greta Mueller
To: Federica Sosa

Did you just knock on my door? I'm awake, I must not have answered fast enough.

Wednesday, 23 May 2018, 01:59 GMT
From: Federica Sosa
To: Greta Mueller

Sorry, hon. Dozed off, am totally wiped out.
And sorry if I sounded harsh before. I just know that
you've got so much talent, G, and I want this to be
huge for you.

See you at breakfast x

PS No not me, you must have a midnight admirer ;)

21

2016

After lunch, Leanna and Sadie walked through town together. Leanna kept pace with Sadie, who had never been able to walk slowly, making small talk about the weather and their girls. Sadie just wanted to get away. All she could think of was the email she had found in Miles's inbox. *And I won't tell.*

They came to the end of the high street, where their paths would naturally separate. Leanna hugged Sadie goodbye, with her citrus-sharp smell and her dark hair silky against Sadie's cheek.

'Thanks for lunch,' Sadie said, because Leanna had insisted on paying. Sadie's pasta had been too salty and now sat in an oily slick in her belly.

'Anytime.' Leanna took a step back, frowning against the weak afternoon sun. 'Take care now.' And then she turned and walked away, glancing back once with a small wave, the two slender silver bangles jangling on her wrist.

Sadie's mind was already worrying at the email again, cat-pawing at it from every angle. He could have been having an affair – who would blame him, after everything? – 'SomeoneSpecial' could have been a colleague, or (no) a student. She could only assume that Miles had had sex with someone else at some point over the previous sixteen years, though he was pathologically faithful and she found it difficult to imagine. She remembered arriving on his doorstep and seeing there on his face, beneath the surprise, a sense of relief – an *I knew it*. He had had faith and it had been rewarded.

Even so, she didn't think it entirely impossible that there had been *someone*. A fling or a friendship or something in between or beyond. That would be understandable. Normal – if anything that had happened between him and Sadie could be described as normal. And he had needs like anyone else, she supposed, though it had taken him months to touch her properly when she returned – even now, he was hesitant and frustratingly gentle, as if she'd been away because of a consumptive illness or serious injury. But perhaps that was because he had been with someone else in the intervening years, had forgotten how to be with her, how she liked to be touched. Though the image made her hot with envy, she thought she could bear it.

But then there was the last part of the email: *and I won't tell*. A threat. That could point to a student, she thought (for the fiftieth or sixtieth time) as she reached the station and climbed the steps to the platform. The pasta threatened to make a reappearance.

And all the while there was that murmur from somewhere deeper and darker. *He has a secret*, it told her. *And someone knows.* 'SomeoneSpecial', whoever they were, knew. Special. How the sight of that word had frightened her when she first saw it in his inbox. This person declaring it so proudly, though Miles would have no idea of its significance, of what it could mean. *Or would he?* asked that same part of her that she tried so often to tamp down. It was Miles who had the secret now, after all.

(Her thoughts were looping dangerously, she knew that.)

She found a seat on the train, facing backwards, and watched the town slide away from her. She turned her attention to Leanna's warning. Amber and a *new friend*. She pictured a man appearing out of the shadows one night, taking her daughter's hand. She could imagine him whispering in her ear, running a finger over her cheek. She could imagine him telling her she could be *special*.

It didn't have to have happened that way. It didn't have to have happened at all, she reminded herself. She had led him away, kept her daughter from danger.

There were other dangers of course. Not everything that could hurt you lived in the shadows – Sadie knew that. But would it really be so bad for Amber to be hurt; to have her heart broken by an irresponsible older man, if that was in fact what was happening? Perhaps it was a rite of passage of sorts – Sadie had no idea. By the time she'd met Miles she'd had no female friends to compare notes with. The only other girl in her life had been small and prone to whispering in the dark, jewels of blood on her dress and a smell of rotting meat coming from the terrible dark crater at the back of her head. And meeting Miles had meant the shadows abandoned her – perhaps falling in love, or lust, or whatever these things were, would in fact protect Amber, once and for all; would mean that she would no longer be able to hear those whispers even if the Tall Man chose to speak to her.

She reminded herself that Amber was different to her. Not fragile, Sadie thought, and with a better sense of self-preservation. Who was to say any man *could* hurt her? Perhaps this man, whoever he was, was pursuing her and she was letting him – perhaps she and Billie giggled together about the poor, feckless guy throwing gifts and his heart at her feet. That could be true, couldn't it? Sadie would have to tell Miles, obviously, because he knew Amber best. He would know what to do. He always did.

She rested her forehead against the cool glass of the train window and pictured him on that same journey every day. It was easy to imagine him sitting there, worrying about Amber and such simple everyday things as an inappropriate boyfriend.

Now she had an everyday worry of her own: she was imagining him exchanging messages with this unknown someone. *Special.* She mouthed the word, trying out the syllables for size. Its familiar shape in her mouth sent a fresh stab of fear through her heart.

She couldn't help it. Every time she thought of that email – *And I won't tell* – it was there. The same image each time (before she stopped the thought, patiently (resignedly) like a border official) – the baby in the basket beside her bed. *The Tall Man takes daughters. But sometimes he needs help.*

No. She closed her eyes, pushed it all away. *Amber is my daughter and she is safe. I can trust Miles.*

But trust was a funny thing, wasn't it? It required forgetting, rewriting. She knew that all too well.

And all the time, the dreams pursued her. A small, warm palm enclosed in hers. A flutter inside a slowly swelling belly. Walking into woods, the birds singing. She woke every night, sweating, purging the thoughts through every pore.

She was sweating now.

She opened her eyes again, watching the fields flash past. Someone a couple of seats in front of her stood up and opened a window, air rushing in. She studied the ghost of her face in the glass. It was strange, sometimes, to see it and remember that she was an adult woman. She had spent so long recently thinking of Amber, thinking of herself at Amber's age. In her head, the gap between them had closed and it was disconcerting to realise that Amber's image was not hers.

The train went into a tunnel, the other windows in the carriage blown open. The glass turned black.

A pale face beside hers in the reflection. Mouth twisted into a scream.

And then the daylight hit again, the window closest slamming shut. She pulled back from the glass, turned round to the seat beside her. Empty. She pressed a hand against her chest and wondered if the sinking feeling there was fear or disappointment.

The train was slowing, her stop ahead. She mustn't panic. This, at least, she had learned.

Being around the university made her think of her own freshers' year, of first meeting Miles. That heady, swelling feeling of being away from the farm, of breathing city air and being able to talk to anyone; tell them anything. It had lasted at least a day or two, before the dread began to seep back in, before she started leaving her curtains drawn each morning. By the time they met, two weeks after she moved into her room, she was thinking of leaving. Because leaving home didn't mean leaving things behind. She was who she'd always been, no matter what she told her new flatmates. And there were nightmares even then, in that single bed with its plastic-wrapped mattress and the sheets that smelled of home. Even with the ugly bright tube light which lit every corner with a forensic and welcome intensity. She was just waiting. Waiting for that face to detach itself from the shadows and creep across the wall towards her, waiting for that little girl's fingers to link through hers.

She'd decided very quickly that she wouldn't have friends. That people couldn't be trusted – and that they also – more so – shouldn't be needed.

Miles had had other ideas.

He'd always claim that he spotted her first at the Freshers' Fair, a week before they actually met. He'd say that she caught his eye because – pause for emphasis, party guests smiling – she was the only first year who wasn't actually *at* the Freshers' Fair. Whilst everyone else milled around the stalls, primping their hair and eyeing others across the courtyard, Sadie was simply stomping past, her weekly rations stuffed into flimsy Happy Shopper bags.

This was so firmly entrenched in the legend of them that Sadie now thought of it as memory – remembered herself that afternoon with her plasticky cheese and her half-loaf of bread, her five packets of instant noodles and her own-brand energy drink. It had become true because he had said it enough, and that made her afraid, now.

Their first real meeting was at the student union's sandwich shop, a grotty, white-countered place with half-emptied mayonnaise sachets turning gluey on the tables. She was queuing between lectures, a new ring binder digging into her hip, when someone tapped her on the shoulder. She'd turned around and there he was.

'Hi.'

'Erm . . . hi.' She returned her attention to the counter, only a couple of people ahead of her now. She wasn't interested in conversation.

'I'm Miles,' he said, undeterred.

'Sadie,' she said, through some kind of ingrained politeness, though she barely turned her head in his direction, pulling the folder from her side and hugging it in front of her.

'Nice to meet you, Sadie,' he said, and though she heard the smile there, he said nothing more.

Often, when Miles told the story, he'd talk about how he wanted to write his number on a napkin; slip it into her bag or her paper-wrapped sandwich. Sadie would play down the fact that it felt less like a meet-cute and more like a pick-up, and she'd never mention how she had marched home after her lecture, bristling at the fact that this floppy-haired boy had dared to touch her (still afraid that she would open the door to her room and find that little figure sitting there).

But then they were assigned the same personal tutor, and he in turn assigned them neighbouring slots for their first meetings with him, and so, on a sunnier day, in a stuffy corridor, they met again and somehow – she wasn't sure, even now, how – he convinced her to meet him for a drink. From that day on, the only visitor to her room had been him. She'd finally been free.

Temporarily, at least.

And now a different woman (maybe) had persuaded *him* for a drink. A different woman knew his secrets when Sadie had always considered him an open book. She stood outside the pub, wondering. Was it even her right to pry?

He never asked her questions, those first years. He seemed to know instinctively that she had come to university to leave it all behind; to forget the farm, to forget the place she had grown up, the things that had happened

225

there (*The Tall Man made us special*). Instead he told her facts: the speed of a star, the depth of an ocean. All of these wonders, all of the things he wondered about. She started to trust him, started to unfurl in his warmth, just a little. Gradually she let him persuade her to things, to clubs and crawls and outings. He showed her that their three years there didn't have to be something she simply endured; that they could be enjoyed, savoured for what they were: a chance to truly start again, to be whoever she wanted to be.

She took a step back, afraid of herself. She had jumped on a train at the first sign of something being wrong – wasn't that exactly the mistake she had made at every possible juncture in her life? (Or was it, a small, insidious voice inside her head asked, the only thing she had ever done right?)

What was she hoping to find here, at some anonymous pub on campus, no shadows in sight? There were things, there were secrets between her and Miles, but perhaps that was inevitable. Perhaps this was another thing she should leave undisturbed; should let the layers of their life slowly settle over it until it sank away. He'd never asked her questions. It was important she remembered that.

She turned and walked away, before she could change her mind. Made her way through the campus, angry with herself and dizzy with memories. The two of them in that single bed, clothes and lips cider-sticky, and the smell of his skin left behind on her sheets. Leaving a lecture and finding him leaning against the wall outside the theatre, one foot pressed against the bricks, hands thrust in his pockets.

When she found herself behind a group of undergrad girls, she almost expected to recognise them – and then she remembered that almost twenty years had passed; that she had a daughter closer in age to these girls than she was.

Amber. The thought of her like a jolt to an exposed nerve, everything flowing back. *And I won't tell.* What had he done?

'Who's doing this one? Dave the Laugh?' one of the girls asked, smoke from a rollie drifting back towards Sadie.

'No, thank God,' one of the others said, and then she turned and smirked at her friend. 'It's Magic Miles.'

'Yes!' the smoking girl fist-pumped the air. 'I love a good Banner lecture.'

Sadie's heart contracted hard. Miles's students. Tall and lean and dressed in painted-on jeans and ballet shoes, their hair long and tangled and tumbling. The kind of girl who might end an email with a winking emoji.

Before she knew it, she was following them into one of the lecture theatres, newly refurbished and smelling of plastic and paint. It was bigger than the one she remembered, the seats sloping endlessly down. The stage seemed so far away, so many students filing into the rows, that she felt suddenly nervous on Miles's behalf. Did he really do this every day?

The curiosity was irresistible and so she took a seat in

a corner near the back, sinking low behind a group of laughing boys. She watched the way they all settled into their places, notebooks removed from bags, laptops opened, phones fiddled with. The last lecture of the day, yawns unstifled.

And then Miles came in. He entered from the back of the room, surprising her – she'd expected him to walk out from backstage, like a rock star – and bounded down the stairs, tossing a wave of his hair back as he went. She shrank into her seat, afraid, but Miles bounced down and down and then loped across the stage to the lectern, a stack of papers under one arm, his satchel slapping his hip. All around her, students watched him. Conversations carried on but their eyes tracked him as he took off his bag and organised his things, their lips turned up in the little involuntary smiles that tended to follow Miles places. Her own mouth felt dry and rigid.

A silence fell with a raise of Miles's hand, and he stood there, a metre or so from the lectern, and smiled up at them all. 'I never get tired of that,' he said, his voice magnified and made wrong by the mics at the edge of the stage. 'OK, so. We're nearing the end of your first year: the very first step in your long careers in Sociology, am I right?'

The wrongness was not just the microphone, she realised. Up there, he was stagey, contrived. He was the Miles who might tap a girl on the shoulder in a sandwich shop, who might assume a conversation began simply by saying his own name. She recognised him and yet she didn't, and

228

she couldn't stop her gaze from travelling to the back of the stage, where the lights cast a long and thin version of him against the wall.

'So, come on,' Miles said, taking another step away from the lectern and grinning at his audience. 'Let's talk about deviance. You know you want to.'

A polite wave of laughter rose up and as it did, she felt it. The breath on the back of her neck, slow and even. Cold. The pressure of a hand on her shoulder, though she did not turn her head to check.

She waited. She had always been waiting.

The voice, when it came, was so familiar that she ached, her eyes filling with tears. Soft and smooth, each word stroking the hairs on her skin upright.

I can make you special, it said. *If you ask*.

22

2018

It's 7 a.m. when Federica calls, the phone whirring against the glass-topped bedside table in time with the bleating of the alarm clock. Greta answers, swinging herself upright and pushing her vest top back down over the soft rolls of her belly. Too many doughnut breakfasts and midnight hotel room beers; no time for walking anywhere. Federica doesn't bother with greetings; gives the essential information and then is gone, leaving Greta to process the news as she fumbles for the alarm clock.

Miles Banner has agreed to talk to them.

They arrive at his flat, third floor of a sullen high-rise in an unloved estate in Battersea, two hours later. Federica and Greta and Tom all shuffling into the narrow hallway, laden with equipment, while Amber spends the morning being interviewed by a Sunday paper's magazine, any cameras other than theirs banned. In the lift on the way up, Federica frowns at her notes, hair pushed back as usual by her sunglasses despite the cloudy day.

'This is going to be a tough one,' she says, for perhaps the third or fourth time that morning. 'You saw him outside that courtroom. He's a broken man.'

Tom gives a shocked laugh. 'Is that any surprise?'

'It's not a surprise but it's no good to us. I need him to break down, to tell us something real. It's no use if he's got nothing left. I'm telling you, I saw him in that stand. He was empty. Dull. It won't translate on film.' She shrugs. 'Maybe that'll be interesting.'

'Does Amber know he changed his mind?' Greta asks.

Another shrug. 'He might have told her. Or maybe she persuaded him, I don't know.'

'I don't get the impression they talk all that much.'

Federica's eyes shoot sideways. 'Did she tell you that?'

'No, not exactly.'

'Probably worth asking her on camera. That could be a way in. She was a daddy's girl, right? She had to have been. Definitely a heartstring worth plucking.'

Tom turns away, eyebrows raised, and checks his phone. Federica carries on, oblivious. 'I think I finally talked her into filming at the school, though. So we can do that when we go to interview the teacher. Is that Thursday, Greta?'

'Yeah. We're meeting her after school finishes.'

'Great. I like the idea of empty classrooms, empty hallways, Amber walking around and remembering her old life. Before, you know? If we wait 'til dark, that'll work well.'

'We'll have to hire better lights,' Tom says.

'Yeah sure – whatever you need, we'll get. We'll tell Amber it's a night shoot and she can have the afternoon off or whatever. Keep her sweet.'

'OK.' Greta scribbles this down in her notebook. 'I'll speak to the school about later access and costs too.'

Tom looks at her. 'Isn't Thursday your mate's birthday dinner?'

'Oh. Yeah—' She glances at Federica. 'It is, actually—'

The lift clunks to a stop, doors grinding open. 'Right, follow my lead,' Federica says, stepping out into the corridor and leaving them to bring the bags.

'You're taking that night off,' Tom whispers to Greta. 'Don't let her take the piss.'

She smiles at him. 'Yessir.'

Federica knocks on a door halfway down the hall. 'I'm dreading this,' Tom says in a low voice, and Greta nods. She is not looking forward to meeting Miles, broken or otherwise, either.

And then he is opening the door, allowing Federica to kiss him on both cheeks, standing aside to let them in. The man she has seen in the dock and in newspapers (though the photos of him were always small, tucked halfway down articles, the headline images always reserved for those of his tragic and terrible wife and daughter) is smiling politely at her, thanking her for coming. Offering to take one of the bags.

'I'm fine,' she says. 'Thank you.'

'OK,' he says. 'Sure.' He closes the front door and stands facing it for a moment, as if he's hoping that when he turns around they might magically have disappeared. Greta backs away, following Tom into the flat.

It's a dim, dingy space; its windows shadowed by the next block, many with the blinds drawn anyway, and there is a strong smell of starch – of boiling pasta and ironed shirts. The hallway leads past a bathroom, its door patterned opaque glass and open; the room inside compact and bleached-clean.

The living room has its blinds at half-mast, a pair of mismatched sofas at right angles to the two skinny windows. Miles sits in one, Federica sinking down beside him, her knees clicking. Tom sets up the camera, checking the light while Greta fiddles with the laptop, butterflies circling in her stomach. Miles is not as she expected; he seems diminished somehow. Without the flashes of paparazzi cameras, his skin has a yellowish tinge, his eyes small and watery.

'Thanks so much for seeing us,' Federica says, swirling a large, brown-stoned ring around her index finger. 'I know it hasn't been an easy decision.'

Miles smiles weakly and nods. 'I'm sorry I couldn't commit before. It's been difficult . . . the press attention —' He trails off, glancing at Greta and Tom. 'Can I get anyone a coffee?'

'We're fine, thanks, Miles,' Federica says. 'Now, are you OK if we start rolling? As I mentioned on the phone, we're going for quite a natural feel, so don't worry about looking into the camera – but don't worry if you do, either. Just relax. This is your chance to put your side of the story out there with Amber's.'

Miles licks his lips, his eyes darting around the room in search of a natural place to settle. It makes him look nervous, which Greta knows Federica will like. She likes long pauses and comments made when the subject isn't sure filming has begun, rarely edits footage down. *My Parents Are Murderers* was full of them – online commenters often rave about a section when Danny, asked about the day police raided their house, the day the diggers came rolling in and began tearing up the lawn where his swing-set sat, trailed off mid-sentence, his eyes on his lap. Off-camera, you can hear Greta ask 'Danny, do you need a break?' before Danny looks up, looks past the camera at her, and nods, the first tears rolling silently down his cheeks. They talk about the scene with the next-door neighbour, a grizzled old woman who sat on her porch for the interview, looking out at the house. The same neighbour who watched as those police officers pulled the first severed limb from the dusty ground, and who, when Federica asked her 'Did you ever suspect the Millers were different? That something terrible might have happened there?' answered simply 'No. They were normal people.' And then looked into the camera for a second, two, three, before her puckered mouth spread into a smile.

Greta doesn't think they can expect any unplanned moments with Miles. She was right there with Federica when he testified in court, his voice low and controlled, his hands folded in front of him. Greta wouldn't have described it as dull the way Federica did, but she agrees it was empty. The only word that came to mind when she saw him there was *drained*. She saw him leave the courthouse, when a woman in a zipped-up duffle coat came pushing through the crowd of photographers and threw a paper coffee cup at his face, the liquid arcing out and splashing across the pale pavement. His face never changed, his focus always locked straight ahead. This, here, with his shifting eyes and his lip-licking, is the least composed she has seen him.

'OK, let's start at the beginning,' Federica says. 'Why don't you tell us what Amber was like, growing up?'

Miles looks down at his hands. 'She was . . . bright. Quiet, when she was very small. We spent a lot of time together, obviously.'

'Yes. That must have been hard.'

'It was . . . a turbulent time. For both of us. But Amber is very resilient.'

Federica frowns. 'Is she?'

Miles coughs. 'It was a difficult childhood, with me working and trying to care for her alone. As you might expect. But she did well at school; she made friends. I suppose I rather thought I'd gotten away with it.'

The words hang on the air. Miles shifts in his seat, eyes flicking to the camera and then away again.

'And Sadie,' Federica says, when enough of a significant pause has passed to satisfy her. His wife's name slipping out so casually even Greta feels winded. 'Perhaps you could tell us a bit about what it was like to have her home again. It must have been quite a shock, her reappearing like that?'

Miles blinks at her. 'Of course. Of course it was.'

Greta tries to picture it. The house, late at night, Sadie Banner staring up at it. Her hand raised to knock at the door, hesitating. Wondering whether or not to step back into her life. Wondering whether it was safe.

Stop that, she tells herself. *Amber was never in any danger. Not the way Sadie thought, anyway.*

But she can't stop herself from shivering, imagining Sadie on that threshold. The door held open by Miles, welcoming her and everything she brought with her into his home.

'I was happy,' Miles says, more to himself than to Federica. He closes his eyes. 'It was like something out of a dream.'

'I can imagine,' Federica says, her voice gentle now. 'It must have taken some adjusting to, though?'

'We got on with things. We were a family again.'

Greta sees Federica's mouth purse. She is not getting what she wants from him. She really is going to try and break him, even when it's clear that that ship has long since sailed.

'Did she tell you much about where she'd been?'

Miles twitches. 'I asked, of course I did. Sometimes . . . Sometimes if she was drunk, she might mention a place or a job. Mostly she asked me not to talk about it.'

'And so you didn't? Weren't you curious? She'd been gone for nearly sixteen years.'

Slowly, Miles lifts his gaze from the floor. 'Sometimes,' he says, red-rimmed eyes on Federica, 'you learn to be thankful for what you have. You learn not to go digging around in the past.'

Greta shivers again, and to her surprise, it's Federica who looks away first. It must surprise her, too, because her next question is sharper, her cheeks beginning to flush.

'Surely,' she says, 'you had some questions about the fact she'd told you your baby daughter was cursed?'

Miles licks his lips again. 'I asked her. Yes. She told me that she'd been wrong.'

'She no longer believed in the Tall Man, then?'

He clears his throat, once and then twice. 'I want to believe that, yes. It's difficult, now . . . Looking back . . .'

Federica waits. The silence draws on. Greta, crouched beside the laptop, can feel her feet turning numb beneath her, but she doesn't move. If she moves, she'll draw his attention away; she'll remind him that they are there, that the camera is there, that he doesn't have to keep talking – and Federica will be furious. Tom is still too – Greta tilts her head, as slowly as she can, and looks up at him. His face, watching Miles's in the monitor, is rigid, his mouth twitching at its corner. He looks at Miles as if it's taking all he has not to walk over and punch him, and it makes her afraid.

The silence and its promise has curdled. The air in the

flat is thin and there is a draught from one of the windows. Outside an alarm sounds.

'Tell me about the trial,' Federica says, relenting. 'Tell me how you feel about the verdict. You testified for Amber in court.'

Miles stares at her. 'Of course I did. She's my child.'

'She *did* do it,' Federica reminds him. 'Surely you more than anyone understand the price of that.'

Miles looks at his hands again. 'None of us were innocent,' he says. 'If there's one thing I've realised over these last months, it's that.'

Greta can see the boredom on Federica's face, the frustration in the room turning the air taut. She knows what's coming next, knows Federica won't be able to resist. She shifts her weight, keeps her focus on the monitor.

'You blame yourself then?' Federica asks. 'For everything you've lost?'

'Federica—' It slips out before Greta realises she's spoken but her voice is hoarse from air-conditioning and a restless night's sleep; neither Federica nor Miles even glance in her direction.

'Because you lost your wife, Miles,' Federica continues, and she doesn't even try and stop the smile from tugging at the corners of her mouth. 'But you also lost Amber, really, didn't you?'

And Greta was wrong after all. Miles begins to cry.

23

2016

The sun had slipped into the window behind Miles, its heat fierce on the back of his head, his neck. His shirt was growing damp against the leather of his chair. It was his last seminar of the day – his third-year Criminology students – and he had had enough. Their long limbs, their blunt and inelegant arguments, their unending beliefs – it all seemed suddenly too big for the room, a tangled, noisy mess of youth that pressed at him like a headache.

'What a simplistic way to put it,' Declan was saying, arms folded, freckled face red. 'Sorry, Deepti, no offence, but that's ridiculous. There's diminished responsibility and then there's playing the system.'

Deepti, who was generally Miles's favourite, leaned forward, her breath drawn to retaliate, and Miles found himself pushing his chair back, the clap of his hands surprising even him.

'You know what,' he said, reaching for the cap of his pen (a gesture they all recognised; bags already picked up, papers gathered before he finished speaking), 'I think we'll leave it there for today. Go out and enjoy the sun.'

They shuffled themselves together, stretching, yawning, fuming (Declan). They left in dribs and drabs, saying goodbye to him, wishing him a nice evening – a thing only his third years did, the gap between him and them closing, closing. He waved them out, he wondered when he could go home.

Emily was the last to leave, packing her things into her bag slowly, pretending to read something on her phone. When the two of them were alone in the office, she lingered by his desk.

'Thanks for a great session,' she said. 'This really is one of my favourite modules.'

'I'm glad to hear it.' He crossed his arms in front of him in a flimsy attempt at protection.

She half-turned but her feet remained in place, her fingers trailing across the desktop. 'You know, I'm struggling with my coursework though. Is there any chance I could come in one afternoon and show you what I've got?'

He tried (and succeeded, mostly) to keep his voice level. 'Of course. My office hours are on the door.'

She smiled sweetly. 'Thanks, Miles. Have a lovely evening.' The door closed softly behind her with a blessed breath of cool air from the corridor outside.

It was not the first time this had happened with a student, though Emily was more persistent than most.

It was also not the first time he'd been tempted. And it hadn't always been as easy to resist as it was now. But he *had* always resisted and he always would. He loved Sadie and he believed in his vows, he'd believed in them for all the years she was gone. He'd known that she'd come back and that he needed to be waiting. He'd told himself that every day.

But yes. There had been temptations.

And now he had his family to focus on. He thought of the previous evening, Amber lying on her bed watching a film on her laptop, he and Sadie downstairs watching their own. How good it had felt, her socked feet curled up beside him, the last of the wine in their glasses – though she had been quiet, her attention drifting from the screen. He hadn't been able to stop himself remembering that terrible morning, baby Amber crying on the bed and his new wife staring at something only she could see in the corner. And so he had sipped his wine and set down the glass, taken her feet into his lap and begun to rub them. Determined to keep her with him this time.

'How was lunch?' he'd asked her, and that had been enough. She'd looked at him and taken a sip of her own wine. 'I'm worried about Amber,' she'd said, and she'd explained about Leanna and Billie and this mysterious older man who had supposedly befriended his daughter. It couldn't be true, Miles reasoned. He'd know. Amber would never keep something like that from him.

He swivelled round to his computer and woke it from hibernation. Sweat beaded on his back again as he waited for it to chug into action. A Hoover whined from somewhere down the hall as the cleaner began making his way through the empty offices, but the rest of the building felt heavy in its silence. As if someone was in the room with him, their breath held.

It was him who wasn't breathing, he realised, his fist clenched around the mouse. He forced himself to exhale as the screen loaded.

As expected, another email awaited him in his inbox. The message was more threatening than the last.

> Come on. You know you want to. I know your
> secrets. Don't make me tell x

A chill passed over him, the sweat forgotten. He thought immediately of Sadie, as he always did – always had. She had come back. He had hoped and wished and whispered – and she had come back.

At what price? A needling voice asked, and he stared at the email again. *You know you want to.*

He made himself delete it without replying. He reassured himself, just as he had done the first time. This person – whoever they were – couldn't know anything. It wasn't possible (he couldn't allow it to be possible).

And so he wouldn't go; he wouldn't meet them. He'd say nothing, and they would have nothing to say. Because there was no evidence. He was sure of it.

Wasn't he?

The computer bleeped with another email. He crossed his inbox away without looking at it.

It was time to go home.

From the diary of Leanna Evans [Extract C]

I spent the days when I did not see you doing those things which I had told you I would. I finished clearing the previous tenant's belongings from the loft – dusty boxes of junk, nothing of any worth. I imagined you doing the same as I worked. I wondered if you cowered from dark places still, or whether you had taken your first steps towards the shadows again. I have never let myself be afraid of them. I sang as I cleared one wall and then the other, and when I was done, I looked at the open space and was pleased.

It was lonely work, as mine often is. I searched out other things to keep me busy – resealing the shower, attacking the kitchen extractor's vents with a toothbrush. Fiddly, time-filling jobs which only made me feel lethargic and dull. Usually such tasks fill me with purpose and I knew then that this was not the place for me. I did not look for a job. I knew by then that there would be no need.

I spent one long day driving around aimlessly instead. Out, away from the town and through the fields, letting the road spool out behind me. Just to see how it would feel. By the time I could persuade myself to return, it was almost time for the final bell to ring so I drove to the school and waited in the car park, happy at least to have the opportunity to give Billie a lift. Perhaps it's silly of me to worry about her walking the fifteen-minute journey home, but I do. I'm sure you understand. I often find myself making little excuses to collect her, reasons to conveniently be in the area.

And I was in luck, because she brought Amber with her too. I watched the two of them strolling across the playground, heads bowed together over something on Amber's phone. When they were closer, I beeped my horn and I saw both of them look up and smile.

'Can Amber have a lift?' Billie asked and I nodded, all of my fear dispelling.

Well. Not all of it. It never completely goes, does it?

I listened to them burbling away to each other as I drove, marvelling at how much they had to say to one another, even after a whole day at school. Billie has always been a chatterbox but Amber wasn't like other girls have been with her in the past, boring easily and talking over her, dismissing her. Amber listened carefully, responded thoughtfully. I thought again how unexpected she was.

Perhaps that's why I agreed when Billie asked me if she could go to a party that Saturday. Their happiness was infectious, both of them beaming at me from the back seat. I felt light, my previous bleak mood forgotten.

I said yes. I knew the party would likely have alcohol, boys. I said yes anyway, because I felt suddenly sure that Billie would be safe with Amber. Because I knew it was time for me to let go of her, just a little. To start concentrating on me again, and the things which I had come to this place to find.

And I hoped I would see you again, Sadie. I thought that perhaps I might finally be able to help you.

24

2016

Amber skipped school on Friday afternoon to visit Leo. She had begun to think she wouldn't see him again. A text she sent went unanswered, and then another (how she hated herself for sending the second), and she kept on remembering that day when he asked her to leave so abruptly, the way his eyes had travelled over her body and how he had turned away.

But it was all right, because he'd called. He called, and he was being attentive, an arm around her as they watched the end of the film she had put on, his finger stroking the bare skin near her shoulder. He'd pulled her to him and whispered in her ear that she was beautiful, that he'd missed her. Normally, it would make her squirm – to have someone close, to have someone want her so nakedly – but with him it was different. Special. She leaned closer and breathed in the smell of him, earth and smoke, the patch of damp on the wall growing larger behind them.

The film finished, the credits rolling for only a second before he hit the remote, leaving them frozen on their journey up the screen.

'I should get ready,' he said, and then he leaned in and kissed her chastely on the temple. 'I have to go out soon.'

She was disappointed but it was also a good thing – now she could be home in time for dinner without having to choose an excuse from her roster to send to Miles. He probably wouldn't care, anyway. He was so busy watching Sadie now that she wondered if he'd even notice. She listened to Leo pad out to the bathroom, the shower thundering against the bath. And then the door closed and the sound quietened as the water slid off his skin.

She got up and wandered around, hungry already for more of him. There was something about him, something unreachable, which frightened her – because it made her want him. She felt unlike herself, felt a hole of need open up in her chest, and so to close it she looked. She surprised herself by thinking of Sadie. She had come into Amber's room late one night, breath hot with wine, after Miles had gone to bed. Sat down at the end of the mattress, lips stained black, and asked Amber to be careful. Because obviously Billie had blabbed to Leanna about Leo – that wasn't especially surprising. What had come as a surprise was Sadie's attempt to have a birds-and-the-bees chat about it, if that had been what that was. Amber wasn't sure. She'd been too embarrassed, too blindsided, to do much more than end the conversation as quickly as possible. But now it came back to her. *You need to be careful with him.*

Amber couldn't help thinking that Sadie was right about that. And so she looked.

There wasn't much to find in the sparse flat, with its jaundiced false wood surfaces and its crackling carpet. A single, empty cup standing sentry on the bedside table, no telltale lipsticked rim to betray it. In the drawer beneath it, a paperback *Carrie*, its cover scratched and peeling, its pages deep yellow.

She ran a hand over the sheets of the bed, moved over to the desk. The varnished top layer was peeling at one corner, its scabby chipboard exposed. His laptop sat in the middle, but she already knew that it was password-protected, and even though it was one of her skills, she hadn't quite been able to map it out as he typed it; he always seemed to manage to angle the keyboard out of sight. Beside it were another couple of paperbacks; *The Girl Who Loved Tom Gordon*, and a battered old guide to the local area (Amber couldn't imagine what the author had drummed up to fill that many pages).

She opened the first drawer – a lonely pad of paper and a couple of bitten biros rattling around inside. She opened the next two in quick succession: both empty, with a smell of pencil and dust.

Or were they? She crouched and opened the bottom drawer again, sliding it shut fast and then slow. Yep: definitely a rattle. The sound of something sliding back and forth inside, even though there was nothing there to see.

She straightened up and listened. The water was still hissing, there was the faint sound of Leo soaping his hair. She opened the drawer fully again and ran her fingers around the inside of it, until she could get a grip on the loose base. She pulled it up, the metal runners like tendons exposed. And nestled in between them, a slim digital recorder like the one Miles used to record his own lectures sometimes, or his thoughts while he was researching a paper or grading essays. An affectation, really – she knew full well his phone could do the exact same thing.

She picked it up, gooseflesh breaking out across her arms. Underneath it was a manila folder, the same drab shade of beige as the drawer. She looked at it, her fingers resting on its surface. She was afraid suddenly, to open it.

Instead she found the play button on the recorder, tapping the volume right down with her thumb.

His voice played back sounded less appealing than it did when he spoke to her. A slightly higher pitch, less of his carefully applied drawl.

'Wednesday fifteenth,' he said, sounding flustered. There was the sound of traffic in the background. 'Miles stopped outside library by unknown female. After a short conversation, he led her back towards his office.'

She had to reach out to grip the edge of the desk. *Miles. Dad.* Why was Leo talking about her dad – *watching* her dad? The recording rolled on, a car horn blaring, but her breath caught suddenly in her throat, her heart seizing with panic.

The shower was no longer running.

When had it stopped? She needed to turn around but she was frozen in place, a draught cold on the back of her neck, sure that he would be standing there in the doorway if she turned—

She heard the toilet flush and let her breath out in a rush. She clicked off the recorder and slid it back into the drawer, her fingers fumbling the false bottom back into place. As the bathroom door's lock clicked open, she slipped silently back into the lounge, where the TV was still showing the frozen credits.

She flicked on a game show and willed her heart to slow down. *Miles stopped outside library by unknown female.*

By the time he came back into the room, his hair wet and the collar of his black polo-shirt turned up, she'd folded the blanket and placed it across the back of the sofa. She sat in her usual spot, relaxed, a foot tucked under her while a hand played idly with her hair.

'God, I needed that,' he said, smiling, and she smiled right back, her heart tripping wildly in her chest.

25

2018

Greta slept badly again, feverish dreams of a Texas back-yard; a child digging, their hands and face streaked with soil. A baby crying and a dark, dark wood. Amber; Amber's face in a car window, looking back at her. Smiling. Screaming. Clothes black with blood. She woke – or thought she did – to the cool pressure of a hand around her throat, a dark shadow bent over her, but then she dragged herself out into full consciousness, the room empty and her phone buzzing on the bedside table. She spent the next ten minutes blinking at the ceiling, wondering why her heart was racing.

They'd been scheduled to film Amber on a lunchtime chat show today, but at the last minute she was bumped for a soap star recently outed as pregnant by a married co-star. Federica, unusually quiet at breakfast in the hotel, disappeared to her room before the plates had been cleared and a text arrived on Greta's phone shortly after.

Had to go out. Tlk later. Entertain A for the day?

A minute later, in quick succession:

extra footage would be good. filler stuff
just chatting?
take tom out with you

Three minutes later:

tell him to just take the DSLR to film. keep a low profile
xxx

And Amber, without noticing that Federica had gone or that Greta was pulling faces at her phone, speared another segment of tinned mandarin and asked 'If there's no interview today, can we go shopping?'

Greta noticed the *we*. Not *I*. She's noticed that a couple of times, now, and it bothers her. As if Amber has gone from the custody of childhood to actual custody and now, in a surrogate kind of way, to theirs. It doesn't seem to occur to her that she is an adult (legally, at least) and that she can go wherever she pleases, whenever she likes.

And yet instead of sending her off, Greta simply said, 'Yes'. Luca had already disappeared too; she assumed to Skype his pregnant girlfriend back in Cardiff. And so she and Tom and Amber went back to their rooms, collected their things and took a taxi from the concrete underground lobby.

Now, in the fierce white lights of Westfield, she feels more exposed than ever. Amber wanders around, chatting idly, checking her phone, as relaxed as she was when it was just the two of them at Disneyland, even though Tom has the camera constantly pointed at her. They've ended up in a shop on the first floor, lights blazing and walls backlit lilac against the endless white of the floor and the carousels and the mannequins. 'God, these DMs,' Amber says, laughing, waving the phone so Tom (and the camera) can see. 'Do these guys actually think I'd date some randomer sending me creepy messages? I mean, hello? I have trust issues, guys.'

She flicks through a stand of jewellery, heavy chokers clinking hollowly on their pegs.

'Do you?' Greta asks.

'Well, *obviously*.' Bored, Amber moves on to the next rail. 'The last time I actually liked someone, I found out he was more interested in my dad than me.' She glances up at them. 'Shall we go eat after this? I'm starving.' She walks on without waiting for an answer.

'But how did that feel? With Leo?' Greta persists, following her.

'What, that my boyfriend was spying on my parents?' Amber holds a top up against herself in the mirror; scraps of silky white chiffon wrapped improbably into a halter. 'Come on, Gee. What kind of question is that?' She glances at Greta and then sighs, thrusting the top back on to the rack. 'It felt shitty, obviously. I knew he'd played me. I just didn't get why.'

She flicks through hangers, moving on to the next rail. 'I kept replaying it to myself, you know? "Unknown female" – I wanted to know who she was, why this guy cared enough to record it. I *needed* to know. I needed to know what was in that folder. It probably sounds stupid now, like, why didn't I grab it, take it with me, right?'

'Or ask him about it,' Greta suggests.

Amber, busy swirling around with a scarlet velvet slip in front of her, stops. She looks at Greta, her eyes beginning to narrow, and then she turns away. Greta understands that she has disappointed her. Breached an unspoken contract she didn't know she had signed. 'What was I supposed to do?' Amber asks, bunching up the dress and tossing it into the pile she's amassing near Tom's feet. 'Go up to him and say "Hey, how come you're stalking my dad?" like he'd give me a straight answer?'

Tom's eyebrow quirks up reflexively. Greta knows what he's thinking: *Yeah, exactly that*. She tries to catch his eye, wanting to share the joke. Wanting, more than anything, to step out of the circle of Amber's attention, even for a second.

Amber shrugs, returning her focus to the rail of clothes. 'I had to be smart about it,' she says, and then she plucks out a ragged-looking T-shirt and adds it to the pile. She glances at the camera. 'I guess that doesn't sound very believable,' she says, looking from Tom to Greta, and then, with another shrug, she looks at the pile of clothing. 'I should pay for these. Hey, want to go to Nando's for lunch?'

In the queue for the till, she picks out a blue dress from

a rack. 'This would look great on you, Greta,' she says, and she moves in close to hold it against Greta's body. Her flecked green eyes move rapidly over her, returning constantly to Greta's own. She is close enough for Greta to smell the cigarette on her breath, the last evaporating traces of mandarin. And then, just as quickly, she pulls away, the dress offered out on a finger.

And Greta, surprising herself, takes it.

They sit in a corner booth, Greta picking restlessly at a wing while Amber attacks a corncob, butter running down a wrist. Tom, a vegetarian, eats Greta's rice and sips his second beer. He and Amber have bonded over a love of *Game of Thrones* and the conversation has devolved into the occasional quote thrown at each other between mouthfuls. He's set the camera on the table, angled back at them, though they must be moving in and out of shot as they lean forward to eat.

'So come on, Amber,' Tom says, draining his beer. 'What will you do now?'

She stops chewing and looks at him; that same betrayed look she gave Greta earlier. Greta looks at Tom but his face is relaxed, his interest genuine. He considers the empty beer bottle in his hand and then stands it on the table.

'I don't know,' Amber says, putting her corn down among the orange-streaked bones on her plate. 'I guess I haven't thought about it much.'

'You must have some kind of plan, though?' Tom asks. 'Like, what did you want to be when you were a kid?'

'Rich,' Amber says, sliding a nail between a gap in her teeth. 'And looks like I kind of ticked that box, right?'

Tom shakes his head. 'You're smart. You know this won't last. People will forget, life will go on. And you'll have to, too.' He considers the carcass on her plate. 'You can't dine out on this for ever.'

Amber laughs. 'Yeah, thanks, Tom. Don't worry about me. Like you said: I'm smart. Hey, Gee – you gonna finish those chips?'

Greta shakes her head, slides the bowl towards her. 'We should probably think about going,' she says, and she thinks she might have diverted them both, diffused the moment. But as Amber slides a finger with its spiked nail through the greasy traces of salt at the bottom of the bowl, Tom says softly: 'It's never going to go away, you know. All of this will only last a bit longer, but what you did will stay with you.'

Greta's head snaps up, her mouth opening though no sound comes out. As if she might be able to stuff Tom's words into it before they reach Amber.

And Amber gets up without saying a word. She walks out of the restaurant without looking back, and Greta and Tom watch her leave.

They met after school though it was almost winter now, the air turning sharp and the daylight already disappearing as the bell for home time sounded. Next to the school was a children's playground and Sadie waited by the railings with Helen, watching the toddlers playing inside as their parents waited for their brothers and sisters to appear through the gate. She wondered if any of the tiny girls would grow up to be special, if any of them would be taken. The scar on her palm was nearly healed and it itched as the skin knitted together, the line of flesh turning white. She glanced at Helen's hand but Helen was wearing gloves, a scarf wrapped up tight around her throat and a bobble hat pulled down over her ears in an attempt to ward off the first of the many illnesses the winter was guaranteed to bring her.

Hers was just a scratch anyway, *Sadie thought unkindly, though it was true that Helen had pulled away when Justine put the knife in, her eyes filling with tears. It* probably wasn't enough to be special, *Sadie decided. She'd never really believed Helen would be chosen anyway.*

Marie appeared first, a neon yellow bubble blown and cracked in her gum as she made her way over to them. She had her Walkman clipped to the edge of her school bag, the headphones hooked round her neck like a necklace, though Sadie knew they were banned at school. Before they'd even heard of the Tall Man, Marie had known she was special.

'Hey, losers,' she said, leaning against the railings beside Sadie.

'Hi,' Sadie said. Marie didn't intimidate her any more.

Justine still did. But though they waited until the road was empty and the first stars were beginning to appear in the dirty sky, Justine didn't show.

That night Sadie sat up in bed, listening as the house fell silent around her. Her parents were long asleep and the neighbours' lights had all gone out too, only the occasional headlight of a distant car flickering across her wall. She knew now was the time. She couldn't let Justine be the only one.

She traced the scar on her palm with her finger, over and over, and then she closed her eyes and thought of the woods. I want to be special, *she thought, each time she touched the scar.*

There was a rippling sound in the room, a scratching in the walls.

She thought of Justine holding the knife, thought of

Helen crouching to scrabble dirt over a photo of herself and Marie, pushing it deeper into the ground. Please let me be special.

The springs of her mattress squealed, the bottom of it sinking under a sudden weight. Another set of breaths joined hers in the room, his cool and deep and smelling of tree and dirt and ash.

Sadie opened her eyes.

26

The sun came out again for Jamie's pool party, after two days of drizzling grey. It pierced through the torn-cotton clouds and the wind scuttled their remains away, letting the light bounce off cars and play through windows. Children freewheeled past houses with their laughing voices and teenagers ventured out into fields, milk-pale skin exposed.

Amber was getting ready round Billie's, hair half curled, the straightener smoking beside her left ear. She'd learned to time it perfectly; letting the hair heat until it was almost burnt, pulling the iron through the way her grandmother used to curl ribbon with scissors when she was little. Billie, lingering in the mirror behind her, glanced down at the two phones nestled together on the bed.

'Leo's calling you,' she said, smiling.

Amber shrugged. 'He can call back,' she said, the words

feeling hollow, and she winked at the reflection of her friend even though she didn't feel like winking at all.

Billie laughed and went back to poking at a spot on her chin in the small, smudged mirror inside one of Amber's palettes of eyeshadow. She watched Amber wind another section of hair around one of the straightener's blades. 'Should I curl my hair?' she asked, uncertainly. 'Won't all the curls fall out once it gets wet?'

'Probably,' Amber said, dragging the straighteners through with a hiss. 'But I've got no intention of getting wet. I'm going to sit in the sun and spike Jamie's mum's punch.' *And think about my dad being stalked*, she thought. *Think about Leo creeping around, watching him.* No, she wouldn't think of those things. She had promised herself. This was a day to have fun, to forget about the many ways her parents and their mistakes crept into her life and her thoughts and her feelings. Her dad was being stalked? His problem. Her mum was completely losing it again? Fine. She was so done with all that. She just wanted to have a good time and be sixteen and not care about either of them.

But Leo kept calling and she'd have to answer soon. She didn't want him to realise something was wrong. Or, worse, stop trying before she had time to find out exactly what he was up to.

'Jenna's calling you now,' Billie reported, looking at the phones again.

'So get it,' Amber said, annoyed and trying to disguise it as something nice. A privilege: you can take my call. Step into my shoes. Be me.

'Tell her I'm busy,' she remembered to mouth, last-minute, Billie wide-eyed and nodding. 'Hey, Jen!' she said, bouncing up from the bed and walking over to the window. She often walked around when she was on the phone, Amber noticed. Like Miles did when he was on a work call and uncomfortable.

'Oh, Amber's . . . um, in the middle of something,' Billie said, face reddening with the burden or the excitement of the lie. 'Yeah, she came over to get ready.'

Amber could picture Jenna's face as this information computed.

'Ams, what shoes are you wearing?' Billie asked, coming right up beside her so that Amber could smell the Johnson's baby lotion she'd smeared all over her legs.

'Just flip-flops,' Amber said, neglecting to mention they were wedge ones which made her legs look long and thin. Jenna could show up in plain old Havaianas.

'Just flip-flops,' Billie sang into the phone, skipping away to rifle through her wardrobe.

The only people (apart from Miles) who Amber had ever seen actually use Dictaphones were people in eighties movies and journalists.

There was a scandal at Miles's university once when one of the lecturers slept with a student. Two students actually, which was how he got caught out. They found out about each other and decided to get revenge – smart girls, if you asked her – by telling the papers all about their pervy teacher and how he promised them good grades as he burrowed into them with his wet mouth pressed against their necks and all those promises leaking out into their hair.

Amber thought it was funny at the time; the pictures in the paper of the lecturer looking old and sweaty and ashamed. Now she couldn't help wondering if her dad had made the same mistake; if the woman was a student and Leo a journalist writing a story about him. *Would he do that?* She loved her dad, but she'd long ago given up the idea that he was perfect. He was only human, she knew, and it wasn't exactly like he'd been getting any action from Sadie for all those years.

God. Don't cry, *Amber, for fuck's sake. What are you, ten?* She pulled the last strand of hair into the straightener harder than necessary, enjoying the needling feeling in her scalp. She didn't cry. She never cried. Crying wouldn't fix anything; it was for weak little babies and she would not be weak.

'OK, byeeeee,' Billie said, hanging up and tossing the phone back on the bed. 'Jenna's getting there for two,' she said.

'Cool.' She released the last curl and clicked the straighteners off. A full stop. *Don't think about it.* 'Is your mum still all right to give us a lift?'

'Yep!' Billie pulled out a T-shirt dress in red and white stripes. 'Will this look OK?'

'Yeah, that's nice.' It actually was, she realised, her heart sinking. 'What colour's your bikini?'

Billie yanked up her top to show her. Navy blue with a white bow in the middle. Cute. Amber smiled at her. 'Perfect.'

She turned back round and looked at herself in the mirror again. Orange dress with flowers on, skin tight, exactly how she liked them. Black bikini underneath – a triangle one that she'd stolen from Sadie (wherever Sadie had been, Amber mused, she'd obviously needed a bikini at some point. It couldn't have been all bad). The bottoms were a bit big on her but they were fine tied slightly tighter at the sides. She'd been pleased with this outfit when she left the house and yet now, looking at it on, she wasn't so sure. She couldn't put a finger on what was wrong with it but there was a word that kept circling in her head as she studied herself: *Cheap*. It was a word Sadie – or actually Leanna, definitely Leanna – would use, not something Amber would ever say or think. But it was there in her head and it fitted. Billie's outfit looked properly chosen, like something out of a catalogue. Amber's, now (so perfect before), suddenly looked like stuff she'd shoved together off a sale rack.

'You look so sexy,' Billie said wistfully from behind her. 'I wish I looked like you.'

And so Amber smiled at her again in the mirror, and applied another layer of lip gloss. 'Come on,' she said. 'Let's go.'

Jamie's house was on the other side of town, in a big, wide cul-de-sac where the houses had long, sweeping drives and pillars framing the doors. The cars sparkled and the windows gleamed; the walls were uniformly white. Any sound from the rest of the street was drowned out by the thumping dance music coming from the Donnollys' back garden.

'Give me a call when you guys want to come home, OK?' Leanna said, looking anxiously up at the house, its windows mirror-flashed with sun.

'Thanks, Mum.' Billie leaned over and kissed her on the cheek; a childish smack of a kiss which made Amber roll her eyes in the back seat. But there was a weird feeling in her chest that was suspiciously like jealousy. If things had been different, would she have been the kind of daughter to kiss Sadie like that?

She got out of the car in the hope that it would dispel the feeling. 'Thanks, Leanna,' she said, clunking the door shut and letting the sun warm her skin. The purple polish she'd carefully applied to her toenails that morning was already chipped.

Leanna didn't drive off right away. The car sat idling and she watched them as they went around the side of the house. Amber didn't look back, linking her arm through Billie's as they let themselves through the garden gate.

Jamie's parents weren't in, she'd lied to Leanna about that. They were visiting family somewhere for the day, his little brother taken with them, and in a couple of hours, the small gathering he was given permission for had sprawled predictably out of control. The pool was full of people, all splashing and laughing and drinking, girls on boys' shoulders, boys holding each other under. Every edge of it was lined with girls, sitting with their legs dangling in until every now and again a boy came and pulled one of them in with a scream and a splash. Muhammed from her Maths class had brought his decks round and set them up on a picnic table near the house, with a huge set of speakers that vibrated every time the bass kicked in, plastic cutlery on the table rattling. People were dancing on the grass, their drinks spilling, sofas and chairs pulled out of the house and marooned on the grass, legs sinking into the soil. Two boys were having a fight with the ketchup and mustard bottles, arcs of red and yellow flying through the air and splattering on the pale patio stones.

The Donnollys' huge chrome barbecue had been taken over by two boys from her form, Kenny Wu and Justin Staniland, while Ona Fitzgerald and Casey Lafountain from her English class watched and criticised, wobbling on their wedges.

'Hey, guys,' Kenny said, glancing up and seeing them. The smoke from the barbecue spiralled in front of his face, his sunglasses steamed up. 'Want a sausage?'

'Nobody wants your sausage, Kenny,' Justin said, elbowing him.

'Soft and juicy,' he said, waggling his eyebrows.

'I'm gonna pass,' Amber said. 'They look pretty raw. You get some kinda tapeworm from raw pork, right?' She shot a look at the half-eaten sausage in Casey's hand. Casey squealed and dropped it immediately.

'I really want a burger,' Billie said from over her shoulder. 'Do you get worms from burgers?'

'Nah.' Amber eyed the smoking, black remains of the burgers. 'I reckon they'll be fine.'

Justin slapped one into a floppy-looking bun and handed it over to Billie with a wink. He liked her, Amber could tell, but Billie blushed and looked away. Amber wondered if she was looking for Jake. She had forgotten to ask if he had ever replied to the message she'd convinced Billie to send him, though she hadn't really thought that he would. He was probably too busy wondering why Amber never replied to the messages he sent *her*.

'So what's been happening?' she asked the boys, trying to catch a glimpse of her hair in the rainbow lenses of Kenny's sunglasses. 'Urgh – who is that?' A girl emerged from behind the shed, vomiting a spray of orange down the fence and then staggering against it.

'Oh, that's Deena Jordan's cousin,' Kenny said. 'Someone spiked the punch.'

'Oooh.' Amber scanned the garden again – there it was, a big glass bowl with murky pinkish-orange juice inside. 'Come on, Bill.'

They made their way round the pool, careful not to get close enough to the grabbers and the splashers. Billie took a bite of her burger and pulled a face. 'It's really burnt.'

'Yeah, no shit, Sherlock.'

'Hey, guys!' Jenna appeared out of the crowd. 'You're here!' And then, in the same breath, 'Ohmygod, Billie, your dress is *adorable* – you look so cute!'

'Thanks!' Billie flushed again and tugged at the fabric like a child, though Amber could tell Jenna hadn't meant it as a compliment. She ignored her and pushed through the crowd to the table. The punch was even more dubious up close, with several blades of grass floating on its surface, but she ladled some into two plastic cups anyway. She pressed one on to Billie, who looked at it suspiciously, both it and the burger held awkwardly in front of her without making the journey to her mouth. Amber took a big gulp of her own. Despite its colour, it tasted of vodka and orange juice and not much else. She took another sip, noticing (without caring) that she had forgotten to get Jenna a cup. That didn't seem to matter though; Jenna was unsteady on her feet, eyes glazed as she looked around.

'This is *so* cool,' she said, flipping hair out of her face, and Amber smiled. She didn't think it was all that cool – in fact, it was kind of a mess. Noisy and dirty and childish. She tried to imagine what Leo would think if he was there, and then she remembered that she didn't care what Leo thought about anything (such a lie!). She sighed and drained her punch. This was supposed to be the perfect thing; getting drunk and being silly and wearing a bikini, all eyes on her. Glossy and sunny, music video cool. Instead it was all ketchup on the patio and grass in the punch, boys burping and the constant explosion of chlorinated water as yet another person cannonballed into the pool. Jamie himself was nowhere to be seen – probably escaped upstairs with Katie Barrow, his sort-of girlfriend – and that was a shame too, because she'd always wondered what it'd be like to kiss him.

She went back and filled her cup again, accepting an extra slosh of something clear from Kenny who had apparently abandoned his post at the barbecue.

'Sick dress, Banner,' he said, staring at her, and she knew then that he was very drunk. Kenny was like most of the boys in their year; he treated Amber like the sun. Like he liked having it around but it was dangerous to look directly at it.

Wary of getting burnt.

'Thanks, Kenny.'

She glanced back at her friends. Billie was still looking anxiously at her drink, and Jenna, laughing, put a hand on her arm and said something in that insistent, screechy way she did, until Billie, nose wrinkled, put the cup to her mouth and gulped the rest of it down in a rush. Jenna crowed triumphantly and turned away, bored already.

Amber filled another cup and went back over to them.

'Need a refill?' she asked Billie, handing the new drink over, and this time, Jenna glanced down and pouted.

'Hey, where's mine?'

Amber shrugged. 'You have legs. I only have two hands. Get your own.'

Jenna stared at her, her face set hard, and Amber felt something stir inside her. She couldn't work out if it was fear or excitement, but she'd learned long ago that they were similar enough that usually it didn't matter.

'What is your problem?' Jenna said after a moment, her mouth twisting, and the thrill turned sour. This was not how things were supposed to go. And words were still coming out of Jenna's sloppy, drunk mouth. 'You've been *such* a bitch for months now.'

Amber kept her face straight. 'I've always been a bitch, Jen. Did you only just notice?'

Jenna laughed, too loud and sharp, people around them turning to look. Billie took a step back.

'Oh God, I am *so* sick of you!' Jenna said suddenly, louder still, her breath yeasty and hot. 'You better watch out, Billie. You might be her favourite right now but she'll chew you right up and spit you out – you won't last a week.'

'You're drunk,' Billie said quietly. 'You should stop talking now.' And Amber loved her.

But Jenna was laughing again. 'She's a bitch!' she yelled. 'You wait! She's a crazy fucking bitch, just like her mother!'

Everyone was looking, the music still blaring and the water shushing against the sides of the pool and nobody talking. And Amber, coming to in a kind of blur, realised that she didn't have to stand there. She scrumpled her plastic cup and tossed it aside, then drove a fist right into the centre of Jenna's face. It didn't hurt, even when she heard knuckles crunch against nose; even later when her hand was red and swelling. Instead it sang through her, that feeling, as she watched Jenna stagger back, blood pattering on the mustard-spotted patio. She staggered back, and she stared at Amber, and nobody did anything.

Nobody ever did anything.

27

2018

Amber doesn't go far. Greta, snapping out of her stunned paralysis, runs through the crowds, panicked (already imagining what Federica will say if they don't return to the hotel with their star in tow) – but there she is, sitting on the edge of an oversized stone plant pot, watching Greta with her arms crossed in front of her chest, phone clutched in one hand.

'I'm sorry,' Greta says, when she's close enough, and Amber gets up with a toss of her hair. She glances behind Greta at Tom, who's just caught up, camera slung round his neck like one of the paparazzi who so far have not found them here, and simply says, 'Let's go.'

It's only when their taxi pulls up to the hotel that Greta realises the bag containing her blue dress is lying abandoned under the table in Nando's.

*

Amber doesn't come down to dinner and when Greta goes to knock on her door, she answers in a dressing gown, a fug of fast food and TV sound behind her. Her new purchases are flung in various positions across the bed, a supersize paper cup on the bedside table next to abandoned ketchup packets.

'No offence,' Amber says, her hair slowly unwinding from a knot she's wrestled it into at the top of her head. 'But I just want to be by myself.'

And so Greta goes back down to the restaurant, which is empty save for a couple in shorts and Buckingham Palace T-shirts, and then, before she can sit down, she changes direction and goes into the hotel's small and sticky bar. Another windowless room, several of its spotlights need replacing – the effect, though, is generally softening, casting a favourable (non)light over the peeling wallpaper with its satin-effect stripes; the cube stools in their faux-leather.

She buys a glass of wine and chooses a spot in the corner of the room; the light from a muted TV dancing across the shiny table. The wine tastes faintly metallic but it's cold and she drinks quickly, watching the silenced news reporters delivering the headlines. She tries not to think of Amber upstairs. Soon, this shoot will be over; soon, she can look for new work. She can tell stories she wants to tell, the kind of stories she wanted to work in film-making for. She thinks of the day she found out she'd been given a place at Goldsmiths, that she'd be moving to London. She'd been sure then that she'd work in fiction, remembers telling her friends from school that one day she would work on films that changed people, changed the world. Remembers calling up her boyfriend Marc and telling him, the words spilling out uncontrollably, Greta unsure whether to laugh or cry. *I'm doing it*, she kept saying. *I'm going to live in London.* It was only when he went quiet that she realised she'd also be leaving him behind. That the thought hadn't even occurred to her since she'd opened the email. He added her on Facebook last year. She looked through photos of his wedding, of his two baby boys. So good to talk to you, he'd written after they'd exchanged a couple of messages. How's it all going?? Seems like you're doing amazing.

It's not too late, she reminds herself. She saw a post on Facebook about a screenwriting class the other day – one of those tailored ads – and was surprised at how deeply it appealed to her. Perhaps she should take it as a sign. Maybe the stories she actually wants to tell are her own.

And yet she can imagine, even now, the people at parties who will rave about how much they love this project, how they love 'that bit' where Miles cries or when Amber does that creepy laugh. They'll ask her what it was like to meet them and she'll think back to these sleepless nights, the echoing cries of a child ringing in her ears, the feel of breath on the back of her neck when no one is standing there. *Do you believe in the Tall Man?* they'll ask her and maybe, by then, she won't feel like saying *yes*.

She finishes her wine and orders a new one. A

businessman, jacket over one arm, takes a seat at a table in the opposite corner to hers, paper and pint in front of him. The barman carries on polishing glasses, his own half of beer at his elbow. And she drinks, and she tries not to think about the Millers or the Banners or blood spreading on a forest floor.

'Want another?' She glances up and Tom is at the bar, gesturing at her empty glass as if they've been here all night together, as if this is merely another Friday at the local. But she does want another, and so she nods.

'You upset her,' she says, when he puts the drink in front of her.

He pulls out the stool opposite her and sits, setting his gin and tonic down on a coaster. 'I know,' he says. 'I shouldn't have. I'm sorry.'

'I could have filmed her myself,' she says, tongue slow on some of the words, 'You didn't even have to come.' She takes a sip of the new wine, and then, petulantly, adds, 'I know you don't like her.'

He considers this, his eyes on the newsreader above her. 'I don't,' he says eventually, and then he repeats her own words from a week ago back to her. 'Am I supposed to?'

'She's only a kid,' Greta says. 'Why did you have to try and make her feel bad? Why am I the only one who can see that she already does? Why am I the only one who can see that she can hardly live with herself?'

'Maybe because you're the only one who wants to.' His voice is gentle but that only annoys her more.

'Yes, exactly!' She puts her glass down. 'Everyone else wants her to be bad because it fits better with the story.'

'I don't want her to be bad. But that doesn't mean I can pretend I see any good in her.'

'Do you realise how horrible it is to say that about a teenager? Especially one who's had such a . . . fucked-up start to life.' It feels good to swear. She wonders why she doesn't do it more often.

'That's it though, Greta. Yeah, she's had this life that none of us can claim to understand – she's done a thing that none of us can even start to comprehend – but you're projecting on to her, you're imagining how you would feel in her place. That isn't what's sitting in front of you. She isn't like you. And she isn't like the Miller kids, either.'

She doesn't answer.

'You're starting to feel too much for her, mate. I can see it.'

A headache pulses at her temples. 'I don't want to talk about this,' she says.

He smiles sadly at her, nods. 'What would you like to talk about?'

She takes another gulp of wine. The businessman finishes his pint, the dregs foaming against the glass, and stands up to leave. 'You,' she says. She looks at Tom. 'Let's talk about you.'

He laughs. 'All right. What would you like to know?'

'You met Federica on *Bleak House*, right?' The wine is making her confident, the words easy.

'Yup. But actually I'd met Millie before that. I was

camera assistant on some awful reality series about freshers' week, and she was there doing research for one of her books. Federica hooked her up.' He takes a sip of his drink, the ice clinking. 'I was pretty much the only one who talked to her; that whole crew was full of arseholes. So, when I ended up on *Bleak House*, I mentioned Millie to Federica and then all of a sudden she was my best mate.'

Greta nods. 'Yes, I remember her telling me that now. That Millie liked you.'

'You know what's going on there?'

'With Millie? No. It seems serious this time though.'

'There was that woman in Cannes . . .'

She drinks some more wine, surprised at how little is left in the glass. 'I think there's always been other women. I don't know. I don't understand their relationship; Millie isn't like that.'

She pauses, her cheeks heating. She feels guilty, talking to him about Federica this way: another surprise.

'Has she even thanked you for taking charge in LA?' he asks, tipping back the last of his drink.

'Yeah. Well, kind of. I guess I should be flattered she trusts me.'

'I think there's a fine line between "trusts" and "takes advantage of" in this particular case.'

She points at his empty glass, ignoring the comment. 'Want another?' She gets up from the table before he can reply. She doesn't want to think about the many ways in which Federica Sosa and Amber Banner are probably taking advantage of her. The ways in which they trust her, either.

At the bar, she checks her phone – nothing from Federica all day, and nothing from Luca either. She wonders if she should send Amber a text, tries to imagine something casual, friendly, something that doesn't immediately translate as *Just checking you're still locked in your room.* Instead she flicks through emails, things she's read and forgotten to reply to – a chain between old university friends about getting together for dinner or drinks, Lisette asking whether Hetty and Greta think it might be a good idea to switch internet provider. It's happening again, the same way it did with the Millers – her life fading into the background, feeling like a fiction, a triviality. *The story is everything*, Federica likes to say, but that's what Greta's afraid of.

She takes the drinks back over to Tom, who's also been checking his phone. 'Nothing from Luc,' he says, as she sits down. 'Wonder where he's been all day.'

'I hope Elke's OK,' Greta says. 'She's due soon, isn't she?'

'Next month, I think.' He tips his head back to drain his first drink. Greta glances up at the TV, where the news is finished, the weather girl waving expansively at a section of coastline.

'So, what'll you do after?' he says. 'When this is done?'

'I'd like to go visit my parents for a while.' She tips the glass, watching the wine rush up it, then moves it to her mouth. Delaying. 'And then I'd like to go back to fiction,' she says, placing it carefully back down. 'No more documentaries for a while, I think.'

He nods. 'I get that. So back to America then?'

'Maybe.' She tries to imagine herself back in Dearborn. Married with two baby boys. 'I'd like to travel at some point too. What about you?'

'I've been thinking about going away, actually.' He stares into his drink. 'I've saved some money. I mean, I know we get to go to some great places, but I want to look at stuff without being behind a camera for a change.'

She glances up at him. 'Yes. To just *see*. I'm so tired of looking for the shot, looking for the story. I want to *see*. To appreciate things without wondering what the best angle is.' She's drunker than she realised, embarrassed at how earnest she sounds.

He smiles, lifts his glass to her. 'To getting away,' he says, and they both carry on looking at each other.

Her phone vibrates against the chipped varnish of the table. Federica.

Her voice is hoarse and traffic roars through her open car window so it's hard for Greta to hear (the wine doesn't help) what she's saying at first.

And then she does hear. She does understand.

'Sadie,' Federica is saying. 'Sadie's agreed to talk to us.'

From the diary of Leanna Evans [Extract D]

I collected the girls from their party at 9 p.m. as we'd agreed. They were waiting for me on the kerb outside, just where I'd dropped them, though it was obvious the party was still going on – music thumping out, people calling from the windows as a couple kissed on the front lawn. I wondered what kind of parents would let something like that go on in their house, and I was glad that our girls were different. They were quiet in the car, Billie asking if we could listen to music while Amber studied her hands in the back seat, and I thought that they had not had a good time. I was glad I had made the effort for them back at home.

They dressed in Billie's pyjamas when we got in and then we all sat in the lounge and discussed which film to watch. I took blankets from the cupboard – the night had turned cool despite the sun that day, and it felt nice to be inside all together. In the kitchen I served up the lasagne I had made, sliced some crusty bread to go with it. We ate in front of the film, the blankets across our laps, and afterwards, I prepared hot chocolates the way I did when Billie was small; whipped cream weeping down the sides, marshmallows heaped on top.

I enjoyed the evening very much, as I have every other

when Amber has been to stay. I like the sound of their laughter filling the house, like having another person to cook for again. I don't suppose Billie remembers what it was like before Ralph left, but for me, having a third person at the table feels good, it feels right. I get the sense that you have never really thought that; that a part of you – perhaps you don't realise it – even now pines for the days when it was just you and Miles.

You. My mind won't stop worrying at you; analysing the way you looked the last time we met, the way you spoke. I know that something has changed. I can't stand not knowing. Even as the film's credits were rolling, I was wondering about you. Wondering if you were sitting in front of your own television with your husband or if you were alone somewhere with the shadows.

I tried to remind myself of all the careful planning that had got me this far. I reminded myself that it was me who was truly special; who had found you, found Amber. I had proven myself when you have done nothing but run from what belongs to you. As I kissed our girls goodnight, I told myself that I did not need to worry. I thought of you, alone, and I knew that the time would come soon. I was not afraid as I turned out the light.

28

2016

There was a man (*the tall man the tall man*) outside the house. Sadie knew she was not imagining it. She'd looked and checked and considered and she knew it with a cold finality: he was there. Standing watching the house, his face in shadow.

She stood at the bedroom window, half-hidden by the curtain, and checked again. She told herself it was her imagination playing tricks, the same way it had done in Miles's lecture theatre, her fear conjuring his voice, his touch.

Still there. She drew in her breath and wrapped her cardigan tighter around her.

The thing that scared her most was the need (the *hope*) that lay under her fear. She thought of the feeling of icy fingers across her arm, breath travelling over her skin. Would it be so wrong to slip back into the comfort of the shadows?

She'd first noticed him when she was on her way down

the stairs, a basket of laundry under her arm. Amber's clothes, all sweet smoke smelling, the collars stained with make-up. She had stopped because a streak on the window had caught her eye; a shimmery smear of moisturiser, the gradual tan Amber used that had dried and turned brown on the glass. She'd paused to wipe it with her sleeve (smudging it further) and through the window she'd seen the figure standing there.

It hadn't always been like this. He was not normally so coy. She had invited him in, all those years ago, and her world had been his after that, her rooms his to walk through, her ear his to press his cool, calm words into. He had left her before, taking with him his shadows, and though he had always come back, he had never taunted her, not like this.

Of course now there was Amber.

He wasn't waiting for her any more.

She drew back from the window, pressed her forehead against the wall. She tried as she always did not to remember what it had been like, slipping from that tiny family housing flat in the milky grey dawn, her baby left behind. Moving quickly, the small bag she'd grabbed thumping at her thigh. Breasts aching, full. And always, always, that feeling of someone behind her. That breath upon her neck.

She'd known as soon as the girl had reappeared, with her dank, metallic smell, that she could not stay. It had only been later, after hours of walking and a sweaty coach journey, that she'd thought more carefully about that moment.

The little girl had warned her. The little girl had spoken without the Tall Man being present.

That hadn't happened before.

The girl, the taken daughter, had more power than she'd thought.

She thought of that again now, feeling her breath bounce back from the wall, her heart thudding in her chest. Could all daughters be taken? Or was there really hope?

That first night – third, if you counted the hours spent with eyes closed and face pressed to a rolled-up jacket against the coach window – she'd been in a friend's spare bedroom up in Aberdeen. She'd trusted them, she'd known she could. They'd never met Miles and they wouldn't tell him where she was, even if he had somehow tracked them down to ask. They had their reasons for not wanting questions. She remembered the mildewy smell of the pillow, the midnight cry of their newborn. She had felt guilty, leading the Tall Man from one infant daughter to another. But her options had been limited. She was learning that in these situations she was the mother she'd always hoped to be. The lioness.

She spent years reading articles she hadn't had when it was her own life at stake, reading forum posts and anonymous questions on sites about the Tall Man and all of the lives he had stepped into. Message board after message board, fan art, news stories, theses. Hours spent reading conflicting theories, the different ways in which people thought the Tall Man had made them special. The posts that said only children were truly pure enough, truly had the potential to become special. There weren't any stories of someone meeting the Tall Man for the first time as an adult. The Tall Man's fans believed that by then it was too late – the gate had closed, or the Tall Man lost interest in letting you through. And she had been relieved; had believed that she truly had protected Amber by leaving. The shadows – though they were slow and twitching, never venturing close – moved with her wherever she went, letting her daughter live in the light, until finally they left her too.

Now she'd returned and so had he. *Be careful what you wish for*. She went to the window, looked out again. In the darkness, he looked back at her. And then he stepped backwards and was swallowed by the night.

When they woke in the morning, Leanna was already up as usual. Standing at the stove, pancake batter made and waiting. And Amber wasn't hungover at all, the alcohol erased by the lasagne Leanna had fed them and sleep, so that the smell of the first pancake crisping in the pan made her mouth water. She took her usual place at the table and idly ate some of the halved and hulled strawberries Leanna had put in the centre. Her hand was swollen, split between two of the knuckles. She thought of Jenna standing there, blood flooding down her face. How she had turned and run back through the party, no one moving to follow her. Amber smoothing down her dress, slipping her arm through Billie's.

Leanna hummed as she cooked until, spatula in hand, she turned to beam at them. 'Now,' she said. 'I've had a wonderful idea. Sit down, Billie, come on.'

Billie was rubbing her eyes like a sleepy toddler, her hair all mussed up on one side. 'What's going on?'

'I feel like going on an adventure. Shall we go to

Scotland? To the cottage?' She flipped the first pancake and turned round to look at them again. 'You too, Amber, if you'd like to.'

'Oh—' Amber blinked at her, taken aback. She was surprised to find that – despite the fact it was obviously a totally lame offer – she actually wanted to say yes.

'Yes! Yay!' Billie definitely didn't think it was lame. 'Today? Oh, Ammie, you'll love it.'

'I was thinking tomorrow,' Leanna said, pouring more batter. 'I thought seeing as it's half term next week we could spend a couple of days up there. I mean, we'd have to check with your parents, Amber.'

As if they'd care. Amber ate another strawberry, stalling for time. There were surely better things to do with her week. She just couldn't, at that particular second, think what they might be.

'Call them, Am!' Billie stared expectantly at her from across the table, all sleepiness forgotten, and Leanna laughed.

'Give her a chance, darling. She might not want to trek all the way up there with us.'

Amber found herself shrugging. 'Yeah. Sounds great. Thanks, Leanna.' Because yes, Scotland would probably be cold and boring but at least these two people seemed to really, genuinely want her to be there.

So she'd go. She ate another strawberry, feeling pleased with herself.

And as Leanna slid her plate of pancakes in front of her, she squeezed Amber's shoulder, almost as if she was saying *Thanks*.

29

2018

Greta wakes at 4:13, the hotel coverlet scratchy on her bare skin. There is a pulsing pain behind her eyebrow and her mouth is gummy and foul. She tries to turn over, tries to pull the blanket with her. But she's on top of the covers, in a bra and nothing else. She scrabbles into a sitting position. The lights are on. She blinks against the pain, a hand pressed against her eye. Reaching for the nightstand (hoping for water), she takes in the two plastic tumblers, the half-empty bottle of whisky.

It floods back – admittedly blurry – Tom's lips against hers, back thudding against door and then wall and then bed, clothes fumbled off, breathless sips of whisky spilling on the shiny quilt. Panic flutters up in her because she remembers now. She remembers asking for ice, throat whisky-burned, and him obediently trotting off, T-shirt and jeans pulled back on. How long ago was that? She finds her phone – twenty-two missed calls, all from him – and knows it was hours ago, that he has given up knocking and gone back to his room. Heat rises to her cheeks and she scrambles for the tangled underwear on the floor, for her T-shirt. She goes to the bathroom and rinses out one of the tumblers, fills it with water and drinks it down. She has to grip the sink to stop herself throwing it back up, and when she is sure she's managed it, she fills it again, her hand shaking, and goes back to the bedroom. She climbs under the sheets and tries (failing) to shut out the jagged snatches of memory, his hands on her, her moan damp against his chest, her teeth sinking into skin.

She manages to drift into a half-sleep, those broken images spliced into a stuttering reel of dream, and so the knocking at the door, at first, doesn't seem real. She dreams she answers it; dreams it's Tom; dreams he kisses her and presses her back into the room. But the knocking persists and she jerks awake, realising.

Tom? She sits up, a plunging feeling in her stomach. She slides out of bed, pulling her T-shirt further down over her thighs. Her breath feels thick and rotten in her mouth, her hands still shaking, and each movement makes the pain in her head beat harder. The knocking goes on and on.

It's not Tom. It's Amber, hair half falling out of a ratty ponytail that's sliding to one side of her head. Make-up smudges under her eyes, a ketchup blob on her vest top.

'This *can't* happen, Greta,' she hisses, pushing her way

into the room, and Greta, confused, follows her, hot with shame, conscious of her sweaty stink.

'Amber, I—'

Amber whirls round, stabs a finger at her. 'I said *no*. You know I did. I said *not her*. Not my *mother*.'

Understanding, Greta fumbles for the robe hanging in the wardrobe. 'I know. I'm sorry.'

'I said that from the beginning. I did! I said I'd only do it if she wasn't involved.'

Greta nods. 'I know. I know. I tried to tell Federica—'

'Did she think I wouldn't find out? Did she think I wouldn't hear about it?' She glances at Greta, who has no answer for her. 'She wasn't supposed to talk to her!'

Greta moves cautiously closer and touches Amber gently on the shoulder, sitting them both on the bed. 'Amber, Federica's under a lot of pressure from the network. She has to make sure we have enough material, and also that we present as many sides of the story as possible. I know that's not what you wanted.'

'I won't do it,' Amber says sullenly. 'If she wants her, she loses me. I'll leave in the morning. I'll go and stay with friends, somewhere she can't find me.'

I'll go with you, Greta thinks, but instead she says 'You signed a contract. They paid you. If you leave now, you'll have to give it back. Can you do that?'

Amber lets out a growl of frustration, kicking the heels of her bare feet against the bed's base with a hollow thud. 'Of course not.'

'I'm sorry.' It's true. It always is.

Amber's eyes have narrowed, her teeth working over her lower lip. 'Fine,' she says, looking up at Greta. 'Fine. I'll do what she wants. If she leaves my mother out of this, I'll do it. I'll go back there.'

'But you said—'

'I don't care. I don't care any more. Call her right now, Greta, and tell her we can go to Scotland. She can film me in that fucking house and I'll tell her everything.'

30

2016

The calls started on Saturday morning; early, while Sadie was sleeping. Miles didn't pick up the first, or the second – sat watching his phone vibrating on the kitchen table, its screen flashing on and off. A silent alarm.

It was an unknown number – it could have been some recorded PPI message, or a cold caller – but he knew. He knew it was the person who had sent the emails. The person who called themselves SomeoneSpecial.

So he turned the phone off. And that worked, for a while. He washed up the previous evening's dishes; scrubbed at the baked-on burn on the casserole dish. Sadie got up and when he heard her footsteps above him, he put the coffee on. Keep things ticking on, that had always been his way. It had been the only way. Act normal; make normal a wall.

But walls could be scaled.

Sadie came downstairs, drawn and pale, and he handed her a mug of coffee. The smile felt lopsided on his face. He was glad to let go of it when she turned away to sit down. 'I'm so tired,' she said, more to herself than to him, and he looked at her hunched frame at the table and he knew. He had let this go on – he had let *her* go for goodness' sake – when he could have taken the burden from her, could have explained. And there would be no running now. The time for running had passed long ago. Their ghosts could not be silenced.

And so he made his wife breakfast. He mowed the lawn, tidied his shed, weeded the flowerbeds. His hands felt shaky and unreliable as he washed off the soil in the kitchen sink, and he couldn't bring himself to look at his reflection in the window. When Sadie came up behind him, a cautious hand placed on his back, he couldn't stop himself from flinching.

With nothing left to tidy or fix, he found himself in his office, his back pressed to the door. He breathed in the soft, woody smell of the room and tried to draw strength from it. When he couldn't resist any longer, he turned his phone back on. It was blissfully silent for a minute, and then it vibrated once, twice in his hand. A text from Amber, asking him to pick her up from Billie's. And a voicemail message.

He thought about deleting it, but what would be the point? They'd only leave another.

He pressed the icon, put the phone to his ear. His pulse thudded like a drum as he waited for it to connect. 'You have one new message,' the automated voice said, and he swiped away more sweat from the back of his neck.

'Miles, it's me.' Her voice was smooth and cool, melodic, like a stream over rocks. It wrong-footed him with its gentleness. He wasn't expecting her to sound gentle. 'I'd really like for us to talk. I—' She lowered her voice; there was the sound of a door closing, a girl talking or a television in the background. 'I know everything.' His stomach lurched, the sandwich he'd half-eaten threatening to reappear. He almost missed the last part, which was low, a whisper. 'I want to give you a chance to explain.'

He deleted it with shaking fingers, tried to draft a reply to Amber. But her voice echoed in his ear. *I want to give you a chance to explain.* As if it could be that simple.

He sank into his chair and looked hopelessly at the computer. If only that first email had never arrived. If only he could go back to those weeks when Sadie was home and work was going well and nothing, nothing (for once) was threatening to breach the wall.

A knock at the door behind him kicked his heart into an even higher gear. He pushed his hands through his hair, trying to straighten out the expression on his face, smooth it away. Sadie turned the handle; rattling it when it refused to open. 'Miles? What are you doing in there?'

He took a deep breath and opened the door. 'Sorry. It sticks. I've been meaning to take the handle off and have a look.'

She looked at him and he thought again about grabbing

her, grabbing a bag and stuffing in a few clothes, driving away. Just driving on and on. As far away as they could go.

It was hopeless of course, because there was Amber.

He pulled his wife into a hug, pressing her into his chest. Tight – too tight; he felt her stiffen against him. He breathed in the smell of her hair, felt the erratic thud of her heart against his.

She moved back from him, her eyes locking on him properly now. 'What's going on, what's wrong with you?'

'Nothing.' He passed a hand over his face, wishing he could leave it there, hide behind it. 'Sorry, I'm tired.'

She pulled away fully and went to the window. 'Still there,' she murmured. 'What is he doing?'

'What?' He looked over her shoulder at the road outside, panic rising through him again. 'There's no one out there, Sadie.'

He wasn't so sure. There was no one there *now* – but had he seen a figure there just a second ago? Sweat prickled across the back of his neck again; beading on his top lip. And then, before he could stop it, he felt the familiar fury rising up. 'You ought to book an appointment with another doctor, Sadie. You're clearly losing it again, whatever the other one said.'

She drew back, the words like a slap, and he was glad. This was all her fault, after all.

Amber was sitting on the low wall that ran around the park, waiting for him. Her head was bowed, phone in hand as always, and the sun glowed behind her, the sky relentless and blue. He pulled the car up to the kerb and pressed the horn to get her attention. Watching her hop off the wall and lope towards him, he remembered her at five, skipping across the playground, pigtails flying. That strange, secretive smile she always had. There was a solid mass in his chest and he had to fight off tears.

'Hey, Dad.' She thumped herself into the passenger seat, slammed the door shut. She was not as tall as Sadie yet, but her legs still seemed impossibly long, her body suddenly stretched.

'Hi, baby girl,' he heard himself say, trying to swallow that pressure in his chest down. 'I would've picked you up at Billie's house, you didn't have to wait here.'

She shrugged. 'They had to go out.'

'Oh. OK.'

'By the way,' she said, clicking her phone to locked. 'Is it OK if I go on holiday with them?'

A car slowed as it passed them at the junction, a pale face turned in their direction, and fear prickled through him, the knot in his chest rising again. Suffocating him. He was hardly listening to her. 'I don't know. When?'

'Like, tomorrow.' She gave an embarrassed, small sort of laugh. 'They're driving to Scotland for a few days. It's half term, remember? Can I go?'

'Erm,' he said, trying to focus on her words. They seemed to belong to a world he no longer lived in – holidays, trips, no ghosts. He could not let Amber see that. 'Yeah. Sure. Why not? Sounds very wholesome.'

'Really?' Surprised – she'd clearly not been expecting it to be so easy.

'Yep. I'll give you some money so you can pay for drinks and food and stuff.'

'Cool.' For some reason he didn't understand, he sensed disappointment in her voice; the lack of anticipated fight perhaps. 'Thanks, Dad.'

'You're welcome. You deserve a break, you've worked hard this term.'

He had no idea if this was true or not. He couldn't remember now any information she'd given him about school, whether or not he'd even asked. All he cared about, at that particular moment, was getting Amber as far away as he could; away from there, away from him, from Sadie. All he could think about was getting Amber to safety.

31

2018

They leave the following morning in a rented people carrier Federica has managed to magic to the hotel in the early hours. She's dressed for travelling, leggings and an over-sized sweatshirt, and greets them all with a grin in the underground car park. Amber ignores her, her hood pulled up, hands shoved in pockets, and Greta is still having to focus a good portion of her energy on not throwing up. Tom is loading equipment into the back, a cap pulled down low. Her stomach twists as she thinks of his hands on her, her naked belly exposed and her faded old bra above it. And then he glances up and sees them approaching, Amber dawdling behind, and she wants to disappear, she wants to turn around and run.

She manages to raise a hand in greeting, murmurs 'Morning' as she gets closer. She wills her face to stay its normal colour. Tries not to remember that first kiss at the table in the bar, her seat moved round next to his. Her hands on his face, his chest, his thighs. Kissing in the lift, the mirror cold against her back. Her stomach lurches again as he raises a hand in return and then turns away.

She's distracted, anyway, by Amber threading an arm through hers. It reminds her of being thirteen, the way girls would walk around the school at lunchtime linked that way. Patrolling the playground like Victorian courting couples, their faces smug and other friends (usually Greta) left to trail behind. Amber's arm feels thin but strong, her elbow sharp against Greta's side. Her hand folds itself round Greta's lower arm and the knuckles are cracked and white, a faint hairline scar between the second and third. Up close, she smells of smoke and shower gel and Diet Coke.

'Good morning, girls!' Federica steps closer, an arm extended as if she might attempt to put it round Amber's shoulders, but it falters halfway, her smile still holding. She waves them towards the van instead. 'Hop in and we'll get on the road.'

'Can't wait,' Amber mutters, removing her arm from Greta's and thrusting her hands into her pockets again.

The van smells of smoke too, its seats threadbare grey with the track marks of a handheld vacuum visible. Greta shuffles her way into the back seat and wishes she'd thought to bring sunglasses like Amber. There's plenty of space but Amber chooses the middle seat at the back, right next to Greta. She pulls her hood further down over her forehead and slouches in her seat, feet up on the cup holder in front of her. Her trainers have glittery neon pink laces; the edges grubby and splashed.

Luca climbs in, pushing up the seat in front of them and closing them in.

'Too early,' he groans, lying across the middle row.

'Don't mind us, Luc,' Tom says, sliding the door closed. He gets into the passenger seat at the front and closes that door too. Greta tries not to think about how they stumbled into the hotel corridor, how her hands fumbled with his belt.

'And off we go!' Federica turns the key in the ignition. 'Road trip . . . Anyone got any music they want on?'

'No music. Too early.' Luca kicks his shoes into the footwell and turns on to his back. He falls (noisily) asleep before they've even left the North Circular. Amber turns her face away from Greta and is silent, hoping for or feigning sleep too. Greta settles her head against the window and watches the steady grey sky start to lighten, the sun bleeding through.

She's seen photos of the house – hundreds of them, actually, during the months of research, those months holed up in the tiny office in Federica and Millie's rented flat. Fuzzy newspaper photos, old online listings, photo exhibits from the trial. It doesn't feel the same way it did back in Texas when she was driving from the hotel to the Miller house the first time – that suffocating heat, her heart pounding. The Murder House, the locals called the Miller home, with its yard dug up and shreds of police tape still flapping in the dirt. Nobody knew what to do with it; it was tainted. Hayley told her a year after filming finished, in one of her weekly calls, that it had been knocked down, the land concreted over. Made into a parking lot for the rest of the barren street, those squat houses with their shuttered windows and their empty porches. The finished film of *My Parents Are Murderers* ended up full of shots of those houses, turned away from the Miller House in its place at the end of the lane, its yard and the things that happened inside shielded by badly planted trees and thorny shrubbery; shots of the empty rooms, a couple of the numbered cards used for police photographs left lying in the dust. The floorboards replaced but their secrets let out.

No, it doesn't feel the same, driving north towards the Scottish cottage where Amber Banner became a killer. It only feels sad.

So she's surprised, an hour later, when Federica pulls into a service station for coffee number three of the day and Greta has to scramble out, suddenly desperate for air. She throws up in the scrubby grass behind the petrol pumps, her back to the car.

From the diary of Leanna Evans [Extract E]

We set off bright and early – arriving to collect Amber by 6:00. Billie complained; she was never one for early starts and unfortunately I was tense and too highly strung to tolerate whining. It was the closest we ever came to arguing, that day, and I think we were both glad when we pulled up outside your house. You were there at the door to wave us off, your face sallow and drawn above your ratty old dressing gown. A state. A mess. I'm sorry to say it so bluntly. You looked beaten, abandoned. You looked as though you would lie down and accept what came next. You would let it happen.

I could have waited for Amber to get into the car and then driven away; I'm sure that's what you were hoping for. Early morning, no need for small talk, pleasantries. And yet I knew this might be the last time we met. I climbed out of the car. I walked up the short driveway, and all the time, my eyes were on you.

The funny thing is, Sadie, your eyes were on me the whole way, too.

I smiled. You smiled. It almost felt as though all the pretences were over, that the end had been reached. But you weren't quite ready. You said, 'Thanks so much for this, Leanna. Amber's so excited to have a holiday.'

And I played along. I said, 'Oh, not at all. We're very excited to have her with us.'

All of it truth. All of it a lie.

You tried to give me money, I remember that. It repulsed me; perhaps you could tell. You retracted it quickly, the notes brought back to your chest before they'd even made it halfway across the gap between us. 'No, honestly,' you tried, your voice weak and unsure. 'For food and things. For petrol.'

'That won't be necessary,' I said, and it was cold, I know that. I saw it register on your face. But I was hurt, Sadie, that this exchange was so pedestrian, so tawdry to you. As if money was the currency within which we were operating.

'Well, thank you,' you said, and the thing that I can't understand is how much you seemed to mean it. You really did seem to be grateful to me; it was clear that this was what you wanted. That you were ready to be left behind again.

I went back to the car. I took the sunglasses down from their propped position on my head and slid them back over my eyes. I turned the radio up and we went on our way. I watched you in the rear-view mirror. You didn't even linger. The door closed behind you and the curtains in your house remained drawn.

And that was that.

It was so easy to take your daughter, Sadie. The Tall Man must be proud.

After ten minutes of driving, they were both asleep,

heads lolling towards each other, the duvet pulled up over their shoulders. It was so beautiful, Sadie. I wish I had a photograph to show you. I wish I could make you see.

They slept for hours, as teenagers do, and in the end I decided not to wake them until we were across the border, almost at Glasgow. They were special, those hours of driving alone. The hills rolled out before us and those two smooth-faced girls slept on and on. When we crossed the border, I felt it as an almost physical thing; a separation. I left 'Leanna' behind. I became – not myself again, but something closer. I could shed those months, those years. I could begin to rebuild things. It was a beginning.

I could have driven for hours and hours, for ever, like that, but I knew that it would be wrong to let them sleep. I knew that they were as much a part of this as me; I knew that they should see it. And so I woke them. I did it gently; I turned down the radio and I called their names. They felt like silk in my mouth, those four syllables in their pairs of two; their wings. *Billie. Amber.* Butterfly girls.

They stirred. It's always something so special, isn't it, to watch a child rise from sleep. That slack face of repose changing as consciousness slowly returns to it, their features reforming and firming until slowly, slowly, those eyes flutter open. I have never tired of watching that.

Of course, you've never seen it, have you? Never held a child and watched them wake? I do pity you that, Sadie. I'm not sure you knew what you were giving up back then.

'Are we nearly there?' Billie asked, *her* eyes still closed, and Amber, who'd hitched herself into a sitting position, laughed through her yawn. I told them that we were an hour away, perhaps, and that we would stop for something to eat along the way.

Amber caught my eye in the rear-view mirror as she stretched her neck and yawned again, and I saw a smile hidden there, her cheeks dimpling. It felt like we were in on this together, if that doesn't sound too fanciful. It was as if she had been waiting for this; as if she knew this was the right thing to do. That this has *all* been the right thing to do.

In the Little Chef, Amber ordered a full breakfast while Billie, as she always does now, ordered pancakes. I opted for black coffee and pushed some fruit cocktail around a chipped bowl. I was too excited to eat. I was like a child, my tummy turning, unable to concentrate. I did my best to conceal it.

'You're going to love the cottage, Am,' Billie said, spearing three segments of pancake on to her fork and pushing them through a pool of maple syrup. 'It's like the cutest place ever.'

It seemed a natural place for me to break my news; that the cottage we usually rented was unavailable, that I had found us a better one. Neither of them seemed to mind. I felt giddy, giggly. I felt free. I looked out at the rolling green hills beyond the road, and I could finally, *finally*, breathe.

*

We arrived at the house two hours or so later, the last thirty minutes of which were spent juddering along a potholed track around the gorgeous, glittering Loch Earn. Both the girls were stunned into silence by the beauty of it – I suppose it's possible that they were both tired and grumpy from being wedged in the car for so long, but I think it truly was the magnificence of the loch. It needs to be seen to be believed, Sadie. Although I'm sure you will, now. It made me happy to think of you standing on its shores, looking out over those endless, silvering waves, and wondering. Searching. Looking for us as I have looked for you.

The house itself is hidden up a steep drive, sheltered by overhanging trees and overgrown honeysuckle, and I had to slow right down to a crawl to navigate it. I was afraid I had got my directions wrong. Then, round a corner, it was revealed; small and whitewashed and perfect. I exhaled, and I caught Amber's eye in the rear-view again. She looked less impressed than I felt, but that was OK. I knew she'd come to understand eventually.

We climbed out, legs stiff, and looked around. The land outside the house sloped steeply, buried beneath gorse and shrubs. And beyond, the loch, vast and churning, the hills gathering at its banks.

Billie clambered on to the small, ancient-looking deck attached to the side of the house, and craned over the railing to get a better view. Amber climbed up beside her. You can imagine my panic. I know I called out 'Careful!', my heart rate spiking as I took in the broken railing, the spiny sea of gorse beneath them. They both rolled their eyes and I knew I had to control my fear, my need to protect them. I turned and busied myself locating the key – the owner had told me it would be beneath a plant pot at the front of the house, of which there were many. Heavy things, fat and ceramic. By the time I located the right one, the girls were down, the danger passed. I could breathe again.

The key retrieved, I unlocked the door, the girls now behind me. It opened smoothly, the air clean and cold inside, a smell of dry firewood and clean sheets. We stepped in together, our eyes adjusting. It was dark, with slate tiles and dark wooden banisters leading up the stairs. Low ceilings and dusty-looking rugs lining the way. But once we made our way inside, the window in the living room gave a perfect view of the loch, the boats on it tiny white dots, and the kitchen was clean and well-stocked. I opened the fridge and found a bottle of Chardonnay in the door. And – you'll like this part, Sadie, it's exactly what you would do – I thought to myself, *Why not?* I took the bottle out and poured myself a glass in one of the small, cheap wine glasses I found in the cupboard. The girls were bouncing across the floorboards above me, laughing, with the occasional thud as someone dropped their bag, a squeak as one of them collapsed on to one of the twin beds in their bedroom. Lovely sounds; normal family noise. It made every bone in my body sing.

I took my wine glass and went back through to the living room, looked out over the water below. So *vast*. I hadn't realised. So dark, so deep; as deep as it is wide, they say. That seemed incomprehensible.

Sadie, it seemed perfect.

I made a shepherd's pie, using the mince left for us in the fridge, the handful of floury potatoes. There were a couple of bottles of red wine left behind, too, and by the time I served the food, I'd finished my white and was ready to move on. I suppose to you that might seem normal, expected behaviour, but for me it was unusual. I was getting too excited, I was counting my chickens before they'd hatched, as they say. It was dangerous and yet I felt more relaxed than I had in years. As a treat, I even poured both girls a glass too.

'Put some music on, Amber,' I suggested, and she plugged her phone into the stereo thing in the corner, surprising me by selecting Frankie Valli and the Four Seasons instead of something poppy and new.

I took my seat at the head of the table, suggesting that Billie served as I stifled a hiccup. I was drunk; too drunk. But there was no risk. It felt, for the first time in a long while, safe.

Billie stood up and started cutting carefully into the dish, suddenly self-conscious under our scrutiny. Such easy tells; the sudden flashes of blotchy colour that strike up across her cheeks, the way her voice begins to wobble and crack. One of the things I love best about her. A purity; no sense of pretence. She picked up the ladle and attempted to scoop up the first uneven section she'd marked out.

'Here you go,' Amber said, noticing and sliding a bowl across in time to catch the portion before it fell. 'Thanks so much for this, Leanna. It looks great.'

I simply smiled at her; I found I couldn't speak. I was overcome by that easy intimacy, the comfort, the beauty of the place. By that sense, again, of an ending; a beginning. She belongs here, we all do. And here we are.

The girls sat down, their bowls full. I took a sip of my wine. I had lost my appetite, but I was content. I moved my fork through the food, occasionally lifting small morsels to my mouth, letting their easy, dull conversation about music and gossip pass over me like the lapping water of the loch.

I had made an error, Sadie. I know that might surprise you. I had let myself relax too far; I had reduced the gap between the things that I think and the things that I say until it was too small to consider, until the words slipped out unchecked.

I called her Anna, Sadie. I wasn't paying attention; I was thinking of you and all those years ago and then I drifted back into their conversation and realised I had been asked a question. They were both there, watching me expectantly, and before I knew it, it was out: 'Sorry, Anna – what was that?'

Amber looked at me strangely though she was too polite to say anything; it was Billie who squealed 'Mum! Who's Anna? She's Amber!'

I laughed it off, I told them that I was tired after the drive. Amber was calm, understanding. I suppose the sight of a drunken mother isn't exactly unusual to her, is it? But Billie kept watching me after that. Unnerved. Amber tried to draw her back into conversation but the atmosphere had changed, just a little, and I tried to repair it, I tried to bring us back to that idle ease. I talked about the things we could do, the walks we could take. Perhaps you wouldn't think that that would interest them, but it did. They seemed younger, there. Happy to be in a small house in the great outdoors, happy to have an adventure. I began to relax again.

The music ended, and Amber got up to put something else on. I was watching Billie, trying to reassure her; I could see that my slip was still bothering her. I heard Amber say 'Oops!', and I turned in time to see my handbag tip on to the floor, its contents spilling out. I must've left it on the counter in my excitement. My brain was slow and foggy with the wine, so when I saw Amber bend down to scoop everything back into it, I kept on sitting, smiling along to the music she'd selected: Madness, this time. Surely not one you and Miles play at home? That seems rather close to the bone. I thought of you and I felt pity again, warm in my gut with the wine.

And then I realised, Sadie. I realised.

I leapt from my seat, my legs unreliable, and pushed her out of the way. I think I managed to scream 'Leave that' as I did, though I can't be sure. I was too intent on grabbing the things that had spilled out and stuffing them back in the bag. I only looked up when Billie said '*Mum.*' She was staring at me, open-mouthed. I glanced at Amber, the bag clutched to my chest. She was watching me too, her face impassive – interested and not yet afraid.

She doesn't scare easily, does she?

I apologised, I gave them a half-baked line about having a surprise for them in there. Billie was instantly appeased, returning her attention to her food. Amber went back to her seat, still watching me. Still watching, and yet not yet afraid. She sees me, Sadie. She sees me and she is here, and everything is going to work out the way it should.

32

2016

Billie had been loudly asleep for hours, flat on her back. The house had long ago stopped settling, its small creaks and taps petering out, and Amber, wide awake, was glad of Billie's snoring. The silence was eerie. It was heavy in its totality, unbearable. It reminded her how far away the nearest town was, the nearest house.

Sadie had once lived somewhere like this – she'd told Amber about it, drunk, one night, when she'd had to ask Amber to log her phone back on to the Wi-Fi. 'I'm not used to any of this,' she'd said. 'I'm used to being in a place where there's only a bus out three times a week.'

Though it hadn't sounded like a brag, Amber remembered feeling slighted, like Sadie was trying to prove how independent she was, how she didn't need gadgets or company to survive. She'd told herself she'd be as good as Sadie in such a situation, better even – but now she was here, she was afraid of the dark, of the silence.

She was not her mother's daughter.

She took her phone – not currently functioning as a phone – out from under her pillow. Still no signal; SOS calls only. It made her feel itchy and anxious, and she checked again in case a random open Wi-Fi network had magically appeared on the list. There was only the one she'd seen the last time she'd looked: Ardvorlich01, password-protected. She remembered a carved sign – Ardvorlich House – a mile or two back down the track, a creepy-looking drive snaking off into the trees. She'd have to trek up that way tomorrow, try and find a signal somewhere. Miles would be going mad that she hadn't texted to say they'd arrived or to tell them the new address, and she felt a twist of guilt that she'd only just remembered, that she hadn't thought to remind Leanna earlier. That until now, she'd only been worried about whether Leo might have tried to call or text her.

Leo. The thought sent a familiar wave of cold dread through her. That Dictaphone with its calm observations: *Miles stopped outside library by unknown female*. Like Leo was David Attenborough, observing a dull but endangered species of bird. And Amber had done nothing. What was Leo doing without her around? Would he be watching her dad again – was he watching him even now? The idea of him outside the house, looking up at its dark windows, made her shiver. She had made a mistake, she knew it instinctively; felt the subconscious knowledge of it start to swirl and press at her. Something was wrong, and Amber had done nothing.

Leanna was kind of worrying her too. She was acting . . . differently, that was the only way Amber could think to describe it. It wasn't that she wasn't being nice – she was, way nicer and more relaxed than usual. Amber had never really seen her have a drink, let alone pound two bottles of wine like she had over dinner. But there was something unsettling about the way she kept smiling at them, smiling and *staring*, always looking at one or other of them in a kind of unfocused, emotional way that Amber couldn't read. She thought of the moment Leanna had called her 'Anna'. Not a big deal, it kind of sounded like 'Amber' – but Billie had completely overreacted and there was something about the whole thing that had chilled Amber; she couldn't put her finger on it. Then there was the way Leanna had flown across the room to pick up the dropped handbag, the way her happy woozy face had dropped for a second. Amber knew what she had seen there instead: panic.

She knew a person hiding something when she saw one.

The more she thought about it, the more her suspicions grew. There'd been something slightly off about both of them since Billie showed up at school and singled Amber out as the friend she'd follow around like a puppy. Leanna equally keen to befriend her freak of a mother, when it was pretty clear to anyone who spent more than five minutes in her company that Sadie was not a lady who lunched; the last person you'd invite round for cocktail hour and sharing recipes.

And Amber *had* seen something, in that neat cascade of Leanna's things as the handbag had tipped over. Of course she had – she didn't like surprises; she had to do what she could to stop people from springing them. She had always been good at spotting the things someone wanted to keep out of sight. Her memory was forensic and she could skip back through it like an Instagram feed, knowing when and how to zoom. So, yes, she'd seen the fat envelope slide out with Leanna's fancy purse and pristine address book, her keys and a neatly clipped bundle of coupons from the local paper, a folded up reservation for the cottage, a receipt for something else. She'd seen it, she'd noticed it, and she'd seen the way Leanna clung to it as she slid it back into her handbag.

Most importantly of all, she'd seen the first line of writing on the envelope: *Sadie Banner*. And she couldn't help wondering why exactly Leanna was carrying around a letter to her mother, when she had seen her in person not one day ago.

She got up with care, the bedsprings squealing traitorously. Billie mumbled in her sleep and Amber froze, a draught creeping round her ankles. When Billie settled back on to her side, Amber kept moving, bare feet placed slowly and carefully, eyes adjusting to the dark.

She tried to tell herself that she was being stupid. That she should get back into bed, try and trick her brain into sleep. But something kept her moving, an animal thing pacing inside her chest. That letter. So fat in its envelope; something solid and hard at its centre. Who sent letters anyway? What would you put in a letter to someone you barely knew and had boring lunches with once a week?

The windowless landing was pitch-black, without even the faint wash of moonlight that had picked out the bedroom furniture. Stepping into it felt like stepping off a ledge, a freefall. She stood for a second, listening to her own breath. Her phone was in her hand but she was too afraid to use the torch on it.

Too afraid of what? she wondered, and she thought again of Sadie. Of the things she saw in the shadows. The curse she carried with her, that she had passed on to Amber. And didn't that corner, where the darkness swirled thickest, look suddenly like the profile of a man? Wasn't there something small crouched there, by the stairs? Something small and rocking, something reaching out to her?

No, she told herself. You are not your mother's daughter. And the prowling animal thing inside her drove her on. Down the corridor, into its mouth. The floorboards remained silent beneath her and she felt weightless, as if she were in a dream.

Leanna's door was ajar, lamplight leaking out and finally breaking up the dark. Amber hesitated, fear suddenly dagger-shrill in her chest. It was an instinct, but she had learned to listen to her instincts. She hesitated. Was that the cool flutter of someone else's breath against the skin of her neck?

Another draught – air creeping from somewhere, from everywhere. She moved forward again slowly, so slowly

313

that the light seemed to expand and loom ahead of her until she reached it. Her hand found the door handle.

And she could hear it now, her heart rate slowing; that wet ratcheting sound with its steady rise and fall. Like mother, like daughter: Leanna was snoring. Confidence growing, Amber pushed the door slowly open. The lamp was on the nightstand, its pale green shade making the light sickly against the frills of the bed and the curtains. Leanna was fully clothed, flopped on her back with her tasteful top riding up to reveal a stretch of skin, wrinkled and red-marked from her jeans. Her feet were bare, toenails painted a pearlescent pink. Amber stood in the doorway, watching her. And then her eyes strayed down the bedspread, where Leanna's hand lay palm-up, fingers half-curled; a spider on its back. Beyond it, that same white envelope, its flap open, a pen abandoned beside it.

Ten steps away; even seven. She looked down at the floorboards, wondering if they could be trusted, and then up at Leanna's slack face, that same thick snore every minute or so. She'd seen Sadie in a similar position plenty of times over the last half year (it wasn't exactly an alien position to Amber, either). Leanna wouldn't wake up. Almost definitely. She'd probably stay that way until morning.

Amber took a step into the room and then another. Suddenly it was the most important thing in the world that she had that letter, that she felt the thick paper of the envelope in her hands and laid out its contents to examine and understand. She was beside the bed, close enough to see the feathery blue veins in Leanna's neck, the crumbs of mascara under her eyes. The air smelled fermented and vinegary, the cottage's mildew and wood beaten back. Something changed and it took her a moment to realise that the thing that was different was the silence.

No snores.

Her eyes flicked up from the letter to Leanna again, certain she'd see eyes open, expectant. *What the fuck are you doing in here?*

But Leanna's eyes were closed, her mouth lax. There was a long second of silence, of total stillness— and then she snorted in her sleep, her forgotten breath gulped in, and the snoring began again.

And then the letter was in Amber's hand. It felt silly, suddenly, anticlimactic. What, really, was she going to find in it? She started slowly to worry that it might be a love letter or gift of some sort, something private; a secret of Sadie's, for once, that had nothing to do with Amber. It was too late now. The letter was in her hand. She could feel that solid form inside the envelope again, squat and thick. She wanted to know. Somehow she knew that she *needed* to know.

She didn't dare to breathe until she was back out on the landing, creeping towards the stairs. At first, she planned to go all the way down, away from Leanna and Billie, but she was so glad to make it to the top step without a sound that she sank down on to it, close enough to hear them both.

She leaned against the banister and pulled out the object from inside the envelope. She fumbled for her phone and thumbed on its torch. It was a notebook, warped slightly with use, its cover soft and leather. Embossed small and gold at its centre: *2016*. A diary. She opened the cover and began to read, her mouth dry with fear.

The pages were packed with dense neat handwriting which occasionally looped erratically, the pen pressed so hard on certain sentences that the letters darkened and bled into the paper. At first, she was confused. It *was* a diary, but a diary that was addressed to her mother. A diary that focused on the mundane details of the ways in which their lives had intersected. Who would take the time to note such things down? To record them as if they were special or important?

Then, like a cloud passing over the sun, the darkness of the words reached her. The hatred she could tell had been inked on to the pages, tied up tightly in the knotted, swooping words. By the time she reached the account of the previous evening, she was shivering. Those last words (scrawled: wine) – *She sees me* – stuck in her like darts. She turned the page, but Leanna's words ended there.

Other people's words took over.

'The Tall Man spoke to me again last night,' Justine said.

They were sitting in their place by the river. There was no one else around, the wind biting at their faces, the low sun almost invisible in the white sky. Sadie fiddled with the metal cuff she'd bought from the market, already pinching the top of her ear.

'He says it isn't enough,' Justine said, hitching herself off the bench and skipping the couple of steps to the river's edge. She sat down on the low wall there and faced them, hands resting under her thighs. 'He says he should take one of us.'

Sadie felt a bolt of fear travel through her. He had not told her this when he visited her in her dreams. Was it her he planned to take? Maybe Justine was the only one who was special. She clenched her fingers into a fist, traced the edge of the scar tucked into her palm like a secret.

'What are we supposed to do?' Marie asked, though her voice was flat and she was looking sideways at Helen.

Sadie had noticed that Marie was not as enthusiastic about being special as she'd once been.

'It's time for us to prove ourselves,' Justine said, standing up. 'We have to give him what he wants. Now come with me, all of you.'

They trudged away from the river, towards the woods. The clearing was mulchy underfoot. The air iron-scented. Sadie thought of the letters she had written to the Tall Man, the letters they continued to write and burn here, their words turned silver and lifted up, carried away. It wasn't enough. She thought of the cat winding its way between Justine's legs, the sound it had made as she grabbed it by the head.

Fingers grazed the back of her neck, gone almost immediately. He was with them. He was with her, *as he often was when she had doubts or felt afraid, and the thought warmed her. She longed to step away from the clearing, to move into the embrace of the shadows. To feel his hand slide into hers. His voice in her ear, telling her she was special.*

But perhaps it was Justine he had come for, Justine he had made special. Perhaps Sadie would be left behind, left alone – a fate even worse than being taken, she thought now. She glanced into the trees, thought she saw a figure move there.

'A long time ago, the Tall Man killed his daughter,' Justine said. She always enjoyed telling this part of the story the best. 'He knew that, even though she was still small, she was very bad.'

'I don't want to do this,' Marie said suddenly, arms crossed in front of her.

'We have to!' Helen looked frantically from Justine to Sadie and back again. 'Tell her!'

Justine stepped closer to Marie, studying her face. 'He told me you were weak,' she whispered. 'He'll take you, you know. When you're alone and asleep at night—' She clicked her fingers in front of Marie's nose, and Sadie jumped, her insides clenching. 'Poof. Gone.'

A bird fled from its tree with a shriek, wings ripping at the air. Helen let out her own scream, her hand clutching Marie's.

'You have to do it,' she said. 'Come on, Marie, he only takes the bad ones. We have to be special now.'

'No, we don't.' Marie pulled her hand free from Helen's. 'Let's go home.'

'I'd stay here with us if I were you, Hel,' Justine said, still watching Marie. 'Your sister is making him very angry. He'll punish her.'

'Shut up, Justine,' Marie said, but her eyes had filled with tears and her voice quivered. 'He will not.'

Justine smiled, glancing behind Marie at the dark space between the trees. And then she took a step closer to her friend, put her face up close to Marie's. 'Wanna bet?' she whispered, and her eyes flicked to the trees again.

Marie spun around and for a second Sadie thought she saw the shadow there again, a figure standing tall at the edge of the shadows.

'Are you scared yet?' Justine whispered in Marie's ear,

and then she shoved her, hard, sending Marie sprawling to the ground at the edge of the clearing.

'Hey—' Helen took a step forward but Sadie reached out and grabbed her hand, holding her back. Her eyes stayed on the figure though Marie did not seem to see it – she pulled herself up, looking down at her grazed and bleeding knee. A tear spilled out and trailed down her cheek and Sadie felt disappointed. Marie was not special at all. Marie was weak.

'Better run along, Marie,' Justine said, still smiling. 'You should lock your bedroom door tonight, if you think that'll save you.'

And Marie did not stay to argue. She turned and ran, the leaves scattering as she went.

Justine turned back to the others and shrugged. 'We can't all be special,' she said, and from her pocket she pulled the knife. 'We have to give him what he wants,' she said to Sadie. 'I know the exact right place.'

'Is the Tall Man going to take Marie?' Helen asked tearfully.

Justine shrugged. 'She isn't special any more.' She glanced at both of them, her eyes settling on Sadie's again. 'The Tall Man takes daughters,' she said, and Sadie felt her own lips mouth the words along with her. 'But sometimes he needs help.'

As they walked through the woods, leaves shushing madly at their feet, the sound of a child laughing drifted through the trees towards them.

33

2016

The first sheet was cut out sentences and paragraphs, the newspaper yellowing. They overlapped each other, packing the page, and the effect in the bright white light of her phone was dizzying.

. . . survived by parents Debbie and David Weatherall, and older sister Lucy . . .

. . . Lucy Weatherall, sister of murdered toddler . . .

. . . joined in court by teenage sister, Lucy . . .

. . . Stacey Frederick, the youngest, held the child's hand and sang . . .

. . . baby-killers, pure and simple . . .

She turned the page. She was afraid and didn't understand and so she turned the page.

A single article, neatly clipped and pasted to the paper.

Anna Lou's killers released

In a statement today, the Crown Prosecution Service announced that the so-called Westborough Witches will be given new identities. The three girls were found guilty of the murder of a toddler five years ago.

Two-year-old Anna Louise Weatherall was found dead in woodland near her home in Westborough in 1990, after going missing from a playground near her home. She had been stabbed twenty-seven times and her skull had been crushed. CCTV footage from the area led police to three local girls, aged 11–13.

A search of the girls' homes found a bloodstained sock belonging to the child, along with a daisy hair clip. The girls told police that they were 'just playing' with the toddler but an unnamed school friend testified in court that the group had become 'obsessed' with an urban legend that involved making sacrifices to a satanic figure. The jury was shown photographic evidence of a 'ritual' they had carried out on the body of a cat found in the school field.

The eldest of the girls, Justine Jones, was described by a police psychologist in the dock as 'a very angry girl' with 'a high IQ, and the power to manipulate', while the youngest, Stacey, was described as 'a dreamer; highly susceptible and very pliable but equally a persuasive and formidable personality'.

Now the *Sun* can exclusively reveal that all three of the

girls have been released to the custody of their parents, and have been given new identities to protect them.

Meanwhile, Debbie and David Weatherall, along with their surviving daughter, Lucy, arrived in Manchester today to give a statement to the press. They said that they felt 'sick to learn that our baby's killers are free to start again, when she will never have that opportunity'.

There was a picture alongside that paragraph and Amber leaned closer, the phone almost touching the page. A man and a woman, both haggard-looking and dressed in black, and beside them, a moody-looking teenage girl, her blond hair cut in a weird bowl shape.

She looked very different – a nose job, definitely, but Amber thought there was more work there, fillers or some kind of reshaping, her face now more refined, more designed. And yet she was recognisable because Amber saw that same thing in her eyes, that thing that scared and repelled her and which suddenly she understood. The nakedness of her loss, her need.

Leanna. Leanna was Lucy Weatherall, sister of poor murdered kid Anna Louise.

Amber's hands were damp with sweat as she turned the page. And there it was. A neat triptych, the pictures cut out carefully and now fading. The first a photo of a round-faced toddler, her fine hair clipped back from her face with a plastic daisy slide. Fat hands clutching a doll against her round middle, an uncertain smile on her face. And then an image cut from a newspaper: the body of a cat, splayed open on the grass. The picture was black and white and grainy, but she could see where the blood had seeped into the grass, where the fur and flesh had been unevenly hacked away.

And then the last photo, this one an old Polaroid. Four girls, skinny arms round each other, grinning at the camera in their crushed velvet dresses and their Doc Martens. The flash had bleached out their faces a bit, the photo sun-worn too, but her eyes were drawn to the smallest, the youngest. That face, so carefree and familiar. *Stacey.*

Sadie.

Mum.

She felt the breath on the back of her neck before she heard the floorboard creak.

'I put that one in for you,' Leanna said.

34

2018

They arrive in Scotland just after lunchtime. Amber, who
seemed to sleep most of the way – though Greta, now, is
never quite sure – is suddenly awake and alert, her leg
crossed up under her, foot tapping against the seat. She
scrolls through her phone, sunglasses still on. Greta,
glancing sideways, notices how her eyes keep flicking to
the window. She's glad of Amber's glasses – if Federica
notices the nervous way their charge is watching the
distance between them and the cottage disappear, she'll
almost certainly suggest they switch on a camera.

Greta managed to get some sleep too, in the end. But
it was a restless sleep, dreams of herself naked from the
waist down, a man stepping out of the shadows to lay
cold fingers on her skin. Long, filthy nails piercing it,
digging out handfuls of flesh. Hayley Miller holding her
hand the whole time while a little girl swung her legs in

the hotel chair beside her. Tom stepping out of the shadows, Tom knocking on the door.

Tom calling her name.

She'd jerked awake and he'd been holding out her phone, left charging on the dashboard.

'Your dad's calling.'

She hadn't answered it in time, a voicemail left in her dad's cool tones. *Sorry to miss you. We are out now for dinner but perhaps you could call us tomorrow. We'd like to hear your voice.* Perhaps it's the hangover, the sour taste in her mouth, but the sound of *his* voice brought tears to her eyes. She follows Amber's gaze to the fields and the hills beyond and tries not to think about what her parents might make of this film. She remembers a Christmas two years ago, she and Sebastian both free and able to fly back to Dearborn for the first time since he'd finished school. How she'd gone into the living room one day – a room they never used, all family dinners and TV time taking place in the basement her parents had converted into a den – and found, among the framed articles her brother had written from Kabul, Baghdad, Damascus, a review of *My Parents Are Murderers* from the *Washington Post* online. Printed out and trimmed and pasted on to the board backing of a chunky silver frame, hung in pride of place over the fire. The living room was a room for guests and there she and Sebastian were, their achievements laid out like rare treasures her parents couldn't quite believe had come into their possession.

Federica hunches forward in her seat, the car slowing. 'Is this the turning?'

Tom consults his phone. 'Can't get the map to update – no signal out here.'

'Yeah, this is it.' The tapping of Amber's foot more rapid on the seat. 'It's like a mile up that way.'

Greta's parents have never seen *My Parents Are Murderers*. If her brother has, he's never mentioned it to her.

'You doing OK, Amber?' Federica's voice heavy with faux-concern, though she is already turning to Tom, checking whether he has any of the equipment in the front with him.

Greta remembers a phone call she received from Danny Miller a year or so ago, his words thick with drink. 'You made me say those things,' he'd said. 'I liked you and you got me to say those things that I didn't mean to tell. Now everywhere I go everyone knows my face, they know about my mom and dad and what they did. They treat me like I'm a freak. How am I ever gonna get a job, Greta? How am I ever gonna get away from it all?'

The car thumps over the rutted road. Trees enclose them, blocking out the sun. Amber's head snaps to the side, watching the woods pass. 'Yeah,' she says. 'I'm fine.' Greta wonders if she's the only one who hears the way her voice trembles.

She thinks again of Tom last night. *You're starting to feel too much for her. I can see it.* Later, after the fourth glass of wine but before the first kiss, she had called him out on it again, irritated and afraid. *What's so wrong with feeling anyway? Isn't that what makes a film great? Caring about it?* He'd shaken his head, looked away. *It's not the film I'm worried about. It's what it's going to do to you.* And then his eyes had returned to hers. *That family is dangerous. It's not like it was with the Millers. There's nothing worth saving here.*

She glances at Amber as the car slows, Federica swearing as she tries to navigate a steep turning off the main track. She misjudges as she tries to shift down a gear, the engine whining. Amber is still watching the woods through the window, her bottom lip bleached white as her teeth push into it. *Nothing worth saving here. It's what it's going to do to you.*

The Tall Man takes daughters.

'I've got no signal either,' Luca says, waving his phone around above him as Federica slows the car to a stop. 'Shit, I hope Elke doesn't need to call. Is there Wi-Fi in there?'

'There are patches of signal in the woods,' Amber says, not turning away from the window. 'If you go in deep enough.'

Luca glances nervously at her. 'Right. Yeah.' As Federica turns off the engine he slides the door open and wanders back towards the track, phone in the air again. His back to the woods.

Tom hefts the seat forward to let them out, his eyes meeting Greta's as Amber brushes past him.

'You OK?' he asks, and she nods.

'You?'

'I've felt better,' he says, grinning. 'At least I got an early night, eh?'

She flushes, glancing at Amber ahead of them on the gravel drive. 'Yeah . . . I'm sorry about that—'

'Greta.' He cuts her off, the brim of his cap casting a section of his face in total shadow under the sun overhead. 'Don't worry about it. We were both wasted.'

'Yeah.' She tries to smile, tries not to remember his hands sliding her jeans down, the way his T-shirt caught in his mouth as she tugged it off. Tries not to imagine what it might have been like to wake up with him this morning, whisky fug lifted and daylight flooding in, all her flaws exposed.

And then, stepping around the corner of the drive, she takes in the cottage for the first time. The loch is wide and calm, a few houses dotted on its far shore. On this side she can see only wilderness; trees and gorse knotted together, vines rambling up the cottage's faded walls. It's no longer rented out, she read that somewhere. The owners can't sell it either. Not so much the crime – if anything, that's of interest to a certain type of buyer – but because of the market. She thinks idly that she would like to live here, so far from anything else, bricks being pulled under by earth. The house slowly shrouded with green.

And then she sees Amber, looking up at it too. She is very still, rigid – if Greta touched her, she thinks she'd feel like steel. Fists clenched tightly by her sides, lips pressed together and glasses hiding as much of her face as possible.

Federica walks slowly around her, tiger stalking its prey, and when Tom rounds the corner with the camera, Federica moves smoothly out of shot. The gravel crackles under his feet, the sunlight flashing on the camera lens.

Amber considers the house for a minute or two and then, sliding her sunglasses on to the top of her head, she looks back at the camera and at Greta beyond it.

'It's smaller than I remembered,' she says. And then she turns on her heel and goes inside.

35

2016

'I put that one in for you.'

Amber scrambled away from the words, the hot sour breath on her cheek. She lost her balance and clung to the banister, slipping a couple of steps as she turned to look Leanna in the face.

'What is this?' Her voice sounded strange in her own ears – young and afraid. But the diary had slid from her lap as she caught herself, was now thudding down the stairs. She heard it skid across the floor at the bottom.

'I knew you'd want to know.' Leanna clasped her hands in front of her, still kneeling on the top step. 'You are so clever, Amber. So suspicious, too. You aren't how I expected you to be.'

'That was you,' Amber said. 'That was you in the picture. It was your sister they—'

'It was, I'm afraid,' Leanna said, and Amber didn't wait

to hear the rest. She pulled herself up and stumbled down the stairs, bare feet slipping on the wood.

'Amber, stop!'

But Amber didn't stop, didn't even turn to see Leanna hurry down the stairs after her. She reached the hallway and ran for the door, wrenching the security chain off so quickly that she ripped a nail in half. She threw the door open as Leanna made a grab for her, her fingers snatching at the fabric of Amber's T-shirt.

'Amber, please—'

Amber pulled herself free, the T-shirt tearing, and ran out into the night.

Miles couldn't sleep; he hadn't slept at all. He sat in his usual place on the sofa, listening to Sadie pacing around the floor above him, willing her to lie down. He pressed his fingertips against his closed eyes, trying to force back the headache throbbing there.

Someone was watching them. Sadie had been right and Miles knew he should not be surprised.

It was almost 3 a.m. and Miles got up and went to the window for the twentieth or thirtieth time. There – stepping more fully into the circle of amber streetlight until he could *almost* make out the face, just hidden from him by the shadow of a hood as rain continued to bat against the window. And then gone again, melting back into the night.

It was surprising (it had always surprised him), the way the rage flooded through him after hours of unease and fear. His feet were moving before he even realised it, anger burning in the back of his throat. He looked around for a weapon – something filmic and satisfying; a baseball bat or a poker, neither an object they owned – and then he was in the hallway, heading for the door. He yanked it open and stalked out into the moonlit road.

This was not him. He did not behave this way. And yet it felt right, this rage: it felt like a homecoming.

He plunged into the darkness between the streetlights, a beat pulsing blindly behind his eyes where the headache once was – and grabbed hold of fabric, flesh, surprising himself. He heaved the figure against the side of a parked car, out in the light. There was the sound of jagged breathing though he was no longer sure if it was his own.

He pulled back the hood.

A man around his own age, dark hair slicked back, uneven stubble edging his jaw. His eyes dancing nervously across Miles's face and the empty street. 'Let go of me,' he said.

The rage was still pounding through him, the words forced out. 'Who are you?'

'You can call me Leo. And I *said* let go of me.'

'You've been watching my *house*. My *wife*.' But Miles released him, hands shaking.

'Yeah.' Leo straightened up, smoothing down his top. 'I have.'

'Why?'

'I was asked to.'

Miles's heart kicked up a gear, blood thundering in his ears. 'By who?'

Leo smiled, just a little. 'I think you know. She's sent you emails too.'

SomeoneSpecial. Miles reached out to steady himself on a parked car. He forced himself to speak, wondering when the rage had abandoned him. 'Who is she? What does she want from me? From us?' Everything was tumbling down, he could feel it. It was over. The wall had been broken, their ghosts flooding in.

'It's not what she wants, it's what she has.' Leo looked around again, pulled his hood back up over his head. 'I'm not here to hurt you, I came to warn you. Amber – she's in danger.'

The adrenaline surged through him again, the street beginning to spin. 'What have you done to my daughter?'

'Nothing. Nothing. She told me to watch her, to find out about her. About all of you. I never thought it'd go this far. I thought it was about Sadie, I never thought she'd do something to Amber.'

'Amber's not here.' Hands numb and frantic, he searched his pockets for his phone. He would call the police, call his daughter.

'You don't get it.' Leo stepped forward, his breath malted and foul. 'She's with her. She's got her. She sent me this message this morning, saying she didn't need me any more. Said it was almost over.' He shakes his head. 'She said the debt was about to be paid.'

Understanding went through Miles like a knife. 'Leanna? Leanna is behind this?'

Leo was already backing away. 'You need to find Amber. You need to warn her.'

'Who is she?' Miles reached out and grabbed hold of him again, suddenly afraid that he might disappear, fade back into the shadows. 'Is she one of them? One of the Westborough girls?'

'You *knew*.' Leo's face twisted as he pulled himself free. 'She thought you did but I didn't believe it.' He spat the words out. 'How could you marry *that*?'

'You don't know her.' Miles was surprised at how steady his voice became. The hope draining from him. 'That isn't her. She isn't Stacey any more.' *I thought I'd saved her*, he wanted to add. *I thought I could*. The great Miles Banner with his degrees, his published papers on deviant behaviour and its roots, on the social rehabilitation of criminals. With his young wife, his first true love. His first case study.

'Get your daughter back, Miles. She doesn't deserve any of this.' And his visitor turned and jogged away.

Miles turned back towards his house and saw Sadie standing there.

Out by the loch, Amber made it to the edge of the woods, her feet bleeding and the wind ripping at her torn T-shirt. The shadows reached out to swallow her but Leanna drew closer. Leanna followed her in.

36

She sits on the step and they crowd in beneath her. Federica and Tom closest, faces turned up to her like worshippers in a Renaissance painting, Luca stretching to angle the boom. Greta at the bottom, a light and reflector held up like a beacon. Amber is crying and they all pretend she isn't. Amber is crying and they carry on.

'So you ran,' Federica says. 'When you realised that the woman who'd been calling herself Leanna was behind you—' She glances (they all glance) into the cavernous dark space cast by the spotlight. 'You ran for the woods.'

Amber nods.

'There was another page of the diary, wasn't there?' Federica says, and her voice is unbearably soft, her words sinking into the dark like silt. 'Did you know that?'

'I didn't read it. I was too busy fleeing for my life, funnily enough.'

'I have a copy here,' Federica says, a folded sheet of paper produced with a flourish from a pocket somewhere. Greta feels her blood turn to ice. Where has she found it? The diary was lost for a long time – its absence one of the biggest holes in Amber's defence in court until finally, at the eleventh hour, her legal team managed to discover its hiding place here, in these woods. Guarded by this tainted house, along with all the rest of its secrets. And yet now here's the most important page, photocopied and obtained by Federica from who knows where.

Photocopied and obtained and brandished in front of a camera, like some kind of magic trick. Or just a trick, Greta thinks, a plain old dirty interviewer's trick, designed to get a reaction. To manipulate. Exploit. She feels her mouth opening, the breath drawn in. It doesn't have to be this way. She won't let it be this way.

But Amber doesn't flinch at the sight of the paper the way Greta does. She leans forward and takes it. Though the tears are still making tracks in the make-up on her cheeks, her eyes widen hungrily at the sight of the words printed there. 'Could you read it aloud for us?' Federica asks, her eyes hungry too. Greta wants to hurl the light at the wall. She wants to leave.

She wants to hear what the page says.

37

2016

The darkness of the trees was different to the darkness inside the house. It lived, its shadows shifting and breathing all around her as she ran, branches and stems reaching out to snap and slap against her skin, to draw her on and pull her deeper. The forest floor was damp underfoot, her skin so bone-cold by now that the roots and stones that snagged the soles of her feet went unnoticed.

And always, always, as the ground sloped upwards and the trees knotted closer, she heard Leanna behind her, that harsh breath and the snap snap of the branches as she crashed on.

'You have to come with me, Amber,' she'd called out as Amber first ran into the woods. 'You must see that. It's the only way.'

But the only way, right then, was up and onwards, into the shadows.

Billie stood at the open bedroom window and listened to the sound of her mother and her friend thrashing through the woods. She knew she should help.

She was surprised at how calm she felt now. Prepared. She already had thick socks on and so she slid her feet into her boots, unlaced at the end of the bed. She pulled another jumper over her pyjamas, found the torch. And then she walked slowly down the stairs and out of the open front door.

She had always known the story of Anna Louise; growing up, it had a fairy-tale slant in the telling, often whispered to her in the pink light of her bedside lamp, ended with a kiss to the forehead. Anna-Lou and the witches. Anna-Lou and her avengers. She remembered realising, wide-eyed beneath her Mulan duvet, that she was supposed to grow up to be the character in the story; the daughter who was meant to slay the witches alongside her mother.

She knew her mother thought she was stupid. Naïve, maybe. She also knew that her mother was not herself, or not *right* somehow – that she didn't think the way other people thought about things. Obsessed was the word. And Billie knew that this meant too that Leanna had always underestimated her, had always thought that she understood less than she did. It meant that she had never considered that Billie might have ideas of her own about how to extinguish the fire that had burned inside her mother since longer than she, Billie, had even been alive.

The night was cool but not cold, not with her preparations. She clicked on her torch, sliced the beam through the trees. There was a cracking sound, followed by a scream and the swishing sound of someone sliding down the slope.

Billie stepped into the woods. She knew she had to make this stop.

She knew, most of all, that the ending of the story had changed in the telling. But the ending had finally arrived.

Sadie stood looking at her husband, seeing him for the first time. She watched him try and call Amber's mobile, watched him finally give up and call the police. Watched him search through his messages with the operator still on the line and then repeat the address of the cottage, which Leanna had emailed him. When he hung up, he looked at her, his face drained and pale.

'You knew,' she said, and he nodded. 'How?'

'Sadie . . .' Miles reached out a hand to her and she stepped back sharply, her heart thudding and her mouth dry.

'Tell me.'

He nodded, helpless. 'It's not why, Sadie, I swear to you. I loved you anyway. I loved you straight away and I could see that you were holding something back and I wanted to know you. Know everything. So . . .' He pushed a hand through his hair and looked away. 'Sometimes I'd look through your things. When you were in the shower or when you left me in your room to go to lectures. I wanted to soak up everything about you.'

'You went looking for my secrets.'

'It—' He seemed to think better of it. 'Yes. There was an old birthday card. *To Stacey, love Mum and Dad.* And a few weeks later when you were drunk, you mentioned growing up in Westborough. And it all started to fall into place.'

'Why didn't you tell me?'

He looked up at her, his eyes wet and wide. Pleading. 'I hoped you'd tell me eventually. I hoped you'd learn to trust me.' He looked as though he might reach out to her again but when she took another step back from him, her stomach churning, he looked away. 'And then you became pregnant, and knowing became something special to me. It was . . . I don't know. It was like it was this secret you were keeping to protect me – and yet *I* was keeping the fact I knew about it a secret to protect *you*. Do you see? It was our bond, Sadie. It was the thing that made us closest.'

'How could you want a *child* with me? Knowing—'

And then it was too much. She looked down and she was Stacey again, eleven and invincible. She looked down and the girl, Anna, was beside her. The girl's tiny hand was in hers. She knelt down beside her and the road turned to grass. Those big blue eyes with their blond lashes looked into hers. Her head intact, her dress clean again.

The Tall Man takes daughters. A child's whisper, breath against the back of her neck, though the girl beside her looked back, unblinkingly, and smiled. A bird sailed high above them on an airless sky and Sadie pointed up at it until the child smiled. She stood and led the girl into the woods where the others waited. Where Justine's laugh scared more birds from the trees.

Alone again, Sadie felt those small cold fingers slip from hers. She felt Miles's hand close over her shoulder.

'I laughed,' she said. 'I stroked her face, and I laughed as the knife went in.'

'You didn't kill her, Sadie,' Miles said, though they both felt the limpness of the lie. He looked at his phone. 'I should call the police back.'

And Sadie was herself once more, her new self, her not-Stacey self, and a coldness was closing around her heart, panic prickling over her skin. 'Why would she give you the right address?' she said and she thought she heard a sound. The faintest of little girl giggles, from somewhere in the shadows.

38

2018

It's time, Sadie. I can't wait any longer. I don't want to wait any longer. I'm ready.

I can remember her so clearly. Can you? The way her eyelashes were blond at the tips. The way her mouth puckered and pursed when she was sleeping, as if she were still giving her little kisses in her dreams. The way her hand felt in mine. I wonder if you remember that too. Poor Anna, led into the woods by you.

You were not the only one, I understand that. I searched for all of you. I wanted to find you, to see what had happened to the girls who killed my sister, destroyed my parents. Because destroy them it did. They never got over Anna, never stopped thinking of the things you did to her. My father spent every night of his life after that screaming his way through nightmares that tormented all of us. My mother only found sleep at the bottom of a bottle and the drink made her see things when she was awake which no person should have to bear. And I lived my whole life being the daughter who couldn't make up for that; the sister who couldn't protect the only person she was supposed to. The sister who turned her back one afternoon for just long enough for you to creep in and destroy it all. All because the three of you were so desperate to believe in some playground tale.

And I did find you. I put my mind to it, like any homework task I'd been so good at in school. And over the years, the leads turned up. Forwarded mail, a forgetful elderly relative. Contact with an old friend. It was all so easy, in the end. Do you want to know what the Tall Man did for your friends, Sadie? The prize for my sister's life? The girl you called Helen is living in a council flat with a hoarding compulsion and crippling agoraphobia. Her sister Marie is twice divorced and an alcoholic at thirty-eight. And the girl you knew as Justine, the girl you were all so afraid of, died of a heroin overdose at twenty-two.

But you. You tried to live. You found love, you had a child, even knowing what you did about the rottenness that lives deep inside you. An act so despicably selfish that even your parents cut their ties with you. An act – another act – which cannot go unpunished.

And now here we are, this small perfect house in its place deep in the woods. I will get the knife from my bag. It's not the cleanest way but it has a certain sense of balance.

I think that's what you've been searching for, all this

time. I think you know that that day, all those years ago, you tilted the scale in the most monstrous way. And every day since that, in your own twisted manner, you've been trying to right things; to repay that debt. You've tortured yourself with it, more Macbeth than Lear. You were a tiger daughter for sure, Sadie, but now you are just a woman with blood indelibly on her hands.

The problem is that you are impossibly, pathetically, despicably weak. You always have been. Little Stacey the sheep. Little Stacey who wanted to be special. You could never repay your debt; you could not right your wrong.

I can.

I will free you, Sadie. I will take from you what you took from us and you will be free. I hope that, as you read this, you will begin to see that. This ending is a beginning for all of us. You believed in the Tall Man once, but the Tall Man does not take daughters. You did. And I will too.

And so it's time for me to put down the pen; to pick up the knife. I am writing this so that you will truly understand, so you will know, without doubt, that your daughter's death is an event which belongs to you. A balancing.

We will both be free now.

The words of the diary echo through the house and Greta stalks from one dark room to another, her hand hesitating at the lights. She feels poisoned by what she's just heard, even though she knew all of the facts, knew everything that fills the gaps, too. It wasn't the hatred in the words that repulsed her. It was watching them leave Amber's mouth, watching Amber's knuckles clench white at the edge of the photocopied sheet. Watching Federica's fingers whiten on the banister too, her glee barely contained, while Tom's mouth turned down at the corners, his face blank and polite, like someone given something curdled and turned at a dinner party.

She stands in the doorway to one of the bedrooms and listens. Amber has made her excuses and gone outside to make a call, though Greta saw the way her hands were shaking as she fumbled with the front door. She can hear the others downstairs making tea; the rattling of the kettle, Federica talking excitedly in a low voice. She is pleased with herself for the letter stunt. Amber reading the words of a woman who planned to murder her, in the place it almost happened – Greta knows that it'll be one of the scenes people post about online, one of the scenes reviewers will love and hate and share. Luca murmurs in agreement with whatever Federica is saying, there is the clink of a spoon, the creak of the fridge opening. And up here, around her, the house creaks and settles too. A cool gust of air whispers at her neck from somewhere. She lies down on the bed where Amber lay and didn't sleep two years ago and stares at the ceiling.

She can't stop picturing Federica's face when she pulled out the letter: *Surprise.* Can't stop thinking of Tom's words back in LA, gulls screaming around them. *You know what's going to happen. You know Federica's going to do something to pull the rug out from under her. She always stitches them up, you know that.*

She'll do it, Greta knows she will. Federica will not be content to let Sadie Banner stay protected in the shadows; she won't rest until she's pulled her into the light, considered her from every possible angle. She doesn't understand, as Greta has come to, that Amber is trying to protect her mother in return for the protection Sadie has given her. Because Sadie giving up her anonymity – going to the tabloids herself – is what alerted the world to the terrible truth behind the murder and its connection to the Westborough Witches. It's what changed the tide of public opinion from disgust to some kind of sympathy for ice princess Amber Banner. And by giving up the second life that was given to her when she was a thirteen-year-old girl called Stacey, Sadie Banner has given Amber a chance at one of her own.

A floorboard creaks in the hallway, the sound of the others downstairs drifting up to her as they take their tea outside. Federica snorting with laughter at something Luca has said. The gruff sound of Tom's voice, the words muffled. Everything carrying on. And that draught of cool air again, licking at her skin.

She thinks of an email forwarded to her from Federica five minutes ago. Nothing said aloud, Federica continuing her conversation even as she pressed send. A random address, someone claiming to be the man Amber knew as Leo. He'll talk for the right amount, he says, as long as his face isn't shown. It'll be up to Greta to validate his claims, figure out if this really is the man who slept with and stalked a sixteen-year-old and her family for cash. His connection to Leanna has never been corroborated though during the trial a tabloid claimed to have identified him as thirty-seven-year-old Lee Mitchell. Wanted in connection with an armed robbery charge and one of sexual assault, he once worked at a garage owned by Leanna's father, David Weatherall. He's still wanted for questioning regarding his part in the Banner case too. Greta wonders whether, should this person prove to actually be him, Federica will hand his information over to the police or if she will film him first.

She gets up and goes to the window, pulls back the flimsy curtain. No view of the loch from here – only the sullen woods; a tree torn from the ground, its roots knotted with moss. The woods seem to stretch endlessly on, the trees pale and the sun not reaching through them, everything still and silent.

She rests her head against the glass, thinking – trying not to think – of Amber's voice shaking as she read that last page of the letter to them; Leanna's last words to Sadie. *We will both be free now.* She watches a figure creep through the trees, moving in and out of the weak light, and wonders if that might ever be true.

39

2016

Amber had tried to hide the light from her phone with her sleeve, her fingers too shaky to be fast enough. She had heard Leanna fall but she must have gotten up, must have caught a glimpse of it, because now Amber could hear her heading up the slope, twigs cracking loudly in the dark. She scrambled further into the woods, bare feet scrabbling against the steep incline, thumb stabbing at the screen. She didn't know if the call connected, didn't dare speak. She walked blindly into a bough and cut open her forehead, her cheek; a bruise that would purple over her eye like a passing storm in the coming days. A scar that would stay far longer.

And behind her, always, the footsteps.

'Come on, Amber,' Billie called, her voice playful. 'It's *so* dark for playing hide and seek. Scary.'

She almost slipped down a sudden gap, her hands

freewheeling out in the darkness. Billie. Goofy, clumsy Billie, out here looking for her. Like real life had crept into a nightmare, made her realise she needed to wake up. She could turn and call for help—

'Ammmmber.' Billie's voice tight and strange. Her footsteps calculated now, as if she were listening for Amber's, trying to track her. No goofing now, another mask shed.

Her breath ragged in her chest, she slid a bare foot over the ridge. It was deep, cool air rising from it. Billie crunched through a shrub nearby and Amber crouched, lowering her body over the edge. Her hands felt ridges like bones; the roots of a tree. And then an absence, a rift in the ground where water had found its insistent way through, streaming towards the loch. She pushed into the bank, into the hollow between two broad roots, a rigid embrace with the stream running icy over her feet. She glanced at her phone but the call, if it had ever connected, had been ended.

Then came a footstep overhead – closer than she'd expected, fear knife-sharp through her – and soil crumbled down the bank and on to her head, her shoulders. Billie, with her snuffling breaths, her heavy tread. 'I know you're here, Am,' she said, softly. 'You should just come out now.'

There was a flaking, metallic sound, nails on a blackboard (blade against a tree). Amber didn't move, didn't even breathe. Around her, the leaves began to whisper – though Billie did not seem to hear them.

'Do you want to hear a story, Am? It's a good one. It happened years ago, when two girls walked into a wood a bit like this one. One of them was just a bit younger than you and me, and the other was only a baby.' The scraping noise again, the bark flaking softly into the air like ash. 'They walked into the woods, hand in hand, but only one of them came out again. You'll know which one obviously, Am, because a few years later, you came out of *her*, right?'

Amber's hand crept across the damp ground beneath her, searching for something sharp or heavy. Moss, pebbles, something feathery and damp. Nothing that she could use and yet something was building inside of her, something louder and more powerful than the fear. Something that stilled her shaking hands; that felt new and yet somehow deeply familiar. That felt unspeakably like anticipation.

There was the sound of a branch breaking somewhere further down the slope, the wind hissing through the trees, and Billie took a step or two in that direction, boots squelching into the ground. The silence seemed to last for ever and Amber still could not breathe.

'No,' Billie said, thumping upwards again. 'You won't get away that easy, Amber. I have to put this knife in you. That's how this ends. That's how I free her.' She took a step forward, stumbling on the edge of the bank, loose soil tumbling down.

Amber stood up, locked a hand around Billie's ankle. 'You can try,' she said.

And then she pulled Billie down into the gully with her.

40

2018

Greta finds her sitting on the edge of the gully, the shadow of a branch spreading its fingers across her back. The air is dank, a smell of belligerent, unstoppable growth, and a bird twitters hesitantly somewhere high in the trees.

'There were wolves here once,' Amber says, without looking round at her. 'My dad told me that.'

Greta sits down beside her.

'I don't sleep much,' Amber continues. 'I told you that, right? I guess after what happened, he didn't either. He'd call me and we'd talk all night.' She glances down the slope to the house. 'I used to have nightmares about these woods if I did sleep.' She shrugs. 'Not sure how he thought knowing the wolves thing would help.'

Greta smiles. 'He'd moved out by then?'

'Yeah.' The bird is joined by another, this one shriller and more insistent. 'She said she'd hurt him too much already. But I guess really she couldn't forgive him,' Amber says. 'For never telling her that he knew, or helping her face it. Helping her see that those things she saw in the shadows couldn't hurt her. I don't know.'

'Do you forgive him?'

Her lips purse, her eyes narrowed as she considers this. 'I guess so,' she says eventually. 'They both fucked up. It's like that poem, right?'

'Larkin?'

'I don't know, probably.' Amber leans back against a tree and looks at Greta. 'I'm never going to give you what you want, you know.'

'And what do I want?'

'You want the tears, you want to hear how my mum was bad and my dad would rather she was mad, and how they ruined my life. You want me to perform for you. But guess what, Greta? The cameras aren't rolling. You don't get to hear if I'm sorry or sad and you don't get to feel better about this whole thing.'

Greta gets up and studies the tree Amber's leaning against. Its trunk bears faint scars, criss-crossed lines level with her shoulder, and she runs a finger across them. It's time for her to leave, she thinks. Germany, maybe. Or Jordan, if her brother will have her. Fiji. Hong Kong. Anywhere but these fervent, fetid woods, the stream brown with clay.

'I didn't have to kill her,' Amber says, looking down into the gully. When Greta doesn't reply, she looks up at her, eyes narrowed again. 'I didn't. Billie was clumsy and screwed-up. She wouldn't have hurt me. I could've just pulled her in and run, she wouldn't have followed.'

'You don't know that.'

Amber smiles. 'Come on, Greta, you've seen the coroner's report, I know you have. You've heard what the prosecution said in court. Does it sound like self-defence to you?'

Greta resists the urge to close her eyes, to push away the memory of those photos of Billie's blue-tinged skin, all twenty-seven of the livid knife-marks. 'I think,' she says, 'that you'd rather be anything than a victim, Amber.'

Amber laughs, a half-hearted sound that echoes through the trees. 'Maybe you *do* know me, Gee.'

Greta's fingers go to the scars in the bark again, imagining Billie standing there two years ago, the last minutes of her life.

'I went to visit her,' Amber says. 'Leanna – Lucy – in prison.'

'Why?'

Amber shrugs. 'I guess I wanted to see her. One on one. Not exactly the same when there's a whole courtroom between you, is it?'

'She was going to kill you.'

'But she didn't.'

'Because she fell and broke her leg in two places.'

Amber shakes her head. 'You almost sound like you're on my side, Gee.'

'What did she say? Lucy?'

Wind whips through the trees, leaves shivering. Amber

glances up at the branches above her, her hands worrying at the edge of her hoody.

'She asked me if I was special now,' she says. A bird calls from a tree somewhere further up the hill, a round, warbling laugh.

'Greta?' Federica in the distance, calling them from down by the house. Amber stands up, wiping her hands on her jeans.

'Come on,' she says. 'Best get back to it, huh? I'm starving, anyway.'

Greta lets Amber lead her down the hill. When the bird calls again, she glances back at the woods, its pockets of dark.

A girl in silhouette, peeping out from behind a tree.

And a hand reaching out, gently coming to rest on her head.

Pulling her back into the shadows.

41

They found her at the edge of the loch as the sun came up. Her pyjamas soaked in blood, water lapping at her feet. Red reeling slowly away with the waves. The knife clutched in her hand. She stood with her back to them as an officer was sent into the woods; as he stumbled out twenty minutes later and vomited on to the dirt track.

They found Leanna in another crevice further down the hillside, splintered bone white against her blood-soaked jeans. Face drained and grey, pulse weak. They wrapped them both in silver, bundled them into separate vehicles as the blue lights flickered back and forth across the trees, the sky lightening in bands of mauve.

Doors slammed shut, radios were used, and the chain of cars rounded the loch, their neons violent. A lone fisherman watched them from the rocky shore. A photo on his phone of a girl in pyjamas soaked black, her hands being cuffed in front of her.

They turned, one by one, on to the road, potholes and dirt track left behind, and as they sped towards Crieff, one bar and then two appeared on Amber's phone, still gripped tightly in her bloody, dirty hand. And the phone burst into life with one message after another.

Mum.

Mum.

Mum.

Miles and Sadie were waiting at the police station when she was released. They had been driving all night, long before the call came. Amber had been stripped and swabbed, her fingers pressed into ink and then rolled across official sheets. After that she'd been left to wait, the small station hushed and confused, the cottage combed for clues.

When her parents appeared in the doorway, Amber stood and for the first time in a long while, Sadie saw her look uncertain.

'Baby girl,' Miles said, crying, but Amber didn't go to him. Instead, she looked at her mother for what felt like a long, long time.

And then she went to Sadie and folded her arms around her.

'I did a bad thing,' she said.

Sadie shook her head no. She put her own arms gingerly around her daughter and brought her mouth close to her ear. She told Amber that Amber didn't even know what a bad thing was.

And Amber rested her head against her mother's, her breath silky and cool against Sadie's skin.

'I gave her to him, Mum,' she whispered. 'I gave him Billie.'

It was the two of them, then. Sadie took the child's hand in hers and she walked out into the daylight.

They walked, together, towards the trees.

Acknowledgements

I am so grateful to Cathryn Summerhayes for her support and enthusiasm, her tireless championing of this book, and for being bloody great company at every step of the way. Huge thanks also to Melissa Pimentel, Alice Dill, Katie McGowan, Irene Magrelli, Martha Cooke and all at Curtis Brown.

I feel so lucky that the Banners found a home with an editor as smart and passionate as Kate Stephenson, who has bravely ventured into their many dysfunctions with me and been so inspiring to work with. Many thanks and many wines too to Ella Gordon, Millie Seaward, Alex Clarke and the rest of brilliant Team Wildfire. I'm also incredibly grateful to the other editors around the world who have shown such support for the novel.

A special thank you to Arabel Charlaff, who took me on a fairly disturbing journey into Amber's psyche. I would recommend her couch to any writer.

Ian Ellard and Joey Connolly were the best colleagues

I could've wished for during the writing of this book. Thanks also to Richard Skinner and Joanna Briscoe.

Thank you, Hayley Richardson, for always reading.

My family deserve a whole essay on all the ways they have supported and inspired me, but instead I'll just say: thank you for everything. I love you (and I'm so thankful that you're nothing at all like any of the families in this book!).

Credit: Mark Vessey

Phoebe Locke is the pseudonym of full-time writer Nicci Cloke. She previously worked at the Faber Academy, and hosted London literary salon Speakeasy. She lives and writes in London.